Heartsong

sisterhood
of
shepherds

1

nicola furlong

Mantle Rock P

D1206710

Published by Mantle Rock Publishing
2879 Palma Road
Benton, KY 42025
www.mantlerockpublishing.com

Printed in the United States of America

ISBN 978-0-9859610-7-7

Cover by Roseanna White

Published in association with Joyce Hart of Hartline Literary Agency, Pittsburgh, PA.

The song, *Battlefield,* used by permission from Glynne Turner.

Dedication
To Patrice, Shauneen, Siobhan and Michael, for inspiring my Shepherds.
Nicola

~

Experience

friendship, family and forgiveness –

Join the

Sisterhood of Shepherds.

~

Chapter One

The best place to seek God is in a garden. You can dig for him there.
George Bernard Shaw

Charly Shepherd gasped in dismay at the sudden torrent of raindrops. She tugged a waterproof hood over her long blonde hair. At the first clap of thunder, she broke into a run. Her lime-green rubber boots sloshing, she raced through mud, slip-sliding around the old Cape Cod house and hustling along the grassy track to the nursery.

In mid-flight, Charly glanced up at the roof. Gracie the flying pig weathervane spun wildly, chasing its curly bronze tail.

It was late winter in the small seaside town of Silver Shores, Oregon, so rain wasn't unexpected. In fact, it was welcome, especially in the retail gardening community. The past winter had brought mere dustings of snow inland and lower than average rainfall on the Pacific Coast.

As manager of the Sweet Shepherd Nursery, a five-acre farm specializing in plants for butterflies and hummingbirds, Charly should have delighted in the deluge. And she might have, except for the thunder.

The fertile land behind the big yellow house stretched out before her. It was a familiar sight: three acres of bedding plants, a couple of large greenhouses, and several outbuildings. A vista she had appreciated all her life. Today, it was a muted patchwork of greens and browns, but soon the scene would be braided by startling rows of yellow, purple and pink, a palette favored by hummingbirds and butterflies.

No matter what challenges Charly was facing in her life, this vivid, ever-changing landscape energized her, sustained her, and reminded her of greater things. As her dear father Barry had often told her when she was growing up, "These're God's acres, child, not ours." Bone tired from digging or weeding, and fuming over not being able to hang out with friends, Charly would respond, "Fine. Why isn't *He* here hauling manure?"

Her father usually chuckled and instead of scolding his youngest daughter, offered her a glimpse of heaven. He taught her about spiral patterns as they examined the whorls of the western giant hyssop, and about Greek mythology when he explained that the *achillea*, or common yarrow, was named after Achilles because his soldiers had favored it to treat wounds.

Truth be known, Charly had relished those times alone with her father. No older sisters to compete with or be ordered about by. Just the land and her dad.

Those precious occasions hadn't happened very often while she was growing up. The little nursery, which supported the Shepherd parents and their three daughters Faith, Hope and Charly, required much manual labor. And with their mother's part-time teaching and housekeeping responsibilities, it was up to one or more of the girls to pitch in most mornings, evenings and weekends. There was never enough money to pay for hired help.

As the eldest, Faith had obediently taken her turn in the dirt. Though energetic, the plump strawberry blonde lacked focus and her family quickly learned not to give her tasks requiring patience or precision. Over time, she slipped into the fetch-it and cleanup roles, and as long as the impulsive daydreamer was given free rein, Faith accomplished a great deal.

Hope, on the other hand, was almost too precise, too focused, and quickly developed a love for insects, not plants. She often became sidetracked while working, her slender fingers holding a pupa or spider instead of secateurs, her gardening responsibilities long forgotten. This interest eventually paid off when she studied biology and entomology and helped her family become one of the first organic nurseries in the state.

For Charly, it was simple. One spring afternoon in her late teens, while she was spreading mushroom manure, Charly became conscious that she was humming and enjoying her labors and hadn't given one thought to anything or anyone else. From that moment on, she couldn't wait to get into the garden, to pinch back seedlings or deadhead spent blossoms, for she knew that horticulture would be her future.

Time stood still when she dug or plucked or watered. Now thirty-seven, she still embraced Shaw's words, which her father had carved over the little potting shed, *The best place to seek God is in a garden.* Her mind emptied of all worries and she embraced natural sight and sound, be it a nodding columbine or a hummingbird climbing a ladder of hollyhock blossoms. The only thing better was being the mother of two, nine-year-old Scotty and twelve-year-old Melissa.

Sliding to a stop near a mound of freshly-turned earth, Charly shouted, "No!" She stood by herself in the Sweet Shepherd Nursery. And tried not to cry. The combination of thunder and falling temperatures had changed the rain from friend to foe.

Hail now drilled down, stinging her face and exploding into white shards, as ice pellets pummeled the dark earth, crushing thousands of young green plants. Wiping out a chunk of this year's income.

Chapter Two

*A garden is always a series of losses set against a few
triumphs, like life itself.*
May Sarton

It'll all come right in the end," Barry Shepherd said, gently laying
a gnarled hand on his youngest child's shoulder. "We've seen our
share of drought and pestilence, and we've always managed to
come through. Haven't we, Charly?"

The pair wore their waterproof jackets and boots in the middle of
the planting beds. The rain and hail were finally over, a fresh breeze
carried the rich scent of moist earth, and condensation blossomed
on the greenhouses. Nearby, a mangy gray squirrel darted across the
potting shed roof, and tiny bushtits danced excitedly in and out of the
laurel hedgerow that partially surrounded the property.

"I…I guess so, Dad. It's just so *hard* to see everything ruined. We
had such good luck with germination, especially with the *aquilegias*,
crocosmias and *agastaches*. We could be in real trouble now, 'cause
I didn't order any of those plants."

Although the Sweet Shepherd Nursery could have followed
the practice of some gardening centers—buying all their stock from
wholesalers—both Barry and Charly preferred to propagate as much
from seed as possible. Not only did this guarantee the final product, but
they reveled in the creation of life. Since they were limited by climate,
greenhouse space and available land, the pair exhausted many winter

hours reviewing catalogues and discussing plant attributes and past sales before carefully choosing species that suited both the Oregon coast's semi-Mediterranean climate and the local butterflies and birds.

Charly possessed an uncanny instinct for seed germination and had dedicated many challenging but happy hours to carefully testing soil mixes, heating methods and light intensities. She was an expert in collecting and caring for the mature seeds and understood the various steps required, whether soaking, chilling or shell nicking, to ensure sprouting success with each species.

Now as they eyed the sodden ground, the true extent of the damage to their plants was evident. Row upon row of recently transplanted seedlings lay twisted and flattened in the dark wet soil. Water drops continued to *plink* down from the roofs of the nearby greenhouses, and twigs swirled in muddy puddles dotting the narrow walkways.

Charly sighed and patted her father's hand. "Oh, Dad…all that work—prepping the soil, casting the best seeds, watering—all wasted."

"Hard work's never wasted, child, you know that. Why, only last week you were telling me about your idea for a simpler sowing system. That didn't come from watching YouTube."

Charly had to smile. She turned and looked at her father. Behind his thick glasses, his eyes were a startling blue. "YouTube, Dad? My nine-year-old spinning you 'round the Web again?"

It was the older man's turn to grin. "Heavens to Betsy, why not? Just because I'm into my sixth decade on God's green earth is no reason not to be hip." He frowned. "Or is it cool?"

Charly laughed before reaching up to bestow a quick kiss on her father's fleshy cheek. "As Scotty would say, 'You're totally honking, Dad.' How 'bout a cup of tea? I might even dig out some cookies. The kids'll be home soon and there's nothing we can do here 'til it dries out."

"Now you're the one who's totally honking," Barry replied, his size fourteen rubber boots already on the move.

Chapter Three

There is nothing in a caterpillar that tells you it's going to be a butterfly.
Buckminster Fuller

Soon they were seated at the old oak dining table, chilled fingers wrapped around steaming mugs of tea.

The country kitchen was the heart of the family home. It faced south, and through a pair of broad windows, most of the nursery was visible. The Shepherds rarely ate in the formal dining room, preferring the antique red kitchen's cozy warm ambiance. The chairs didn't match and the fir floors were gouged, but the constants were fresh flowers, lively conversation and a special place at the table for each family member. And as young Charly had often said, "Mom's kitchen smells so good."

It was the room that Eileen Shepherd had also loved best. Whether the Shepherd matriarch was washing dishes, peeling potatoes or sipping tea, her beloved family was often within view. One daughter would usually be helping with housework or meal preparation, while the others worked outside with their father.

Even after her untimely death the previous May, the kitchen remained the Shepherds' go-to place. Charly often thought it was because everyone still sensed her spirit in the cheery glow of the big room. Charly frequently wore her mother's apron, feeling loved and protected as soon as she tied the worn blue strings, and she knew she wasn't the only one to feel that way.

A month after Eileen's death, the family had settled into an uneasy silence as each of them struggled with grief, avoiding the mention of her name for fear of adding to the others' heartache.

Fortunately, Charly's daughter Melissa quashed this approach during one muted Sunday dinner. Hope and Charly had tentatively begun discussing seed germination and the merits of using warm water for misting, but their father and older sister remained gloomy and unwilling to engage.

That is until the skinny pre-teen uttered the prophetic words, "What would Grammie think?"

At first, the reaction was a stunned silence, then all eyes surreptitiously focused on Barry Shepherd. To his family's dismay, the older man blinked away tears. Charly was about to admonish her daughter when a smile slowly lit Barry's wide face, the first genuine smile since his wife's funeral. He said, "That's a good question, Lissa. What *would* she think?"

After that, Melissa's question became a sort of rallying cry, and Eileen Shepherd was reborn into her family.

Charly took a tentative sip of tea, followed by another. "Tomorrow I'll go through our inventory and orders lists and see where we're at." She paused, hearing a rumbling outside the house. "It's only mid-February, I should be able to get some orders in quick to cover our damaged stock." She rubbed the lip of her mug. "I hate losing those plants, though. We had some real beauts coming, especially the peach *agasta*—"

"Please don't tell me it hailed," a female voice shouted.

Seconds later, Faith Shepherd, strawberry blonde locks spilling over her face, stormed into the kitchen.

Charly couldn't help but smile at her older sister's outfit. Charly favored loose overalls and men's flannel shirts. Since she spent most of her time working outside, she was never very comfortable in dresses and high heels. She did, however, have a weakness for colorful silk scarves and always sported one as a neckerchief.

Faith was her polar opposite. Today she wore black tights, a checkered gray skirt and a pearl-gray sweater, topped by a fringed, tan leather jacket. Huge looped earrings, a tumbled-stone necklace and a pink motorcycle helmet completed the look. Charly was never quite sure what to call her sister's distinctive style. Not quite Sunday-school teacher, not quite biker chick, but somewhere in the middle. And the forty-three-year-old carried it off with aplomb.

Faith dumped a pastry box on the table. "Heard it on the radio, but it was so nice in town I thought it must be a mistake." She hesitated. "Oh boy...don't like the look on your faces..."

Faith quickly moved past the table and peered out the window. The others waited in silence.

"Oh noooo!" Faith swung round, eyes bright with worry. "How bad?"

Her father stood and pulled out the chair beside him.

"It'll be all right, dear. Come, sit and have some tea."

He reached for the box.

"What've you got here?"

"Butter tarts. Didn't know what else to bring."

Her father answered by taking a huge bite out of one of the tarts, then added, "Mmm, thank you."

"Where's Michael?" Charly asked, grabbing a mug and pouring.

"Oh, he's just putting the bike 'round the ba—" Faith stopped as a roar filled the air and an old blue motorcycle with attached sidecar blasted into view.

Her husband, Michael Lawless, flicked off the engine and the odd-looking vehicle skidded to a stop nearby. Michael flipped up his dark visor and stared into the nursery. After a minute, he pulled off his helmet, flung his leg over the bike's seat and strode to the back door.

Faith jumped up and hurried to meet him. "Oh, Michael, Isn't it awful?"

"The northern lights have seen queer sights but the queerest they ever did see," Michael sang as he entered. "Was that night on the marge of Lake Lebarge when I cremated Sam McGee."

A brief stint in northern Canada as a game warden decades ago had imbued Michael with a passion for crisp winter mornings, Inuit sculpture and the poems of Robert Service. Recently retired from the local police force, the lanky man kicked off his muddy boots, reached the table in a few long strides, shook his father-in-law's hand, air-kissed Charly's cheeks and then dropped into a chair.

"But I'd say those sorry-lookin' plants come a mighty sight close."

He grabbed a pastry, inhaled it in three bites, then glanced around.

"Any chance a man might have a cup of coffee?"

Charly couldn't hold it in any longer and burst out laughing. Barry quickly followed suit, slapping his knee as he guffawed.

Michael's rugged face flushed and he scowled. "What's so funny?"

That sent Charly and Barry into howling fits.

Bushy eyebrows raised, Michael stared at the pair, while Faith slipped in beside him, smiling anxiously.

Finally, Charly gasped, "Oh, Michael, you're completely nuts."

She stood, gave him a quick hug.

"And I'm so glad. Instant coffee okay?"

Chapter Four

A garden is evidence of faith.
Gladys Taber

S o," said Faith a few minutes later. "What can we do to help?" Her husband nodded while gulping coffee.

"Well..." Charly looked at her father.

"Not sure there's much you two *can* do, but I appreciate your asking," Barry said. "We'll need a day or so to see if any of the plants recover. We'll probably have to talk to the insurance—"

"Don't envy you that," Michael interjected between swigs.

Barry sighed. "No one likes to go begging for a handout."

"But Dad, it's not a handout," cried Faith, reaching across to touch her father's arm. "You've paid into it. It's not like you don't deserve it. You do." She smiled at her sister. "You both do."

"I know, dear. It's just something I hate to have to do." Barry sighed again and jammed his thumbs under the apron of his worn overalls. "Your mother and I were always...reluctant to ask for help. Only claimed once, winter of '75."

His back straightened. "For the most part, we've done it all ourselves, with our own two hands and the help of you girls." Barry grimaced, then burped. "Excuse me. Touch of indigestion. And you know our rates'll skyrocket. We might not be able to afford to make a claim."

"Well, guess we're lucky we just renewed our coverage," added

Charly. "And we have the choice."

"Just?" Faith asked, voice rising in concern. "Then what if—"

"Don't worry," her father said. "We mailed the check a couple of weeks ago." He scowled and then tapped his chest.

"Sure you're okay, Dad?" Charly asked.

Her father smiled ruefully. "Shouldn't have had that second butter tart, is all."

"Well, Barry," said Michael. "If you need any help, just whistle."

"Yes," added Faith. "Please do. Michael doesn't know what to do with himself now that he's retired."

Charly said, "You must be bored stiff, Mikey. No police chases, no late-night stakeouts, nobody to lock up. What're you doing with your free time?"

"Oh, I still get calls," Michael replied with a huff. "Don't I, Faithie?" His wife looked surprised. "You don't just quit being the chief of police like that." He snapped his fingers. "At least, not in Silver Shores, Oregon. Besides, I've got a lot of corporate knowledge, the force might even hire me as a consultant."

"Corporate knowledge? Consultant?" Charly chuckled. "Aren't we suddenly Mr. Wall Street. What happened to perps, BOLOs and the slammer?"

Michael shoved back his chair and stood. "You really don't want to know, missy," he said, offering his sister-in-law an exaggerated wink. "Now, if you folks'll excuse me, I've got an appointment with a piano."

There was a *bang* as the front door flew open. By the time Charly's two children had dragged their heavy backpacks inside the hall, Michael was happily astride the piano bench and the surprisingly professional sounds of "She'll Be Comin' Round the Mountain When She Comes" echoed from the living room.

As always, Charly's heart rose when she heard her children's voices and she sang out a welcome over the music. Then she quickly slipped the pastry box into the fridge and flashed a smile at her sister. "These'll be a great treat later." She glanced from Faith to her father, adding quickly, "Let's keep the hail damage to ourselves, okay?"

The others nodded. Charly immediately realized she shouldn't have worried. The siblings, squawking like hungry baby crows, rushed into the kitchen, demanding her attention.

"Whoa, there!" Charly raised a hand. "Hold that thought. We want to hear all about it, but you're both tired and hungry."

She handed each a large glass of skim milk and a handful of peanuts and raisins.

"Let's get something decent into your stomachs first, 'kay?"

"Thanks." Melissa plopped down beside her grandfather.

Already chewing, her younger brother nodded and jammed himself into a seat near the window.

"Michael, my man!" Faith pulled on her jacket. "Let's ride."

In response, the music suddenly changed into the rising, dramatic phrases common in old western movies. The kids laughed. Michael returned, Faith gave everyone a quick cheek peck, and the pair headed into the yard.

After the motorbike's engine squeal faded, Charly asked the children about their day. Since Scotty was guzzling milk, Melissa took center stage, a favorite position for the outgoing girl.

"Mr. Burgess says kids shouldn't be vegetarians, Stephie got a pink iPod—y'know, I so want that color, Mom, right? Christine's invited me for a sleepover and d'you think Aunt Hope would help me with my science project?"

"My goodness," said her grandfather, exchanging an amused look with Charly.

Charly took a deep breath. "I think Mr. Burgess meant that being a vegetarian takes extra work to make sure you get the right nutrition. That can be hard, especially if you're a picky eater," she said, glancing at her son, who quickly pretended to study a raisin. "Pink's a great color—" Scotty blew a raspberry and Barry tried to suppress a grin. "And if you keep up your chores and babysitting, you'll soon have your iPod moment. Y'know your aunt's teaching full-time this term, but she'd love to help you. Just make sure you give her a heads-up." She paused for a breath. "Now, about that sleepover, I'm not so sure."

"Aww, Mom..."

"We'll talk about it later, Melissa. Okay, Mr. Scott, what's going on in your little world?"

The nine-year-old scratched his spiky dark hair and thrust out his bottom lip. "Did ya know General Robert E. Lee had a pet hen?"

His grandfather gasped. "He had a what?"

Scotty grinned, jumped up and ran around the table, flapping his elbows and clucking.

"A hen, Gramps!" He squealed in delight. "Y'know, a chicken that lays eggs."

When Scotty reached his grandfather, Barry grabbed hold. The two wrestled briefly, then Barry began tickling his grandson. "Bawwk, bawwk, bawwwk," Barry crowed, much to the children's enjoyment.

Charly leaned back in her chair and watched in delight. After a few seconds, she thought of her mother, her heart wrenched, and she wished keenly that Eileen could see these glowing faces. Her pain lasted only a moment, though, suspended by her daughter's high-pitched voice.

"When's dinner, Mom?" Melissa said. "Gotta call Aunt Hope."

Chapter Five

Show me your garden and I shall tell you what you are.
Alfred Austin

A chunk of earth smacked against Charly's calf, followed seconds later by a higher spray of dirt. Bent over and tugging hard on a hoe, Charly didn't pay any attention. After all, she had been kicking up debris all morning, tilling flattened plants into the garden beds. Though her shoulders and back ached, Charly kept working. Her job was only a third done.

She was concentrating extra hard, trying to stop her thoughts from spinning into too many disheartening what-if scenarios. Not one of the hundreds of home-grown seedlings had survived the hailstorm, and she kept blaming herself for having planted out the stock too early. What if she couldn't find good-quality replacements in sufficient volume? What if she couldn't negotiate a reasonable price? After all, her competitors would have placed their orders in the fall, and anything left would come at a premium.

Not for the first time, she questioned the wisdom of having a specialty garden center. Her father's focus had always been on nectar-producing plants, even before it was in fashion, and for the most part his Sweet Shepherd Nursery was a blooming success.

At times like this, Charly wondered if they would be better off carrying a wider, more mainstream selection of plants and accessories, but both she and her father were born specialists, naturally interested in focusing their knowledge and expertise. Besides, they appreciated growing something with a greater purpose beyond mere enjoyment. Providing sustenance to butterflies and hummingbirds was their vocation.

Well, Mom, Charly thought, *I really wish you were here. What do you think? Is this a good time to change our business model?*

Charly knew her mother had always supported the nursery's approach and expertise, but she was a pragmatic woman. For a moment, Charly felt guilty, realizing that her mother's response would have been practical, but delivered from a humanitarian perspective.

I know, I know, Mom. First you'd tell me to thank God that things weren't worse and to count my already ample blessings. Then you'd remind me of how fortunate I am, compared to many others.

Charly sighed, knowing that this was all true. And even if she didn't really feel like accepting it at this moment, she would have given anything to have heard the words directly from her mother.

Though Eileen had wholeheartedly supported her family's efforts, the majority of which were dedicated to plants and animals, she had often said she wished they would devote more time to helping people. To that end, she had organized their active participation in an annual charitable effort, part of her long-standing role in St. Peter's by-the-Sea's outreach activities. Over the years, the Shepherd gang had been involved in a variety of their church's good works, including baking and selling fund-raising cookies, delivering Easter flowers to elderly shut-ins and collecting roadside litter.

Just two years ago, they had prepared and served dinners for a week at a local homeless shelter, and last year, the family had hammered its way through a whole weekend—not to mention a few thumbs—in support of Habitat for Humanity.

As she grew older, Charly began to enjoy these activities, appreciating the warmth she felt from giving of her time and talents to others. Her mother's death brought about an even more profound change within her, and for the first time in her life she found herself considering a previously unimaginable possibility.

Maybe there's a life for me beyond the nursery. But what?

Again, something smacked against her leg.

"Dollar for your thoughts?"

"Oh!" Charly spun toward the familiar voice. "Hope, you startled me."

"Yeah, sorry 'bout that, kiddo."

Charly looked up at her forty-one-year-old sister. A tall, slender woman, Dr. Hope Shepherd wore old jeans, gloves and a scuffed-up field jacket. The attire was typical for Hope, a well-respected and tenured professor in the department of entomology at nearby O'Brien State College.

"Well, you didn't notice the dirt I chucked at you earlier," Hope opened her hand and black earth trickled onto the ground, "so I went to check some overwintering Red Admiral larvae and figured you'd see me."

"I'll take that dollar, if you don't mind. We're gonna need every one we can get."

Hope ruffled her short brown curls and surveyed the garden beds. "Lissa mentioned something about hail on the phone last night, but wow, I never imagined it was this bad." She prodded the dirt with the toe of a work boot. "Where's the Dutch hoe?"

"In the shed. Thought you had classes all day?"

"Boiler trouble," Hope said, as she tramped to the small outbuilding. Moments later she was back, garden implement in hand. "The whole wing's shut down. Figured you could use some help."

Charly smiled affectionately at her. "Always knew your fancy education would come in handy, Doc."

Hope gave her a gentle poke with the hoe then headed across into the next field. Soon the two sisters were contentedly plowing and churning earth and chatting intermittently, just like they had done hundreds of times before.

After forty-five minutes, Charly sneaked a glance at her hard-working sibling and offered a brief prayer of thanks. At least, the "what if I were alone" scenario was one she didn't have to consider. Her father was inside, discussing their options with the insurance adjuster. Hope had given up a free day to pitch in, and Faith had offered to come by later and prepare dinner.

She stooped to dig out a stone. It looked like things weren't going to be so bleak after all.

Noon came and went and the women kept digging. Finally, they finished the second garden plot and stood, breathing heavily and leaning on their equipment.

"Phew!" Hope ran a dirty glove and an accompanying smudge across her forehead. "It's been awhile since I've done this much manual labor." She gave Charly an admiring glance. "I know you've been at this twice as long as I have, kiddo, but you don't seem nearly as tired."

Charly chuckled, pulled free her red and black scarf and ran it over her face and along her neck. "Well, I should hope so. I'm out here practically twenty-four seven." She shoved the piece of colorful silk into the bib of her overalls.

After a momentary pause, Charly continued, "Hey, can I ask you something?"

"Anything," her sister said glibly, while carefully pulling out weed tendrils caught in the cross-blade of the hoe. "I mean, except how a butterfly's DNA can be completely different from that of its caterpillar form." She looked up, then flushed slightly at Charly's solemn expression. "Uh, sorry. Go ahead."

"Have you noticed anything…different about Dad?"

Hope's dark eyes narrowed. "Different? How?"

"He starts to speak and then he just…stops." Charly kicked at some mud. "This may sound a little weird, but he seems…oh, I don't know… wistful, even vulnerable sometimes."

Hope watched her for a few seconds, then asked, "You mean, like when he's talking about Vietnam? That kind of vulnerable?"

"Exactly. Know he's bound to be sad, what with Mom's death, but somehow I don't think that's it. It's like he's…preoccupied. Like he has something to say. And, oh, I don't know. He, he just looks older, Hope." Charly caught her breath. "He…he acts older."

Hope took a step and squeezed Charly's shoulder. "I know, kiddo. It's been a real blow to all of us, but for Dad…" She breathed deeply. "I mean, you don't just let go after forty-three years. Not the way those two loved each other. Give him some time. He'll get back his cheery confidence, you'll see."

Charly nodded. "I'm sure you're right. So, how 'bout we break for lunch?"

"Thank heavens! I was beginning to feel like one of my students on a field survey."

Puzzled, Charly frowned.

"They're always complaining that they never know when we're going to stop." Hope grinned ruefully. "And they're right, because I don't know. I get into a groove and just keep on truckin'."

She took her sister's garden hoe and laid it on the ground. "You're just the same, only your groove's a heck of a lot more work! Come on, kiddo! Race you to the back door."

The pair took off, slipping and sliding in their heavy boots, their laughter punctuating the moist mid-afternoon air. As usual, Hope's longer stride gave her an advantage and she was a couple of feet ahead as they neared the house.

At the last corner, Charly grabbed hold of her sister's jacket and tugged.

Hope lost her balance, slithering sideways.

Charly pounded past, charged up the steps and thumped the door twice in the Shepherd girls' traditional signal of victory.

A second later, Hope burst onto the platform. The siblings fell into one another's arms, gasping and giggling.

The door opened.

Their father stood looking at them, his broad face creased with worry.

"Sorry, Dad," Hope said, when she caught her breath. "Didn't mean to upset you."

"You'd better come in," was all he replied, before turning and moving toward the kitchen.

Hope and Charly exchanged raised eyebrows, then quickly shucked their outerwear and hurried inside.

Chapter Six

*To be overcome by the fragrance of flowers is a delectable
form of defeat.*
Beverly Nichols

Their father was seated at the kitchen table, surrounded by sheets of paper. As she slid into the chair across from him, Charly picked up a page and gave it a once-over. No big surprise. It was part of the business insurance forms that she had earlier given to her father.

Hope glanced over her sister's shoulder before taking her seat. "Is there a problem?"

Before her father could respond, Charly said, "What's going on, Dad?"

Barry Shepherd bit his lower lip and studied his children for a moment. "I'm not entirely sure," he said finally. "Seems there's a hitch in our insurance coverage."

"Hitch?" the sisters exclaimed simultaneously.

"What do you mean?" Charly asked. "We've religiously paid into that every year, in full, on time. Even though the rates are outrageous." She leaned back. "Don't tell me they're trying to deny our claim?"

"Afraid so," her father replied.

Hope shot upright. "But that's ridiculous! There's no way they can do that. You've paid, now it's their turn. I know some lawyers at the college, I can—"

"I don't think a lawyer is going to be able to help."

"Wait a second," Charly interjected. "Let's just start at the beginning, okay?"

The others nodded.

"Dad, we haven't even decided if we're going to make a claim yet, right? I thought you were just calling the insurance folks to check things out."

Barry nodded.

"Well then, how on earth can they decide to deny us a claim, when we haven't even submitted one?"

Barry exhaled. "It's incredibly simple and completely unbelievable."

"What?" Hope asked.

"The insurance guy says he never got our money. And...our coverage expired ten days ago."

Without a word, Hope dropped back into her seat.

Charly couldn't move, momentarily stunned. This wasn't possible. *There's no way.*

"This can't be right, Dad. I remember you writing the check weeks ago. You mailed it, didn't you?"

"Of course I did," her father replied, then his expression turned to one of concentration. "I...now that I think of it, I'm sure I gave the envelope to Scotty to mail on the way to school."

"Well, it must have gotten lost in the company's mailroom," suggested Hope. "Did they say they'd look for it?"

Barry nodded. "They say they've already checked, that they didn't receive anything, and they seem very certain."

"Okay, so it's the postal service's fault then," Hope said. "I mean, I wonder if there's some kind of recourse when they lose someone's mail?"

"I don't understand," Charly added. "It's just got to be some silly mix-up."

"Yeah," said Hope. "I'm sure that's what it is."

But no one, not even Hope, dared believed it.

The trio sat in silence for a full minute, pondering the situation. Finally, Charly jumped up and plugged in the kettle. She turned to the others.

"Right. This is what I suggest. I'll make a follow-up call to the insurance company. I'm not blaming you, Dad. I just think it makes sense for someone else to give it a try."

"No offence taken, dear," Barry said. "I truly pray you get a different answer."

"If, after that, we're still in the same boat, then we'll have to contact the post office."

"I'll handle the tea," said Hope as she laid three mugs on the counter top. "You go make that call."

When Charly returned ten minutes later, she didn't have to say a word. An expression of defeat clouded her lovely face.

Hope reached for the battered silver thermos the family used as a teapot. She poured a cup, added a dash of milk, then slid it toward her sister.

Charly took a sip and sighed. "It's just as Dad said. They claim they never received our check. The guy who handles our paperwork was on holidays and no one noticed that our payment was overdue."

"Can they do anything?" asked Hope. "After all, the nursery's been a customer for years."

"Ever since April in seventy-three," Barry said. "Over thirty-six years."

"Well," continued Charly, "I finally got to talk to the manager. She was very polite and sympathetic—"

Her father snorted. "Is she going to help us if we make a claim?"

Charly shrugged. "She said she'd take it up with their parent company, but unless we can prove that it's their fault..." She fiddled with her mug. "I don't hold out much hope. Guess we'll have to try the post office."

The others exchanged an unhappy glance.

"Uh..." Hope said, "while you were on the phone in the office, I made a preliminary call on my cell."

Charly slumped back in her chair. "Don't tell me. They don't accept any responsibility, either."

"Not one iota," said Hope. "If you'd paid extra to register the letter..."

"But that's ridiculous!" snapped her father. "I've always mailed my bills and we've never had a problem."

Charly said, "I know, Dad, it's not your fault. Maybe we'll have to make a change, start paying online and getting confirmation." She swallowed the last of her tea. "But that's in the future. What we're going to do now is the question."

"I've got some money saved," said Hope. "How much do you think you'll need?"

"That's very generous of you, Hope," her father said, "but we can't take your money."

"Dad's right." Charly nodded. "It's very kind, but we'll figure something out, thanks."

"Well, it's there if you want it." Hope stood. "I should get going. Got to finish a grant application for this summer's research."

"Going Black Checker spotting in Arizona again?" asked Charly.

Hope shook her head. "Y'know how much I've always wanted to study a local butterfly? Well, there's been a shake-up at the college. Now might be a chance to finagle a bit of cash for the *Icaricia icarioides fender*." She grinned. "That's a Fender's blue to you two."

"Sure would be great to have you around in the garden."

"Amen," added Barry.

"Thanks. I can already smell the salmon on the barbeque."

"Salmon?" Charly asked, her eyes twinkling. "I was thinking of another summer aroma."

Puzzled, Hope looked at her younger sibling.

"One of your faves: e*au de* compost."

Chapter Seven

*Last night, there came a frost, which has done great damage
to my garden...It is sad that Nature will play such tricks on us poor
mortals, inviting us with sunny smiles to confide in her, and then,
when we are entirely within her power, striking us to the heart.*
Nathaniel Hawthorne

The next day Charlie sat in the small den, which had been
used as an office for years. The cozy room was highlighted
by an oversized picture window, through which soft north
light flowed. She hummed softly, following the patchy music her
daughter was playing in the TV room, while staring vacantly out at
the large front lawn and past the wide perennial bed that hugged the
property's circular drive.

With its steeply sloping roof, broad covered porch and jutting
dormers, the Shepherd homestead was a classic Cape Cod design.
Painted a rich yellow with creamy white trim, its cheery facade
welcomed family and customers alike. Five years earlier, Charly and
her father had replaced the grass lawn with a variety of flowering
ground covers, including alyssum and pussytoes, each meticulously
chosen for its role as larval host plant or nectar provider.

The massive perennial bed was designed both as a showcase for
customers and a destination for birds, butterflies and other insects.
From early spring through summer and into late fall, a cornucopia of

plants thrived, their vast range of colors, leaves, heights and blossoms a wonder to behold.

Scattered about were a number of *objets d'art*, compliments of Faith. She favored odd-shaped rocks and strips of metal. Her resulting creations, which her family nicknamed "naïve art," were simplistic, original and often wacky. Surprisingly, they were also customer favorites.

Though her eyes took in the pleasant darkening view, Charly's thoughts were focused more on the green of money than that of their front garden. She had spent the morning doing inventory and the afternoon reviewing lists—current stock, planted seedlings and plants ordered—and now, just before dinner, she had a clear idea of their current situation.

It wasn't dreadful, but it wasn't impressive, either. As she had feared, they would have to order hundreds of plants at an inflated cost. On the other hand, one of her highly sought hybrid honeysuckles—which had yet to be planted out and had thus been spared from the hailstorm—was sprouting extraordinarily well, and she realized it would command a hefty premium. Not nearly enough to cover their additional costs, but a help nonetheless.

"Hey, Mom," Scotty shouted from upstairs. "When's dinner? I'm starving."

Charly pushed her long hair off her face, stood and stretched. She switched off the lamp and padded into the hall in her stocking feet.

"Fifteen minutes," she called up the stairwell. "Make sure you wash your hands." She turned to face the hall. "And, Melissa? The music's lovely, honey, but it's your turn to lay the table."

The clarinet squawked loudly in protest and then the music stopped. "Okaaay," her daughter's voice floated in from the nearby room. "Be right there."

Charly was a "just in time" cook, happier growing the produce than preparing it. Though she made every effort to ensure her children ate a tasty, well-balanced and nutritional diet, her collection of dishes was often uninspired and unoriginal. At least, that was what she thought. Her children and her father devoured everything she made and seemed not to notice the lack of variety.

She made up for her perceived failing by specializing in cookies.

Though bored when cutting up vegetables or marinating meat, she enjoyed beating butter or measuring chocolate chips. Who wouldn't, when the latter was so much tastier?

Her mother, an excellent traditional cook, was often taken aback by her family's desire for sweets. Many times she would offer something "healthier," like a fruit salad, only to end up eating it herself, while her husband and daughters munched happily on whatever homemade dessert they had scrounged from the freezer.

As Charly boiled pasta and grated Parmesan cheese for a Caesar salad, her thoughts roamed through her to-do list for the next day. Getting the plant order in was paramount, but it would have to be done in between dropping Melissa off early for band practice, taking Scotty to a mid-morning dental appointment, and picking up a load of organic fertilizer. And she and her father hadn't finished deciding which plants to purchase.

She was still mentally reviewing the potential candidates while rinsing Romaine lettuce when Melissa rushed into the kitchen.

"Sorry," the pre-teen said, grabbing cutlery. "I was just waiting for the show to end."

"No problem, hon, we won't be eating for another ten minutes."

Melissa watched her mother. "Mmm, Caesar salad. Super idea, Mom." She began setting the table. "What's for dessert?"

Charly stopped in mid-rinse and feigned a groan. "Hey now, we haven't even started dinner yet."

Her son ambled in. "Come on, Mom," Scotty said. "Y'know the best part of dinner's dessert."

She handed him several carrots and a peeler. "The sooner you peel, the sooner we eat cookies."

Scotty energetically scraped the peeler along the carrots.

"Oh, by the way Scotty," Charly pointed a lettuce leaf at him, "d'you remember mailing a check addressed to Pemberton Insurance for Grampa a couple of weeks ago?"

The frantic peeling stopped, then started again with abandon. "Uh, sure."

Charly looked at her son. "Are you certain?"

Scotty kept peeling an already stripped carrot. He nodded.

"What's the big deal, Mom?" Melissa asked, reaching for plates.

"Oh, nothing. Just checking. I'll finish that, Scotty. Would you go get your Grampa?"

Her nine-year-old tore from the kitchen, shouting, "Grampa! Dinnertime!"

A few minutes later, Charly was about to place a dish of spaghetti on the table alongside a mountain of Caesar salad when she heard her son scream.

Charly felt her stomach contract. The dish fell from her hand and smashed on the floor, launching strips of pasta and stains of red sauce. Melissa shrieked and shrank back in her chair, trying to avoid being struck by the flying food.

"Go grab me a flashlight, okay?" Charly said.

Scotty screamed again.

Charly skidded through the slimy mess before racing down the hallway to the back door, oblivious to the trail of footprints she was leaving on the beige carpet.

Please, God, she prayed silently. *Please!*

She shoved open the back door and stepped outside. Dusk had fallen and it was difficult to see beyond the glow emanating from inside.

"Scotty! Where are you?"

"Mom!" he cried, his voice distant. "Come quick! Grampa's hurt."

Oh dear Lord, no!

She raced across the uneven ground in the direction of his voice, barely noticing that she still hadn't put on shoes. She found her son kneeling just outside the large greenhouse. His small face, white with terror, gaped up at her.

Beside him, face down and unmoving, lay her father.

"Dad!"

Charly pulled on her father's shoulder. She felt a surge of panic and swallowed hard to suppress it. She turned and shouted toward the house, "Melissa! Call 9-1-1!"

Then she leaned down, gently turned her father onto his back and grabbed one of his hands. "Dad! Dad! Can you hear me? Oh, please Dad, don't go!"

No response.

Chapter Eight

In joy or sadness, flowers are our constant friends.
Kozuko Okakura

For Charly, the next twenty minutes seemed to last an eternity and an instant, experienced through a kaleidoscope of shadows and disturbing sounds. Her father was no longer breathing, so she quickly positioned his body and began CPR. Between chest compressions and breaths blown into his mouth, she barked further instructions at her children.

While Melissa raced inside to call for help and to find a blanket, Scotty stood next to his mother, pointing the flashlight. It wasn't until later that Charly realized that the uneven illumination she had experienced during her first-aid efforts was caused by her son's terrified shaking. In the moment, she was keenly aware only of her father's closed eyes, of the damp earth beneath her knees, and of the harsh throb of her own heart pounding in her ears.

There wasn't time to think or to pray, just to breathe and pump, breathe and pump.

She was so focused that she scarcely heard the wailing siren, barely noticed the approaching lights, and was startled when a paramedic gently touched her shoulder. She turned and for a second, believed she was looking into heaven, until she realized the brilliant beam shining in her face was a headlamp worn by the attendant.

As he expertly took over, Charly fell back, exhausted. Scotty and Melissa dropped down beside her, throwing their arms around her neck and sobbing uncontrollably.

"He's going to be okay, right?" Scotty asked the second ambulance attendant, a young woman who was checking Barry's pulse and heart rate.

"Shhh, honey," said Charly, desperately wanting to ask the same question. "Let them do their work."

Within a couple of minutes, Barry coughed and his eyes fluttered open. The attendant flashed them a quick smile and switched gears, quickly hooking Barry up to oxygen and a heart monitor.

Barry weakly raised an arm toward his daughter.

"Dad?" she said, rushing to his side. "It's going to be okay."

He grimaced and tried to speak.

"Don't talk now, Dad. Save your strength."

Barry shook his head and tried to rise. "Some…thing, must tell—"

"Please, Mr. Shepherd," the male ambulance attendant said, gently holding Barry down and positioning an oxygen mask over his ashen face. "Breathe. Just concentrate on breathing. Okay?"

The female paramedic stopped talking into a cell phone, beckoned Charly over and began asking questions. Charly knew the answers—her father was sixty-two, took no medications, and had neither medical allergies nor any history of heart trouble—but she struggled to shape the words.

The paramedic's smile reached right up into her kind blue eyes. She touched Charly's hand. "It's okay. You're Faith Shepherd's sister, huh?"

Charly nodded.

"She's real good at her job."

"You…you know my sister?"

The woman smiled again. "We get to know all the dispatchers. Your sister's one of the best."

"Oh, I get it," replied Charly, finally understanding the connection. Her eldest sister had been an emergency services dispatcher in Silver Shores for many years. It was how she had met Michael.

"Okay, now," the paramedic continued, "just take a deep breath and we'll go through the questions again."

This time Charly replied easily and the woman jotted down the information. The two attendants conversed for a minute and then adjusted some of the equipment attached to Barry, readying him for transport.

Charly fiercely hugged her children as the paramedics carefully laid her father on a waiting gurney and strapped him in.

The three Shepherds rose as one and hurried alongside as the gurney was carried—the ground too muddy for wheels—to the front yard and slipped into the ambulance. Barry Shepherd lay eerily still, while the female attendant crouched over him and adjusted the plastic mask covering his face.

He looked so vulnerable.

Charly's stomach was in knots. But she called out in a clear and confident voice, "It's going to be okay, Dad. You're going to be fine. Don't worry. We're here. We're right here with you. We love you, Dad. I love you."

"Oh, Mommy," Melissa cried. "Is he going to die like Grammie?"

The ambulance doors slammed and the young girl burst into tears, squeezing her mother's hand.

"No, sweetie," Charly replied automatically. "He's not going to die."

She looked up at the male attendant who was climbing into the driver's seat.

"Is he?"

"Not if we can help it," he replied. "You'll meet us at the hospital?" Charly nodded. "Okay, then," he said and started the motor.

Charly stood, a protective arm held tightly around each child as the ambulance rolled away. A sudden *chirp* broke the air and then the full siren *whooped* into the night sky. All three of them flinched at the echoing blasts and watched in silence until the bulky vehicle disappeared.

That was when Charly whispered another fervent prayer, begging God to save her father's life.

Chapter Nine

*Death has come for me many times but finds me always in my
lovely garden
and leaves me there, I think, as an excuse to return.*
Robert Brault

The little waiting room in the Critical Cardiac Unit (CCU), empty save for the Shepherd family, was dimly lit, sparsely furnished and lacked personality. Charly's eyes slid aimlessly over the bare, bone-white walls and blue and chrome chairs, until finally resting on the pinched faces of her children. She reached across and patted each on the knee.

"Don't worry. He's going to be okay. You know your Grampa's tough."

"We didn't do the tests," Melissa said.

Her brother nodded.

"What tests?"

Melissa dramatically held up her arms, Scotty faked a huge smile and they both replied, "You know, the tests that Aunt Faith taught us."

"Oh, yeah, those tests."

During one Sunday family dinner about a month after their mother's death, Faith had taught them all the three simple tests anyone could do to identify whether someone had suffered a stroke.

"Right. I remember: ask them to smile, to raise their arms and to speak a sentence. Well done, you two." The kids beamed with pleasure. "The thing is, those're for checking for a stroke. Grampa suffered a heart attack. It's not the same thing, so they wouldn't have helped."

Melissa said, "How d'you know the difference?"

Charly hesitated. "Well, honey, I'm not real sure myself. I'll find out, but don't blame yourselves over Grampa. He was unconscious, remember?"

The pair nodded.

"So we couldn't have asked him to do anything, right?" She forced a smile. "We might be here awhile longer. Why don't you two go and get something to eat?"

Scotty leaned forward. "Saw a doughnut shop near the entrance."

Melissa looked hesitantly at her mother.

This time Charly's smile was genuine. "Sounds good, hon." She fished for her wallet and handed Melissa ten dollars. "Make mine a honey cruller."

Still, Melissa appeared uncertain.

"It's okay," Charly said as she stroked her daughter's cheek. "Go on. Nothing's going to happen."

"You sure, Mom?" Melissa gulped and twirled her long sandy hair. "I…I don't like to leave you alone."

A well of love surged through Charly and she blinked back tears. She hugged Melissa quickly, then shooed the children from the room.

A few moments later, she heard Scotty's voice as it floated along the hallway. It was too muffled to make out, but his sister's high voice carried back clearly.

"No, I don't think Grampa's gonna want a doughnut today. Maybe tomorrow."

It was then that Charly let go. She slumped into one of the hard chairs, bent her head and cried. Cried for her father, her children, herself and her mother. The tears raced down her face as she sobbed without restraint and without pause.

After several minutes, her weeping lessened. She reached for a tissue from a box on a small table and blew her nose. Then, holding her face in her hands, she silently prayed.

Please God, no. Not again. It's not fair. Don't take him, too. We need him, I *need him. Oh, please, please…*

"Charly?" whispered a voice.

Through a tangle of hair, tears and tissue, Charly looked up.

Hope stood silhouetted in the small doorway.

"Is…is he…?"

"He's alive," Charly said, her voice breaking.

"Oh, thank God," said Hope.

In one fluid motion, Charly stood and flew into her older sister's arms, grateful to feel Hope's strong body holding her.

They hugged for a long time until Hope stepped back and said tenderly, "Come, sit down and tell me what happened."

"They think he had a heart attack," Charly replied as she sat. "A cardiac episode. They're running some tests. Oh, Hope, he looked so awful. Ghastly white, perspiring…the kids…I…oh, it was horrible! I thought he was, oh—"

She glanced over and lost her breath. Hope, the daughter Eileen Shepherd had nicknamed her strong one, had tears streaming down her angular face.

Charly reached out and took her sister's hands. "Oh, Hopeful, I'm so sorry. It must be such a shock finding out this way. Don't worry."

She reached to offer Hope a tissue.

"He's going to be okay. He is." Charly knew she was saying this for herself as much as for her sister. Just as she had said it earlier for her children. It helped, she was certain, to be positive.

Hope dabbed at her eyes and nodded. She leaned back and took a deep breath. "I mean, the drive here was frightful. All I could think of was Mom and how we never got to—" she trembled and then added weakly, "say goodbye."

Charly's heart rose in her throat, her thoughts rushed into the dark past, and it took all her strength just to nod.

There had been no first aid, no hospital bed, and no doctors that dreadful day ten months ago. Worse yet, no family. For in the middle of a sunny May afternoon, Eileen Shepherd had suffered a massive stroke while sweeping her kitchen floor. The kids were at school and Charly and her father had gone to a nearby town to meet with a new supplier.

The sixty-three-year-old mother of three and grandmother of two had died alone.

For Charly, the moment she and her father entered the front door late that afternoon was seared into her memory like a ragged scar. The house seemed cold and still. Their enthusiastic greetings went unanswered, and when Charly entered the kitchen, her world shuddered to a stop.

No time to say goodbye. To say thank you. To say I love you. It was all over in an instant, and now each member of Eileen's beloved family had a lifetime of emptiness and regret ahead.

It's not going to happen again, Charly told herself. Not now. Not yet. She was sure God was going to spare her father. For a moment her pulse lurched and she felt ashamed. By praying to keep her father with her and her family, she was denying her mother their final reunion.

I'm sorry, Mom, she said silently. *I'm sure you miss him, but it's not his time. We...I need him.*

The sisters sat quietly, each engaged in their own thoughts, until Charly's children reappeared. Melissa rushed across to hug her aunt, while Scotty moved to sit beside his mother.

"Any...anything happen?" he asked.

"No," said Charly. "I think, hon, no news is good news."

"No news is good news," Scotty repeated. "Okay."

Charly glanced at the brown bag in Scotty's hand. "Something in there for me?"

"Oh! I forgot. Yeah, a honey cruller, just like you said." His face fell.

"What's wrong?"

"I didn't get one for Aunt Hope." He looked in her direction. "Sorry."

Hope reached over and ruffled his brown hair. "No problem, Mr. Scott. Your mom loves to share." She winked at Charly and reached for the little bag. "Don't you?"

Before Charly could answer, Hope had plucked free the pastry and taken a huge bite.

"Hey! Gimme."

For a second, Hope pretended to hold the doughnut away from her sister and then she offered it with a flourish. Charly finished it in two bites, then smacked her lips with approval.

"Mmm, that was good. Thanks, Scotty. Just one thing missing."

Her son grimaced.

"The other half," Charly replied, gently hip-checking her big sister.

Everyone laughed.

For a moment, their hearts were lifted.

Chapter Ten

Gather ye rosebuds while ye may, Old time is still a-flying
And this same flower that smiles today, Tomorrow will be
dying.
Robert Herrick

A shadow filled the doorway, blocking the light.

They all turned with a start and stared.

An attractive man wearing a white coat and a serious expression walked into the room.

"Are you the Shepherds? Barry Shepherd's family?"

Both Hope and Charly rose to meet the red-haired man. "I'm Hope, his daughter, and this is my sister, Charly. How's our Dad?"

"I'm Dr. Rogers. As you know, your father has had a serious cardiac episode—"

"Is Grampa gonna be okay?" Scotty blurted, joining the trio.

Dr. Rogers smiled down at him. "You must be Mr. Scott." He said the last words with a decent Scottish accent. The boy looked puzzled. "Your Grampa mentioned you. I think he's going to be just fine, young man."

"Thank God," Hope and Charly simultaneously exhaled.

The doctor studied them for a moment through a pair of sea-green eyes.

"Two of your father's arteries were eighty percent blocked, so

45

we had to perform an emergency angioplasty. That's when we send up a little balloon to open the blocked arteries. While we were in there, we added two stents."

"Stents?" Charly asked.

The doctor nodded. "They're like tiny mesh tubes. They'll prop open his arteries and keep the blood flowing to his heart."

"But he's going to be okay, right?" said Hope.

"Should be. He was lucky someone was there to administer CPR right away and that he was strong enough for the angioplasty."

Charly said, "Can we see him?"

Dr. Rogers smiled briefly. "Only for a minute or so. He's very tired and needs rest."

"We don't know how to thank you, Doctor," Hope said, taking the physician's hand and squeezing it. "You've given us back our Dad."

"Where's Daddy?" a new voice called out anxiously. "Is he okay? Hope, Charly, please tell me he's going to be all right."

A second later, Faith swept into view, filling the room with perfume and color.

Charly held out her arms and embraced her sister. "He's going to be okay, Faith. The doctor just told us."

Faith's eyes were bright with tears as she stepped back. Then, without hesitation, she flung her arms around the startled doctor.

"Oh thank you, thank you," she whispered breathlessly.

Dr. Rogers gently disentangled himself and glanced at his watch. "I have to go. We'll talk again, but for now, a quick visit and then you have to let your father rest." He paused, eyes searching the anxious faces staring back at him. "Just the adults for now. Two at a time."

The sisters nodded and exchanged a quick, knowing look.

"Follow me," Dr. Rogers added.

Hope and Faith were immediately on his heels. After a couple of steps, Faith whirled. "Please keep an eye out for Michael. He dropped me at the door and then went to find a parking spot." She paused and dabbed her eyes. "He...he didn't want me to miss another minute."

Hope put her arm around Faith's waist. "Very thoughtful. Come on, then."

Charly and the children sat and waited.

"Not fair," said Scotty, kicking at the legs of his chair.

"He's our Grampa," Melissa added. "We have a right."

Charly tried to smile. "Don't worry, kids. You'll get your turn."

"Promise?" Melissa said.

The two youngsters watched their mother, eyes wide and worried.

Charly said a silent prayer and then nodded confidently. "Promise."

At that moment, her sisters returned. Charly inhaled sharply, shocked at the look of pain and fear on both their faces. Faith sniffled into a tissue and a feeling of dread seeped deep into Charly's bones.

"He's sleeping," Hope said softly. "Your turn. First room on the right."

Faith sat and pulled Melissa onto her lap. Hope took the chair next to Scotty while Charly walked out and into the hall. She stood for a moment, gathering courage, in front of double doors boldly marked "CCU. Authorized visitors only."

She swung open one door and found herself in another hallway. It was empty and quiet except for the occasional murmur of voices and mechanical beeping. She took a deep breath, inhaling the acrid smell of bleach and urine, and stepped into the first room on the right.

Her father lay alone in a hospital bed, surrounded by chirping equipment, blinking monitors, and snaking hoses.

Charly approached him cautiously. His eyes were closed. He appeared to be breathing easily under the mask, but the stubble on his chin and cheeks stood out against his skin, which was now a sickening grayish color. He looked very drained and very defenseless.

She reached for his hand, noticed it was marred by tape and tubing, and hesitated. She swallowed and lightly stroked the parchment skin, careful not to touch the little device attached to his index finger.

Suddenly, she recalled his efforts to speak while he was being treated by the ambulance attendant.

What did you want to tell me? What could possibly be on your mind at that awful moment? Probably wanted to say you loved us. That would be like just you, Dad.

Suddenly, Charly flinched. *Did I tell him I loved him? Oh dear, did I?*

She couldn't recall a word of what she had said to him. She

leaned closer and gently rubbed his hand.

"I love you, Dad," she whispered urgently. "More than you'll ever know."

Her father remained silent and still, so she quietly watched him for a long time.

Finally, she glanced around and pulled a little stool over to his bedside. She perched, laid her head against his arm and wept.

Chapter Eleven

All my hurts my garden spade can heal.
Ralph Waldo Emerson

Charly sat on an old milking stool, fingering one of the many rust-stained rocks that littered the property, and surveyed the Sweet Shepherd Nursery in the glow of the mid-morning light. At least she was trying to, but her gaze kept returning to the spot where her father had fallen.

Was it only last night?

Still obvious was the hodgepodge of muddy ridges where the advancing and retreating tracks of the ambulance attendants mixed with those of the Shepherd clan. And near the middle, she feared she could see the outline of her father's body.

It had been a challenge earlier that morning to get the kids off to school. They had all been tired, yet so keyed up by sugar, caffeine and worry that none of them had had a decent night's sleep. Of course, the children had wanted to go to the hospital and were bitterly disappointed when Charly dropped them off at their schools instead.

"Please, Mom," Scotty had whined, reluctant to leave the car. "After all, school'll always be there, but, well…Grampa might not."

"Your Grampa's going to be fine."

"Mom, please," added Melissa.

"Come on, guys," Charly said. "He's getting the best possible care. The most important thing is that he rests and there's nothing

49

you can do for him except to stay in school. Y'know how important it is to him."

"Yeah," Melissa said, while her brother just sighed.

"Don't worry," Charly called out as Scotty slammed the door. "We'll go right after dinner, okay?"

Her son's expression lightened, and then he turned and raced up the steps.

As she did every time she dropped them off and every evening before she fell asleep, Charly offered prayers to the Lord, laying her family at the feet of God.

A couple of hours later, Charly shivered and pulled the zipper of her fleece jacket up to her neck.

"What am I going to do?" she asked aloud, tossing the rock into a weedy area at the back and then wiping the rust stain off her gloves.

She stood, picked up a rake and dragged it through the mud. Some of the distressing marks from the night before disappeared.

"Okay," she continued aloud, thrusting the rake up to the sky as she tramped between garden beds, "we're short of money, we're short of stock—" she exhaled peevishly, "short of staff, and given that Spring's around the corner, short of time."

She watched a chubby robin poking its beak into the soil. "Well, little fella, there's one thing we've got a lot of and that's 'short'."

"That's not the only thing," chimed a trio of voices.

Charly spun and smiled to see her sisters, accompanied by her brother-in-law, strolling into view.

"Oh, yeah?" said Charly. "What else?"

Before answering, Hope trotted into one of the equipment sheds and returned with two Dutch hoes and a shovel. She handed the hoes to Faith and Michael and then the three marched over to Charly.

"Okay. I'm waiting."

"You've got a lot of one other thing, little sister," Faith replied. "And that's—" she glanced at the others and then the threesome sang out, "our support."

Charly's heart swelled at the sight of her caring and helpful family. It will be okay. It will. *Thank you, dear Lord.*

Faith thrust her hoe straight in front of her, blade toward the earth. Michael dropped the handle of his over top, and finally, Hope piled on the head of her shovel. With a grin, Charly laid her rake tines against the tangle of gardening tools.

"All for one Shepherd, and one Shepherd for all," the four shouted and then burst into laughter.

"Don't you worry, little missy," added Michael, thrusting an arm around Charly's shoulders. "You're not alone. The man's here."

Faith beamed.

"Hey!" retorted Hope, stepping in front of Michael. "The man's outnumbered by us three fabulous Shepherd women, and don't you forget it."

Michael threw back his head, bald spot glinting in the sun, and laughed. "Think I ever could?"

"All right then," Charly said. "Let's get rolling."

And within a matter of minutes, she had assigned each a simple task and they were all hard at work.

Charly appreciated the physicality of her efforts. As time passed, her muscles toiled and she fell into a familiar routine of exertion and completion, followed by satisfaction. Though tasks like digging and cleaning were repetitious, the mind-numbing tedium allowed her brain to slide into neutral and not obsess about her father's condition or about their financial setback.

As she watched her family diligently laboring nearby, she hoped they were sharing a similar experience. The duty nurse had told Charly the same thing she had later suggested to her children, "At the moment, there is nothing you can do for Barry Shepherd but let him rest." The nurse had even recommended no visitors until the evening, as Barry's condition overnight had remained stable but weak.

By one o'clock, much had been accomplished. The rich soil in all three garden beds was loose, mixed with compost and manure, and ready for planting. The potting tables and dozens of pots had been cleaned and disinfected, every garden tool had been examined, oiled and sharpened, and the windows in both greenhouses sparkled.

Only two mishaps occurred. A rake handle shattered when Michael unwisely used it to leverage a heavy patio stone, and a set of fluorescent-glowing lights splintered under Faith's feet when she lost her balance in one of the greenhouses.

Charly gazed at the outdoor scene, so different from just three hours earlier, and like her Father before her, she saw that it was good. There was much still to do, but the family had tackled several essential tasks.

Though not entirely squelched, her earlier feelings of panic and desperation were diffused, replaced by the feathery stirrings of optimism. She chuckled inwardly as Faith, on her knees in the smaller greenhouse, battled to separate a couple of plastic pots.

"Don't worry about them, Faith," she called, taking a break from inspecting a hose line. "Lunchtime."

Faith glanced up, plump face shining with sweat, and waved. With a satisfied *thump*, she jammed the pots onto a stack and peeled off her gardening gloves.

"Hey Michael, Hope, time for some food," Charly shouted to the pair who were at the far end of the nursery, shoveling compost into a wheelbarrow.

The two stopped instantaneously, pitched their tools and began tramping toward Charly.

Charly chuckled. "Hold your horses, guys! Got to get it ready first."

But they kept coming and soon strode right past her. "We've got it all worked out," Hope offered, over her shoulder. "Mikey's cutting bread and I'm on cold-cut patrol."

"Hey, wait for me!" cried Faith, hurrying past Charly. "I'll do coffee and dessert!"

Chapter Twelve

One of the most delightful things about a garden is the
anticipation it provides.
W.E. Johns

D oes it hurt?" asked Scotty, pointing to the wires attached to Barry Shepherd's chest.

"Yeah, Grampa, does it?" his sister echoed.

"Kids," Charly said. "The nurse just told us he can't answer when he's on oxygen."

She studied her father. Though still gray, his skin appeared less transparent, his blue eyes were clear again and he seemed comfortable, almost comical in his yellow hospital pajamas. For the first time in many hours, Charly felt her body relax slightly, and when she breathed, the air nearly reached the bottom of her lungs.

But she still felt disoriented and on the verge of panic. She was now solely responsible for her family, their home and the business, but was embarrassed to even think this, much less admit it to her father, given the shocking event he had just experienced.

Of course, when she was married, she and her husband Matt Robinson had shared their family responsibilities. They had owned a home a few blocks closer to town, near Matt's real estate brokerage business, and Charly had raised the children and worked part-time for her father.

Charly had believed deeply in their lifelong marital commitment, and while it was difficult at times to juggle schedules and pay all the bills, their shared efforts and goals eased much of her anxiety. When times were tough, the young couple would reassure one another by clinking tea cups and saying, "We'll figure something out 'cause we've got each other."

But somehow, during their fourth year of marriage, things had shifted. Matt blamed his too-frequent absences on client demands, and Charly spent more and more hours alone with her toddler daughter and infant son.

And then one day, Matt had phoned. Not from his office in Silver Shores, but from Hong Kong.

And…it was all over.

He said he had fallen in love with an international client and was giving everything up to be with her.

No more marriage. No more fatherhood. No more future plans with Charly.

The instant she had put the phone down, she had experienced two overwhelming emotions. Disbelief and dread.

Now, as she watched her ailing father, Charly realized those two sentiments were once again fluttering in her veins. And this time, the family responsibilities were hers alone.

Barry shifted uncomfortably in the hospital bed and struggled to raise an arm.

Charly reached for him. "It's okay, Dad."

"It doesn't hurt?" Melissa asked, voice rising with hope.

Barry nodded.

The two children beamed.

"That's epic, Gramps," Scotty said. "Just epic." He hitched himself up onto the bed beside his grandfather.

Barry smiled briefly beneath the plastic oxygen mask.

"You're missing out on some super desserts," Scotty continued. "Folks've been droppin' by all kinds of goodies. Haven't they, Mom?"

Charly nodded. It was true. Word of Barry's attack had spread quickly in the small town, and within hours, friends and neighbors had begun arriving with a variety of fresh-baked goods.

"Not just desserts, Grampa," added Melissa. "Other stuff, like casseroles, salads, bread. Betcha Mom won't need to cook for weeks!"

"Yeah," her brother said. "And Uncle Michael's already got dibs on the pies."

Barry actually laughed, fogging up the little plastic mask. Then he started to cough and the others froze. After a long moment, Barry successfully took a couple of deep, smooth breaths and flashed them a thumbs-up.

The trio of visitors grinned and relaxed.

"D'you think you'll be home by next weekend?" said Melissa.

Barry blinked.

"Honey," said Charly. "We don't have any idea about when Grampa's coming home." She squeezed her father gently on the shoulder. "He's getting better. We want to make sure he has the time to fully recover. Okay?"

Melissa twirled her hair. "Okay, but don't forget our band recital. It's next Saturday night." She pulled her chair closer to the bed. "I'm first clarinet. You promised you'd come."

With an effort, her grandfather raised a hand and placed it over Melissa's. The girl bent and kissed it.

Dr. Rogers walked into the room. "Hello, all," he said.

He stepped over and checked a couple of monitors, jotted something onto a chart, then looked down at his patient. Charly was struck by how gracefully he moved. "How're you doing, Mr. Shepherd? Any pain?"

Barry shook his head.

Dr. Rogers smiled. "That's good." He watched another monitor and then fiddled with a drip line. "Not too much longer, folks. He's doing really well, but he needs rest."

"Thank you, Doctor," Charly said. "Okay, kids. Time to move."

"Awww, Mom!" they both exclaimed. "Not yet."

Dr. Rogers put up a hand. "Don't blame your mom." He smacked the name tag on his coat. "Doctor's orders. You can come back tomorrow."

"Oh, all right," Scotty said.

Melissa kissed Barry's cheek and hugged him. "See ya, Grampa."

Scotty leaned over and gently punched his grandfather's shoulder.

"Later, Dude."

Barry's face brightened and he nodded.

As she watched her two loving and well-behaved children, Charly felt something else stir in her. Hope. She had experienced a similar inkling earlier when her siblings had pitched in to help, though it had quickly fizzled, and vanished completely by the time she had arrived at the hospital.

Now she realized that these new challenges were very different from the shocking breakdown of her marriage nearly nine years earlier.

Yes, with her mother deceased and her father hospitalized, she was solely responsible for herself and her family, but the kids were older, she had more work experience and most importantly, she had proven that she could rise to the occasion. After all, she had successfully survived her ex-husband's horrendous betrayal. She had taken back her maiden name, both for herself and for her children, she had moved back into her parents' house, and she had stepped up to full-time nursery work.

And for the most part, she and her children couldn't be happier.

Chapter Thirteen

When gardeners garden, it is not just plants that grow,
but the gardeners themselves.
Ken Druse

After she had packed the kids off to school the next morning, Charly poured a fresh cup of tea, grabbed the portable phone, a notepad and a pen, and settled at the kitchen table. Dozens of people had left voicemail messages over the past couple of days, expressing shock and concern over Barry's heart attack and wanting information on his condition. Many had offered to help in any way possible, and some had even called a second time.

It was these follow-up calls that spurred Charly into action. She knew from her mother's recent passing that most of the folks of Silver Shores were incredibly kind and wonderfully supportive.

There was a fistful of people, however, who felt that another's tragedy was an opportunity to meddle, and sensing even a whiff of encouragement, these few would march in with a military takeover in mind. If she didn't respond in a timely and poised manner, Charly knew her home would be overrun within a matter of hours. As it had been almost immediately following her mother's death.

At the time, the Shepherds were in a state of shock, numbly going through the motions. This allowed others to step in and make decisions that were clearly beyond their purview. The wrong flowers were ordered, some mourners were unaccountably turned away, and two women spoke, unsolicited, at Eileen Shepherd's memorial service.

By the time Charly and her sisters realized what was happening, it was too late. Any expression of their vexation or hint of their anger would have distressed their already brokenhearted father and further spoiled the arrangements for their mother's funeral.

So she went on the offensive. Her first calls were to those two uninvited speakers, whom Hope had nicknamed the dragon ladies: Millie Peel, the town's head librarian, and Veronica Bergeron, a retired accountant with too much time on her hands. Both women were widowed empty-nesters and sat on the St. Peter's by-the-Sea's advisory council and on the women's auxiliary, as had Eileen Shepherd. That was why they believed they had the right and the duty to rush in and "handle things for poor dear Eileen's family."

Charly targeted the librarian first. She frequently visited the town's small library with the kids and regularly exchanged pleasantries with the wiry-haired woman, who often staffed the front desk.

"Hello, Mrs. Peel? It's Charly Shepherd."

"Oh, Charly, my dear. How is your father? I was just about to come by again. I'm so—"

"I'm sorry," replied Charly. "Again?"

"Yes, dear. I came by yesterday. I'm sure you're at your wit's end and need my help, but there was no one home and the doors were locked."

Mrs. Peel's dry voice was accusatory, as though the Shepherd home should always be open to her, and Charly had to take a second breath so as not to snap back. She shouldn't have worried, as Mrs. Peel rambled on.

"I left the double raspberry crumble on the rocking chair by the front door. You did get it, didn't you? I used my very best fruit from last year. I know how much dear Barry loves raspberries. And as you know, crops were poor."

"Of course," Charly replied hastily, running her mind quickly over the variety of foodstuffs that had arrived. "One of my sisters must have found it. I bet it's in the freezer, and now I'm looking forward to eating it. That was very kind of you."

She heard Mrs. Peel's intake of breath, but plunged on before the older woman could speak.

"Just wanted to let you know that Dad's doing well. We're not sure when he'll be able to come home, but I doubt he'll be up for company for a while."

"Heart trouble, was it? My dear Jake, God rest his soul, had all sorts—"

"Yes," Charly said again, wanting desperately to avoid a long segue into Jake Peel's final days. "But he's had a procedure which should make all the difference. Now, I wish I could chat longer, but I have so many people to call and thank. You know how kind folks are. So if you don't mind, I'll let you go."

"But—"

"Goodbye, Mrs. Peel. I'll tell Dad you asked about him." With that, Charly punched the TALK button on the phone and heaved a big sigh of relief. One down, only one to go.

She took a sip of her forgotten tea, grimaced at its tepid temperature and rose to make another. After it had steeped, she poured while dialing Mrs. Bergeron.

The retired number cruncher answered on the third ring, her voice as crisp as a fall frost. "This is Veronica Bergeron speaking. Who is calling, please?"

"Hello, Mrs. Bergeron," Charly replied. "It's Charly Shepherd."

"Charly! Well, it's about time, I do say. I was beginning to wonder, young woman, if you were ever going to give me the courtesy of a return phone call."

Charly just sat, suddenly blinking tears, unable to reply. She hadn't heard Mrs. Bergeron's voice since her mother's funeral and the sound of the elderly lady's icy tone jerked Charly's thoughts back to that terrible day in May.

Though she still grieved profoundly for her mother, Charly had been able to control her emotions by mentally distancing herself from her loss. She thought of her mother constantly and regularly chatted to her, and for the most part, was able to maintain her composure.

But oh, how she hated to cry. Hated the feeling of loss, of powerlessness, of despair. And these past few months she had tried to avoid anything that would place her in that position of vulnerability. Yet with a mere few words from this woman, she was mentally hijacked, once again slumped in the church pew, reeling from an unimaginable scene. Her beloved father, moving stiffly in a new blue suit, bending to kiss her mother's casket.

"You still there?" Mrs. Bergeron's voice was abruptly in her head. "Hello? Charly? What's going on?"

"I'm sorry, Mrs. Bergeron," Charly heard herself replying automatically. She bit her lip to control her emotions and then added, "Uh…I…I spilled some tea, caught me by surprise. I *am* sorry."

"Weeell," Mrs. Bergeron said doubtfully.

"I won't keep you," said Charly, head aching. "Just wanted to thank you for your calls about my father." She wanted this phone conversation to be over, this distressing memory to drop back into her past, so she hurried on. "He's much improved, but not out of the woods yet. We're not sure when he'll be coming home. Thanks again, Mrs. Bergeron."

"Wait! When can I—"

Charly blurted, "Not at the moment, thanks," and quickly hung up.

Immediately afterward, she felt ashamed. She had been rude and not altogether truthful with either woman. Not the sort of behavior her parents would have expected of her.

Charly pinched her throbbing forehead and stared out the back window. She vowed to apologize the next time she saw the women, and since she expected them to arrive on the doorstep sooner rather than later, despite having asked them not to, she decided to let fate take its course.

After all, there was just so much more that needed her immediate attention.

She made one more call.

A deep voice responded, "St. Peter's by-the-Sea. The blessings of God upon you. How may I help?"

"Hello, Pastor Joe?"

The man replied, "Yes. This is himself, Pastor Joe."

Charly immediately relaxed, comforted by his familiar soft Irish accent and quirky expressions. Although semi-retired and in his early eighties, Pastor Joe Ritchie had recently returned to St. Peter's as a temporary replacement until a new, permanent pastor could be chosen. Since he had been the church's most popular pastor for over fifty years, the members of his congregation were delighted and thankful for his return.

"To whom am I speaking?"

"It's Charly Shepherd, Pastor."

"Charly! How nice to hear from you." There was a pause. "Is there anything wrong, dear?"

Charly bit back her tears and gulped. "Y...yes, Pastor. My father had...he had a heart attack yesterday."

"Oh, my great goodness! Your Da, is he all right?"

"Yes. Yes, we're very grateful, Pastor. It's going to take some time, but I believe he'll be okay."

"Thanks be to God. That's a spot of good news, my dear. What can I do?"

Charly smiled at the elderly clergyman's immediate offer of assistance. She could visualize him sitting in the kitchen of the small cottage rectory. The diminutive and wiry man, wrinkled as the bark on the Douglas firs that surrounded St. Peter's, would be sipping his tea and scanning the sports pages.

"Well, could you visit him in the hospital? I know how much he'd appreciate seeing you."

"Of course, Charly. I'll nip by this morning after I've finished my *cup a scald*. Is there anything else? Anyone I should tell on your behalf? Someone from the women's auxiliary or the council?"

"No," Charly said, a little too quickly.

There was a muffled sound on the other end of the phone line.

It may have been a chuckle, but Charly wasn't sure. "I'm sorry, Pastor," she added hastily. "It's just that I've already spoken to Mrs. Bergeron and Mrs. Peel."

"Straight to the offensive. A fine strategy, my dear. Always used by my beloved Rovers. Now, are you sure there's nothing more I can do?"

"Yes, Pastor, thank you."

"Mind yourself, Charly. Goodbye and my blessings go with you. And remember, everyone lays a burden on the willing horse."

With that he hung up, leaving Charly to seriously consider the accuracy of his last words.

After a while, she rose and looked at her second cup of tea.

Untouched and cold. *That's it! Caffeine. I need caffeine.* She refilled the kettle and plugged it in for the third time. *No more calls, no more interruptions until I've had my own cuppa.*

She smiled, again thinking of Pastor Joe. Then a thundering noise froze her expression. Charly turned from the back window and took a couple of steps toward the living room. Through the wide panes of glass, she watched with dismay as an old motorbike rumbled into view. It stuttered to a stall and her brother-in-law dragged himself free.

So much for a quiet cup of tea.

Charly walked to open the front door. She immediately felt guilty. After all, the guy was giving up his free time to help her. She should be grateful, she knew. And she was, truly.

It was just that she wasn't used to having anyone other than her parents intimately involved in her work. She didn't like the feeling of needing help, nor of being beholden to others.

Don't be so stubborn and ungrateful, she chastised herself as she turned the knob. One minute she was panicking about handling everything by herself and the next she was complaining about not being alone!

"Hey, there, missy!" exclaimed Michael as she pulled open the door. "Figured you could use a helping hand." He air-kissed her cheek and strode inside. "Any coffee?"

Chapter Fourteen

*Among gardeners, enthusiasm and experience rarely exist in
equal measures.*
Roger B. Swain

Y ou've decided *what?*" Charly said as she furiously stirred a
mug of instant coffee.

Michael plunked down at the kitchen table and tossed
his baseball cap, emblazoned with the initials of the Silver Shores
Police Department, onto the chair beside him.

"Helping you with the nursery's my new retirement project.
Faith's idea, and I think it's a doozey." He grinned and looked up
at Charly. "You gonna stir the java right out of that cup, or what?"

Charly blushed. "Sorry," she said, handing over the steaming
mug.

She poured her own coffee and joined her brother-in-law at the
table, wondering how she could politely get him to change his mind.
This was one extra responsibility she didn't want or need.

"That's awfully kind of you, Michael," she started slowly, "but
surely you'd rather do something else. Something fun? It's your
retirement, after all. You've worked hard to earn it."

Michael blew across the top of his mug and shook his head.
"Can't abide golf, Charly. Too early for fishin,' and with Faith still
working, there's no point in going sightseeing."

He stretched his long, denim-clad legs.

"What about your new consulting practice? Thought the good ol' SSPD would've had you back on contract."

It was Michael's turn to flush. He was silent for a couple of moments, staring at his coffee. Then he flicked an embarrassed gaze up at Charly.

"Please don't tell anyone, especially Faith, but. . . it seems they don't really need me."

Ouch. Poor guy.

Michael Lawless was a proud, talented and hard-working man. Though he didn't speak much about his childhood, Charly had learned bits and pieces from Faith. Michael, along with his mother and older brother, were all bright and musical, but their lives were anything but melodic. A violent alcoholic father had created havoc, physically, emotionally and financially. The Lawless family was poor and often shell-shocked, but somehow his mother had managed to raise a pair of trustworthy, law-abiding and loving sons.

A bit old-fashioned and rough around the edges, Michael's language and work ethic always seemed to Charly to come more from her father's era than from a guy in his mid-fifties. Like those of her father's generation, Michael's job defined him as a person. He was a man's man, a cop and committed to his community.

Charly looked across the table, seeing her brother-in-law in a new light. Some of his recent comments and reactions, which at the time had seemed a bit peculiar, even for Michael, now made sense. She realized with a jolt of surprise and pity that the newly retired chief of police had been struggling to deal with the loss of his identity.

"Well, Michael, their loss is definitely my gain." She reached over the table and shook his hand. "Glad to have you aboard."

A look, first of gratitude and then of relief, flickered across his craggy face, and Charly thought she saw him quickly blink away tears as he rose to his feet.

"Now then," he began, then paused to drain his mug before continuing, "This is the law of the Yukon, and ever she makes it plain, send not your foolish and feeble, send me your strong and your sane." He slammed down his mug for emphasis. "This is the law of the Yukon, that only the strong shall thrive, that surely the weak shall perish, and only the fit survive."

Charly jumped up. "Far's I know, Mikey, we're in the fabulous state of Oregon, but other than that I'm with you and Robert Service one hundred and ten percent."

He beamed and jammed on his baseball cap.

"Of course," Charly put her hands on her hips, "so long as you obey *our* family's law."

Michael's bushy eyebrows rose in surprise. "And that would be?"

"Shepherds lead, everyone else follows."

With that, she tugged down hard on the peak of his cap, bleated like a sheep, and hustled toward the back door.

Fifteen minutes later, Charly was banging on the plywood walls of the storage area at the front of the larger greenhouse. In the center of the eight-by-eight-foot space lay a hastily piled jumble of potting mixes, plastic buckets, and an assortment of tools and fertilizers.

"Dad built this addition about a decade ago," said Charly, neatly stepping over a roll of chicken wire before thumping along another stretch of plywood. "At the time, he needed more floor storage space, but now I'd like to hang some cupboards and get a lot of this junk out of the way."

Michael nodded while fiddling with a hand sprayer. He pressed the spray lever, but nothing squirted out of the nozzle.

"Think the construction's strong enough," said Charly, tugging free a tarp to reveal four medium-sized wall cabinets resting on the concrete. "Should be able to have a couple of these along each side. That'll help a lot."

"That's why you're banging on the walls?" Michael asked, peering into the seemingly blocked nozzle.

"Uh-uhh…looking for a stud," replied Charly.

Michael's face reddened and he shot Charly an astonished glance.

Charly giggled. "Not that kind of stud, you goof." She rapped against the wood. "A wall stud. You know, for support."

"Right," Michael replied, eyes again downcast, madly pumping the sprayer lever.

"Think the stud finder's inside somewhere. Uh, Mikey," Charly motioned toward the sprayer, "I'd be careful of that if I were you. It's been rinsed, but there's always a little water—"

At that moment, the nozzle head exploded open, squirting a blast of liquid into Michael's face.

This time, Charly laughed heartily. She had cleaned the sprayer herself, so she knew that it contained nothing harmful, and the sight of Michael blinking, dripping and sputtering, was too much. She did offer him her neckerchief, but seeing her lanky brother-in-law frantically swabbing his face with a coral and teal patterned scarf made her howl even louder.

In the distance, she heard the house phone ringing. She caught her breath and gasped. "I'd better get that. Have a look at how the cupboards're supposed to be mounted, okay? And I'll track down the stud finder."

Charly raced to the back door and sprinted down the hall just in time to pick up the phone mid-ring.

"Hel...hello!" she answered breathlessly. "Charly Shepherd speaking."

"This is Dr. Rogers," the now familiar baritone echoed in the receiver, "from the CCU."

Charly felt what little air she had left in her body implode. She gripped the phone more tightly. "My Dad...is...is my Dad okay?"

"What? Oh, yes, yes, of course. I'm sorry, didn't mean to worry you. In fact, it's the opposite. He's doing so well, we're moving him out of the CCU this afternoon into a regular ward."

"Oh..." Relief flickered through Charly's body. "I'm so glad, thank you."

"You're planning on visiting him this evening as usual?"

"Yes."

"Excellent. Do you think you'd have the time to buy him an electric shaver?"

"Electric shaver?"

Dr. Rogers chuckled. "I know it's an unusual request, but your father's going to be on blood thinners from now on and we don't recommend the use of disposable or straight razors. Too many nicks. He's getting a little antsy about his stubble, another sure sign he's feeling better. Don't worry if you can't get one tonight, within the next day or so would be fine. Well, I've got—"

"I know you're extremely busy, Dr. Rogers," Charly rushed to say, "but d'you have any suggestions? For an electric shaver, I mean.

It's been a while since…uh…" Her voice petered out as she realized how foolish she sounded.

"Sorry," he said cheerfully. "I'm a multi-blade disposable kinda guy." And with that, he hung up.

Charly didn't get much chance to ponder her purchase, as she was startled by a bizarre noise. For a moment, she believed someone was firing a machine gun in her backyard.

Then she heard Michael yelling. And immediately following that, the *rat-tat-tat* noise started all over again.

Charly rushed into the backyard, shouting Michael's name. The noise led her to the large greenhouse, her heart thudding wildly.

Though grim-faced under his ball cap, Michael appeared safe enough. He stood, semi-crouched like a soldier on patrol, clutching a cordless drill in his hands.

"Michael! You all right?" asked Charly, panic waning. "What was that noise?"

"I'm fine," he said, eyes fixed ahead of him. "Just a little argument with the wall."

Charly cocked her head. "What?"

She followed his gaze until her eyes came to rest on one of the plywood walls. Her jaw dropped. The rough surface was punctured by a pointless zigzagging line of small holes, as though someone had lost their balance and sprayed it with an automatic rifle.

Charly blinked in disbelief. She looked at the drill in her brother-in-law's hands and then at the dark perforations in the wall.

"But…but all those holes," she finally managed to sputter. "What on earth were you doing?"

Michael flipped the hand tool, aimed the long skinny drill bit at the sky and punched the control trigger several times. The drill screamed unevenly, like someone gunning a gas pedal.

"A man can only wait so long. I finally tried to find the studs myself."

"You what?!"

The middle-aged man had the good grace to be embarrassed. A dusky blush seeped across his cheeks. He smiled sheepishly.

"When the first few holes found air, I got a little impatient." He jammed a finger on the trigger and the drill whined. "So, I kinda just let 'er loose."

Charly was speechless and stood, slack-jawed, as her brain whirled. This was the guy who just made her nursery his retirement project. Oh dear, what was she going to do?

"Don't you worry," Michael said, as though reading her mind. "I've got jim-dandy news."

This ought to be good, thought Charly. "Okay," she replied weakly. "I'll bite."

Michael jammed the drill bit into a number of holes in quick succession. "I found the studs, and once we mount the cabinets, no one's going see the other holes."

At that, he stood proudly in front of his handyman efforts, crossed his arms and winked.

Charly groaned.

Chapter Fifteen

*One of the most important resources that a garden makes
available for use
is the gardener's own body. A garden gives the body the
dignity of working
in its own support. It is a way of rejoining the human race.*
Wendell Berry

O h, Dad," Charly said, leaning over and kissing him. "It's so
good to hear your voice again."

Barry Shepherd smiled. "It's sure great to be heard."

An elderly man in the next bed chortled. "You don't know the
half of it," he bellowed, fiddling with one of his hearing aids. "He's
been talking to beat the band ever since he arrived." He winked slyly.
"Two lovely women just left."

Hope and Charly looked at their father.

Barry shrugged. "Just your mother's friends, Millie and Veronica.
Very sweet of them to call. Oh, and Pastor Joe came by again."

"Ha!" shouted his bedmate. "That little holy man's a hoot!"
He peered up at the sisters. "You must be the daughters. I'm Stan.
Stantheman Hubenig."

Charly and Hope avoided eye contact and shouted back in unison,
"Hello, Mr. Hubenig."

As she stepped back to let Hope embrace their father, Charly
glanced around the new hospital room, relieved to see that it was

a typical four-bed ward furnished with very little scary medical equipment. Even more rewarding, her father was sitting up, free from tubes and monitors, and actually looked hearty and relaxed in a fresh pair of yellow pajamas.

Hubenig glanced at Barry. "You weren't whistlin' Dixie, my friend. These two're as pretty as peaches."

Hope and Charly blushed.

"But isn't there a third one?" Hubenig boomed, eyes locked on the Shepherd women.

Charly nodded.

"Our sister, Faith, is babysitting Charly's kids." Hope tucked a small bouquet of candy-cane Camellias into a vase on the window sill.

At that moment, a nurse appeared next to Hubenig's bed and shouted, "Hello, Mr. Hubenig." She smiled at the Shepherds and then yanked shut the privacy curtain, blocking their view. "Time to change your catheter bag."

Hubenig hollered back from behind the curtain, "Why don't you just tell the whole floor, woman?"

All three Shepherds burst out laughing, then made even more noise trying to hush each other.

After taking a moment to regain control, Barry managed to blurt, "How's the nursery?" He stretched briefly, then grimaced. "This sitting around in bed's no good for my arthritis. Can't wait to get back into my gumboots. You know, dears, don't think I've ever been out of the Sweet Shepherd's dirt for more than three days running."

"The nursery's fine, Dad," said Charly. "The whole family's pitching in."

"Yeah," Hope added slyly. "Michael's even volunteered to be the nursery's new handyman."

Barry's jaw dropped. "Michael? Handyman?" His blue eyes fixed onto Charly's face. "You're letting that...that klutz handle my power tools?" He fell back onto his pillow in a dramatic exaggeration of anxiety. "Heavens to Betsy, Charly, don't let him touch the chain saw. Faith would never forgive us."

The sisters chuckled.

"It's going to be crazy," suggested Charly. "You won't believe what he—"

She hesitated, uncertain whether she should continue. Though she couldn't wait to tell them all the wacky details about Michael's latest escapade, she didn't want to humiliate her brother-in-law.

"Believe what?" asked Hope, while her father gazed at her with expectation. "Come on, Charly, you're talking about Michael. You gotta tell us. You know you do. Doesn't she, Dad?"

Barry's eyes were bright with interest. "Well, Charly," he hitched himself up higher, "we're a very close-knit family. Interested in what everyone's doing." He paused, features darkening for a moment. "Would Michael be hurt by this revelation?"

That's exactly what Charly had been thinking.

"Hurt?" cried Hope. "Our Mikey? That'll be the day. Bet ya he's as proud as a peacock about whatever he's done." She gazed steadily at her sister. "Tell me he wasn't."

But Charly couldn't. A vision of Michael, positioned self-importantly in front of the wall, popped into her mind.

"Okay, okay," she finally admitted. "You're right. He'd probably be hurt if I didn't tell you."

Hope hiked up onto her father's bed and patted the mattress encouragingly.

"Come on, dear," her father said. "Don't keep me in suspense any longer. After all, you don't want me having another heart attack, do you?"

The sisters gasped.

Barry smiled at their stunned reaction. "Kidding, girls. Just kidding."

Hope exhaled with relief.

"Okaaay," Charly began doubtfully, but after the first few words, she found she was getting a kick out of entertaining the others with the details of the stud-finding incident. By the time she got to the part where Michael was nervously revving up the drill gun while she examined the holes in the plywood, her family members were laughing so hard they were crying and holding up their hands, begging Charly to stop.

She did, finally, and everyone took a few moments to recover.

"Oh, my goodness," Barry whispered, wiping tears from his eyes. "That did me the world of good, that did. Better than any drug.

71

Thank you, dear."

Charly dipped her head in acknowledgement and then added, "Can't take any credit, Dad. It's all down to our beloved, crazy Michael."

"He's a one-of-a-kind goofball, that's for sure," said Hope.

After a few moments, Barry's expression turned serious and he asked, "What's happening on the insurance front?"

Hope and Charly exchanged a rapid glance. They had earlier agreed to spare their father any apprehension by glossing over the nursery's money problems.

"Don't you worry, Dad," replied Hope. "We've got it all under control."

He frowned. "You mean they're going to pay out the insurance?"

"Everything's fine, Dad," Charly added hastily. "We're much more interested in you. The doctors say you're doing real well. How're you feeling? Any pain?"

"Nope. Feel right as rain." He rubbed a large hand across the week-long stubble which darkened his cheeks and chin. "Or I would if I didn't look like Grizzly Adams."

Hope grinned. "We've got that covered, too."

She glanced at Charly.

Charly held up a linen shopping bag. "Belated Happy Valentine's Day, Dad."

A look of surprise filled Barry's face as he hesitantly took the gift. Once he had pulled the box free of the bag, his expression turned to one of pleasure, and he smiled broadly.

"An electric shaver! They told me my days of disposable razors were history." His gaze rested happily on his daughters. "How thoughtful!"

His fingers were fumbling to open the package when the privacy curtain flew back and Stan Hubenig was once again staring at them from his bed.

The old man whistled. "Well, well, well," Hubenig bellowed. "That's one humdinger of a shaver you got there, Barry." He leaned toward them and rubbed together a skinny thumb and forefinger, exhibiting the universal sign for something pricey. "Wish I had daughters who spoiled me like that." He glanced at the Shepherd sisters, eyebrow tufts raised. "You sure are one lucky son of a gun."

Barry's smile grew wider. "I know," he replied. He blinked for a moment as tears glistened behind his eyelashes. He sat up and firmly clasped his daughters' hands in his.

Charly's heart flipped and she felt Hope stir nearby. Charly glanced over. Her older sister's lovely face was taut with emotion.

"I am very blessed," said Barry. "And I thank our dear Lord for it every day."

"Amen," his daughters echoed. "Amen."

Chapter Sixteen

Wisdom is oftentimes nearer when we stoop than when we soar.
William Wordsworth

L ater that evening, while Charly was drying and putting away the last of the supper dishes, she spied Melissa hovering hesitantly in the kitchen doorway.

"Everything all right, Lissa?"

Melissa swallowed.

Charly noticed that her daughter was holding her hands behind her back, as though hiding something.

"Melissa?"

"Well," the young girl started. "I'm not sure."

Charly stopped piling dishes and turned to give her daughter her full attention.

"Not sure about what, honey?"

After another long moment, Melissa bit her lower lip and walked toward her mother.

"Are we in trouble, Mom?"

Charly blinked, momentarily taken aback. "Uh...of course we're not in trouble. Whatever makes you think that?"

As she approached her mother, Melissa brought her left hand

into view. Her fingers clutched a piece of off-white paper.

"What's that?"

"It's a letter. I...I found it in your office." The pre-teen's cheeks flamed, highlighting the sprinkling of freckles across her nose. "I wasn't snooping, Mom, honest! I was just looking for that form for the recital and—" Her eyes dropped. "I found this."

She thrust the paper at her mother.

A quick glance told Charly that it was the formal letter from the insurance company, informing them that the coverage on the nursery was cancelled. Charly berated herself for being so careless as to leave the letter lying about. She had meant to put it away, but had been distracted by a phone call.

She believed in always being honest with her children and making sure that they participated in most family decisions. A mature and thoughtful twelve-year-old, Melissa understood most domestic situations, but her energetic younger brother less so. Sometimes, as a result, Charly confided more in her daughter than her son. Charly feared this might create an imbalance in her relationship with her children, something she didn't like or want, but she believed it was the most appropriate approach.

Finances were one of the few family issues she generally didn't share with her children, and in particular, she had hoped to keep this missed payment fiasco private.

"What's going on?"

It was Scotty's turn to stand in the doorway. He looked from Charly to Melissa and hesitated to enter.

"We're in big trouble, that's what," said Melissa. "Big trouble."

Scotty's mouth twisted. "Hey, don't look at me! I haven't done anything wrong."

"Nobody's in trouble and nobody's done anything wrong," Charly responded adamantly. She gestured toward the table. "Come on, kids, have a seat. Got something to tell you."

The siblings exchanged a glance and then slowly took their seats.

Charly headed to the fridge, pulled out the skim milk and placed it on the table. She added three glasses and a container of freshly made oatmeal raisin cookies. As she poured, the kids each grabbed a cookie and began munching.

Charly sat opposite them and placed the letter on the table in front of her. "I'm sorry, I probably should have told you this sooner, but it's been a bit of a zoo, what with your Grampa's heart attack and all."

Chewing contentedly, her children waited.

Charly took a sip of milk and began, "First things first, I want to repeat what I just said, so that you both understand completely. No one is in trouble and no one has done anything wrong. Okay?"

She looked at the two faces she loved the most. Melissa's expression softened but remained guarded. Scotty licked milk off his lips and began kicking his chair leg.

"Good." Charly tapped the letter. "This's from our insurance company. You understand about insurance?"

"Sure," replied Melissa.

Scotty shot his sister a quick glance and nodded.

Charly had her doubts, so she bit into a cookie, chewed for a moment, then added, "It's pretty simple. We pay a company some money every year and if anything bad happens to the nursery, say the watering system fails and a bunch of plants die, they pay us back to help make it right. Get it?"

"Yeah, yeah," said Scotty, kicking harder now.

"Stop that!" said Melissa, before giving him a shove.

"Hey!" he replied, pushing back.

Charly stood. "Hold it, both of you." Melissa opened her mouth, but Charly held up a palm. She sat back down and continued, "Okay, so we usually have insurance, but there's been a little problem. Somehow, our most recent payment got lost, and well, we didn't have coverage for a few days. But we do now, so there's nothing to worry about."

"Nothing to worry about," repeated Scotty, his small face brightening. He yanked free another cookie and stuffed it in his mouth.

"But Mom," Melissa said, jabbing a finger onto the paper, "the letter says they won't pay for all those ruined seedlings. Doesn't that mean trouble?"

Scotty's heel struck his chair leg.

"Mom!" squealed Melissa. "Make him stop."

Charly reached across and briefly squeezed her son's wrist. "Scott Alexander Shepherd," she said, looking him directly in the eyes. "Please, enough of that kicking."

Scotty slouched back. "Okay, Mom." After a moment, he leaned over the table. "So, Lissa was wrong, right? We're not in any trouble, are we?" He flashed his sister a triumphant grin. "I didn't do nothin' wrong, told ya."

"Anything wrong," Charly replied. "Didn't do *anything* wrong."

Melissa rolled her eyes and twirled her hair in exasperation.

Scotty jumped up. "Can I go now, Mom? Got some stuff to do."

Charly nodded.

Scott headed to the door.

"Wait," Charly called. "You've forgotten something."

"Aww," the boy replied, spinning on his heel. He scooted back to the table, snatched his glass and took it to the sink. Then he offered his mother an impish bow and sprinted out into the hallway.

"Thank you!" Charly sang out after him.

A couple of seconds later, the back door slammed.

"It's dark out," said Melissa. "What's he up to?" She shook her head. "He's nuts, you know that?"

Charly smiled at her. "Just delightfully exuberant, that's all."

The pre-teen played with some crumbs in front of her.

One key parenting attribute Charly had learned early on was patience. So she munched a cookie and waited.

Finally, Melissa glanced up. "They're not going to make us leave here, are they?"

Startled at her daughter's grave expression and serious question, Charly almost choked on a raisin. She coughed, swallowed and then took a gulp of milk.

"Honey, where is all this coming from?"

Charly stood and walked around the table to sit beside Melissa. She took both of her daughter's hands.

"We're not in trouble and we're not going anywhere. Now, take a deep breath and tell me what's going on."

Melissa's sweet face crumpled and she launched herself into her mother's arms. "Oh, Mom," she bawled. "I'm so scared. Grampa's gonna die and I don't want to have to move like Janie Allen."

Charly rocked her gently. "Shhh...okay honey. Your Grampa's not going to die. You believe me?"

"Yes," Melissa whispered.

"Good. Now, Janie's the one whose parents've just divorced, right?"

Melissa nodded against her shoulder.

"And they're selling the family home?"

Another nod.

Charly swept her daughter's hair off her forehead. "Honey, I know it's a terrible thing for Janie to go through, but you've got nothing to be scared of."

Teary-eyed, Melissa stared up at her.

"We're fine. Your Grampa's coming home soon...to *our* home. No one's going to make us leave it. I promise you."

"You're sure?"

Charly kissed her daughter's freckled nose. "Absolutely, positively, one hundred and ten percent sure."

Melissa managed a half-smile. "There's only one hundred percent, Mom. Mr. Burgess tells us that all the time in math class."

Charly squeezed Melissa. "You know what, honey? I'm a hundred and ten percent sure that Mr. Burgess's right."

Melissa giggled against Charly's breast.

Charly held on tightly and prayed that she could keep her promise. Then she silently begged for the Lord to protect her children.

Chapter Seventeen

Half the interest of a garden is the constant exercise of the imagination.
Mrs. C.W. Earle

Charly sighed and leaned back from her laptop computer. It was nearly noon. The spreadsheet on her screen was a blur. She was too tired to distinguish between orders and stock, and no matter how she jiggled the numbers, the nursery was seriously short of cash.

She flipped the screen down and then tapped it absentmindedly. *We'll find the money, somehow.*

"Lunchtime," she called out to the empty house.

She rose and stared out the partially fogged front window. Fat raindrops splattered onto the gardens and stone-crushed driveway. This time the precipitation didn't worry her, as it was accompanied by a warming trend, but she was slightly frustrated about the wetness hampering her outdoor efforts.

Oh well, she told herself. It's a good time to get the books in order and to consider a work plan for the next few weeks. She chuckled ruefully. Normally, she and her father accomplished most tasks by rote and an agreeable and silent understanding of each other's responsibilities. Now that she had Michael as an assistant, she had to keep him busy, and at the same time, maintain the safety of the nursery. No small feat, she was beginning to realize.

Fortunately, Michael was a cheerful and eager helper, and with only a modicum of good-natured groaning and complaining, took on any and all menial tasks. Earlier that morning, he had happily taken the truck to pick up bags of fertilizer. In fact, she realized with a prickle of panic, he should have been back over an hour ago.

He's a grown man, she thought. Capable of phoning if he gets in trouble. He probably just stopped off somewhere for a treat.

At the thought of food, her stomach grumbled and she headed to the kitchen.

Ten minutes later she was settling in at the table, about to tuck into a blueberry yoghurt, a misshapen banana muffin—one of a dozen that Faith had brought the day before—and a glass of skim milk when Hope strode through the front door.

"Hey, kiddo," the tall woman said cheerfully as she entered the kitchen. "Thought I might catch you. Is that one of Faith's?"

She reached for the muffin, and before Charly could react, had swallowed it in a few bites.

"I'm starving. Been all over the place this morning." She paused, wiping crumbs from her upper lip. "Mmm, that sister of ours makes a mean muffin. What's she got in them? Apricots?"

"And pecans."

"Any more where that came from?"

Charly smiled good-naturedly. "Grab a chair," she said, rising and heading to the refrigerator. "Want a yogurt, too?"

"No, but you might."

Charly paused and then turned to see her sister scooping out the last bits of creamy liquid from the small plastic container. She shook her head, pulled out a couple more yogurts, the bag of muffins, and a jug of milk.

"So, what got you running around this morning?" Charly said as she sat down and ripped the lid off her yogurt.

Hope tore into another odd-shaped muffin and took a large swig of milk before replying. "How would you like to rear butterflies?"

Charly looked up in surprise. "*Rear* butterflies? Is that possible?"

Hope nodded. "Not only is it possible, my dear sister, I think the Sweet Shepherd Nursery is ideally suited for it. Want to know why?"

Charly took a bite out of a muffin and chewed for a moment

before saying, "I'm probably going to regret this, but yeah, I'm curious."

Hope pushed the food away and leaned closer. "I mean, the nursery's got two strong assets." She held up a long finger. "One: you've got the know-how and facilities to grow larval host plants." Another finger. "Two: you've got an empty greenhouse that could be a perfect butterfly rearing sun tent." She leaned back. "Make that three assets."

Charly frowned. She was having enough trouble keeping up with her sister's speeding train of thought, much less trying to figure out what she meant by a third asset.

Hope's angular face broke into a broad grin. "Me. As you know, I'm a lepidopterist. I know butterflies like you know plants." She clapped her hands in delight. "In fact, we're a perfect team."

"Not quite perfect," a deep voice said.

The sisters spun to see Michael leaning against the door frame. He grinned at them, his face and hands grimy with dirt and sweat. "Hang on to that thought," he added and disappeared.

A few moments later, the others heard the sound of running water and then Michael reappeared, hands and cheeks crimson from scrubbing.

He dropped into a chair beside Hope. "That looks tasty," he said, eyeing the pile of food in the middle of the table. "Those Faithie's?"

The sisters chuckled as Michael reached for a squarish lump.

"Help yourself," replied Charly.

Hope smiled. "Guess the shape gave it away, huh?"

Michael grinned and took a bite. "Looks aren't everything."

"Okay, so why aren't we a perfect team?" asked Hope.

Michael swallowed yogurt and wagged a spoon in her direction. "You're right, Hope. You're the butterfly queen and Charly's an ace gardener, so you two specialists've got the bugs and the plants covered, but you're still missing something crucial if your scheme's gonna work." He paused to inhale a muffin.

Hope and Charly exchanged an amused glance.

"And that would be?" the older Shepherd sibling asked.

Michael filled a glass with milk and downed it in two swallows. "A generalist. Someone who isn't focused on the minutiae, but on the *bigger* picture."

Hope choked on a swig of milk.

"You mean," Charly pinched off a chunk of muffin, "someone who doesn't know anything about horticulture or entomology."

Michael nodded energetically. "That's the idea."

"I get it," Hope said, rising, "someone who's totally in the dark about what we'd be trying to accomplish."

Michael's expression darkened. "Well, uh... "

Charly smothered a chuckle.

Hope clapped her hands onto his shoulders. "We get it, Mikey. We need someone who doesn't know a Turner's silverspot from a neckerchief—"

"Or an *agastache* from a mustache," Charly added, with a smile. "Some man who hasn't got a clue."

Michael flushed and began worrying his spoon.

"In other words," the sisters finished in unison, "you're telling us we need you!"

"All right, all right," Michael said finally. "Very funny, ladies. But one of these fine days, you're gonna be glad I'm a partner."

"You're a riot, Mikey," Charly sputtered, standing. "A total laugh riot."

Chuckling, his sisters-in-law each gave him a peck on the cheek before returning to their seats.

Michael grinned self-consciously and chomped on another muffin.

A moment later, Charly asked Hope, "So what's involved in rearing butterflies?"

Before her sister could respond, Michael held up a large palm. "Wrong question." He turned to Hope. "First things first: does it pay?"

Hope smiled. "That is the right question, Michael. And yes, it does."

Excited, Charly leaned forward. This might be the answer to her prayers. "You mean we could make some money at this?"

"Uh huh. Not a fortune. After all, we're talking conservation research here, but more than enough to cover all our costs plus a little extra, especially since I won't be taking the salary component."

"We can't let you—" began Charly.

Hope flipped up a palm. "Forget it. After all, you'll be doing most of the work." She tapped the tabletop thoughtfully. "If everything works out okay, it might even wipe out the hail debt."

"Well, that's fantastic!" said Charly. "When do we start? What do we need to do?"

"Hold on," Hope said. "Nothing's settled yet. I mean, I've applied for a grant from the zoo to raise Turner's silverspots, but I'm still waiting to hear back."

Charly felt her stomach flip. "You mean it's not a go?"

Hope noticed the look of disappointment that crossed her younger sister's face. She reached across and touched Charly's hand. "Sorry, kiddo. No, not yet." She leaned back. "Guess I shouldn't have said anything 'til I knew for sure. It's just that I wanted you to have some hope."

"That's okay," said Charly. "It's very thoughtful of you to think that."

Michael asked, "When'll you know for sure?"

"A week, ten days, maybe," Hope said. "Shouldn't be too long, because spring's nearly here and the zoo's under pressure to issue the conservation rearing contracts."

"You mean, other groups rear butterflies, too?" Michael wanted to know.

"Yeah, but mostly for commercial sale. Nobody's doing conservation rearing, except the zoo. Far as I know, I'm the only one who's applied. You see, the zoo's handled the Turner's rearing program since the beginning, about five years ago."

She jumped up. "Tea, anyone?" The others nodded. Hope continued while filling the kettle, "I just happened to hear from a colleague that they might be interested in farming some of it out—I think they want to spread the risk and expand the program—and I immediately thought of our nursery. We could do it, we could rear thousands of butterflies, I'm positive."

"Of course we could," replied Michael heartily.

He and Charly swapped looks and then Charly asked, "Uh... what exactly is involved?"

"Been there, done that, got the zoo T-shirt," replied Hope. She grinned at the others. "Don't worry, when we get the contract—and

I'm pretty sure we will—I'll go over everything in great detail."

"We're gonna need an awful lot of one thing," said Michael.

The two women gazed at him expectantly.

"I'm thinking tons of real tiny diapers."

Nicola Furlong

Chapter Eighteen

*The most noteworthy thing about gardeners is that they are
always optimistic,
always enterprising, and never satisfied. They always look
forward to
doing something better than they have ever done before.*
Vita Sackville-West

After lunch, Hope headed back to the college and Charly and
Michael started to unload the truck.

To Charly's relief, a quick inventory check confirmed
that Michael had picked up exactly what they had ordered. There
were bags of different sizes and fertilizers of various concentrations
and combinations. They toiled quickly and quietly, dropping the bags
onto a wheelbarrow, then taking turns trundling to the storage area
and tugging the rest of the sacks closer to the back of the truck in
preparation for the next load.

After a while, they fell into a natural rhythm. Charly was
surprised to find that they were working together easily, and at a
similar pace. Maybe this'll work out better than she'd ever imagined.
Who'd have believed it?

After the last sack had been dropped into place, Michael
deposited his usual peck on Charly's cheek and then jumped on his
motorcycle.

"Make sure you thank Faith again for the muffins!" Charly
shouted over the engine din.

In response, Michael waggled his visor and roared down the drive.

It didn't take long for Charly's good humor to sour. She was walking by the large greenhouse and noticed a couple of cupboard doors hanging open. As she stepped in to shut them, she was taken aback to find several plastic bins jammed onto the shelves. Even more shocking was that the containers were filled with a jumbled mess of parts.

Before she had found the time to store them separately, someone had collected her carefully organized piles of irrigation fittings and thrown them higgledy-piggledy into the containers. Now gaskets, couplers, latches and heaven knows what else, were all mixed together in each of the bins.

"Michael, you idiot!" shouted Charly as she slammed the doors shut.

It'll take forever to find a part. Well, he's just gonna have to go through and re-sort them all.

She stomped into the house. And to think she was actually starting to believe he might work out!

~~~

"You really think Grampa might be coming home soon?" Melissa asked later that evening as she poured chocolate chips into a measuring cup. "You know my band recital's this weekend and I really want him to come."

"Well, honey, you heard Grampa. That's what the doctors're telling him," Charly replied, plugging in the electric mixer. "They just have to get his medication straightened out and then he'll be home, right as rain. As for the recital, why don't we just wait and see, okay?"

The Shepherds had just returned from the hospital and were in the kitchen making peanut butter chocolate chip cookies. Charly and her sisters had agreed to alternate their hospital visits, thus ensuring their father didn't get too lonely nor too tired, and both Faith and Hope had thoughtfully suggested that Charly and the kids take the earlier just-after-dinner shift to allow time for homework and chores.

Melissa looked crestfallen. "Okay," she removed a couple of

chocolate chips, "but it sure won't be the same if he can't come."

"He'll be home," Scotty said confidently, plying butter onto a rectangular cookie sheet.

Dad did look better, Charly thought, beating the butter and eggs. So much brighter and stronger. Although excited at the possibility of his return, Charly was surprised to find her stomach clenched as worrisome thoughts swirled in her head. What sort of modifications, if any, should they make to the house and nursery? How will he have changed? What about his diet? Would she have to learn a whole bunch of new recipes? Would the kids be afraid and treat him differently? Would he act strangely?

After a few moments, she realized what she feared the most. *What if he has another heart attack?*

Fortunately, the ringing of the kitchen phone interrupted that terrifying consideration. By the time Charly switched off the blender, Melissa had abandoned her measuring efforts and was reaching for the receiver. Scotty glanced up from his greasing job.

"Hello? Oh, hi, Uncle Michael," her voice dropped in disappointment. "Yeah, just a sec, she's right here."

Just the guy I want to talk to. Charly wiped her hands on a tea towel as Melissa turned and handed her the phone.

"Hello, Michael," she tossed the tea towel over her shoulder, "everything all right?"

"If I were any better, Charly," his voice boomed into her ear, "I'd be twins."

Charly groaned at the familiar old refrain. "Faith okay?"

"She's tops. Absolutely tops. Now, are we parents yet?"

Charly blinked in surprise. "Parents?"

"Yeah. We rearing thousands of flying baby bugs or what?"

Despite her desire to blast him for mixing up her irrigation parts, Charly found herself chuckling at the imagery created by the very idea.

"No word yet, but it's only been eight hours since Hope told us. And if we want the job, Michael, I think we'd better bone up on our knowledge. Far as I know, there aren't any *baby* flying butterflies, they're eggs or caterpillars or something."

"Details, details," he said.

Charly barked out a laugh. "Oh, yeah, I almost forgot. You're the generalist." She moved away from the children and lowered her voice. "Hey, tell me something. What were you thinking of when you threw all those irrigation fittings together?"

"Irrigation fittings? What're you talking about?"

Charly hesitated. Michael sounded truly surprised.

"You...you didn't pile up a bunch of irrigation bits and pieces and dump them into bins in the new cupboards?"

"Nope. Why would I do that?"

Charly hardly heard his answer. Her attention was suddenly drawn to her son. Head down in fierce concentration, Scotty was vigorously rubbing way too much butter on the already greased cookie sheet.

An idea started to build in her mind. She remembered hearing the back door slam last night as Scotty inexplicably headed out into the nursery. Usually, he played in the front yard. And then an image of the cupboard floated into view, and she now realized that the offending bins were resting on the lowest shelves. The only ones that could be reached by a nine-year-old. But why on earth would he—

"Charly? Hey! You there?" Michael's voice was shouting in her ear.

"Oh, sorry. Look, let's talk about it tomorrow, okay?"

"Ten-four."

"Love to Faith," added Charly, before hanging up.

Melissa stopped chewing a chocolate chip to ask, "What's wrong?"

Her brother's dark head remained lowered, his fingers swirling on the cookie sheet.

"Nothing's wrong. In fact, I think something real nice has happened. Your brother's made an effort to help me out all on his own."

At that, Scotty glanced up shyly.

"Honey bun," Charly unplugged the mixer, "was it you who kindly put all the little parts in the bins in the large greenhouse?"

Scotty nodded. "And then I put 'em away," he added, face beaming with pride. "Just like you always tell me to do with my toys."

Melissa popped a couple of chips into her mouth then wagged a finger at her brother. "Y'know you're not supposed to touch any equipment or be in any of the buildings without adult supervision."

Scotty's expression blackened. "Don't tell me what to do."

"Melissa," Charly said, "you know, it's impolite to point. Now, would you please stop eating those chocolate chips and stir them into the batter?"

Melissa flashed her mother an injured look, chucked the dark chips into the bowl and began mixing with all her heart.

Charly sat down and motioned for Scott to join her. After a moment, he climbed up onto her lap.

She leaned in and kissed the back of his neck. Oh, how she loved his little-boy scent! Soon, she realized with a start, he wouldn't want to sit on her lap at all anymore. He had already been avoiding doing so in public for over a year now. They grew up so fast.

"That was very kind and thoughtful of you."

"See?" he sneered, sticking his tongue out at his sister.

"Hey! None of that," Charly said. "That's impolite, too."

Melissa's eyes flickered with an expression of satisfaction.

"Now," Charly shifted her son until they were face to face, "I know you meant well, hon, but your sister's right."

Melissa stopped her beating and grinned directly at her brother. Scotty gaped.

"You've always been taught not to play in the greenhouses or fool around with any equipment by yourself. It's for your own safety, you know that."

"I know, I know," he rocked back and forth, "but I wasn't fooling around. I was helping."

"And I'm grateful for it, believe me." She lifted him onto his feet, gently placed her palms on his shoulders and looked directly into his deep-blue eyes. "But in future, honey, just ask me. Okay?"

He heaved a huge sigh and then nodded.

"Now," Charly stood, "we'd better give your sister a hand, 'cause she's doing all the work. And we Shepherds know what that means, don't we?"

"The Shepherd who makes the cookies gets to eat the cookies," the kids shouted.

Charly gave Scotty an affectionate swat on the bottom.

"Well, I'm desperate for a cookie, so let's get cracking!"

Chapter Nineteen

The greatest gift of the garden is the restoration of the five
senses.
Hanna Rion

O h, it's so good to be outside," Barry said, as he watched the
patchwork of sage and umber fields unfurl past the truck's
passenger window. He opened the window a little further.
"Spring's around the corner, red-winged blackbirds're returning,
everything looks so beautiful."

He leaned out and inhaled the fragrant country air.

"Can't wait to smell the garden again. Being cooped up for days
makes a man very grateful to be out and about."

Charly nodded, while keeping her eyes on the narrow, winding
highway. He seemed so happy. So relaxed. *Don't know how he does it.*
I'm in a blind panic. She sneaked an admiring glance in her father's
direction, then patted her jacket pocket to make sure the bundle of
prescriptions the nurse had handed her were still safely there.

That flustered her even further. She had to fill all nine
prescriptions as soon as possible, then sort out when her father was
supposed to take them. Some pills had to be swallowed once a day,
others twice. Some were specifically designated for the morning,
others before bed. And some medications were to be consumed with
food, others without.

It was all very confusing, and Charly was terrified that she
wouldn't remember the instructions and might give her father the

wrong medication, or forget one entirely and kill him. She made a mental note to find some quiet time once her dad was settled in when she could line up and review the medications and create a chart that would help her keep track of them.

He looked good. Looked strong.

Oh dear Lord, I can't thank you enough for returning him safely to us.

Ever since the surprise early phone call from her father saying he was being released, she had been feeling blissfully terrified. Kind of like what a kindergarten-aged Melissa used to call "topsy-turvy" when describing how she felt when her grandfather spun her around like an airplane.

Over and over during the forty-minute drive to the hospital, Charly's stomach had fluttered, her heart jumped and her mind raced, as she made emergency plans. They needed a place to store her father's nitroglycerin pills so that any family member could find them, and a list of people they could call to keep an eye on him if and when the family left him on his own.

Now, her mind was darting ahead to what might be happening at home. After receiving her father's call, she had barely had time to call Faith and ask her for help before heading out to the hospital. She knew her father would have waited patiently for her to arrive whenever it was convenient for her, but she couldn't bear the thought of him sitting alone in the hospital for another minute.

Fortunately, Faith was available and immediately agreed to come by the house and finish setting up her father's new bedroom. At the doctor's suggestion, Barry would now sleep on the main floor, in the Shepherd children's former playroom. Charly and Michael had already spent a few hours moving Barry's bed, furniture and clothes from the large master bedroom at the top of the stairs to the smaller playroom at the back of the house. Thus, Faith had only to make the bed and bring down the rest of his personal belongings.

Charly glanced at her watch. Almost eleven o'clock.

"Past tea time, Dad. You thirsty or hungry? Want me to stop somewhere?"

His pale face brightened momentarily, then he shook his head and jabbed a finger toward his left ankle.

Charly blushed at her blunder. "Oh, Dad, I'm sorry. I...I forgot all about it."

It was another surprise: a urine drainage bag strapped to her father's left leg. Charly had been horrified and her father equally mortified when she had arrived to pick him up and the nurse had matter-of-factly pointed out that he was still attached to a catheter, and would be for a few more days. This wasn't unusual, they were told. The nurse had also informed Charly, who was also embarrassed to be so hugely relieved by the news, that a mobile healthcare worker was scheduled to provide daily assistance to her father.

What were you thinking? she rebuked herself silently. Of course the poor guy would be too self-conscious to go into a coffee shop.

"Don't worry," she reached across and squeezed his forearm. "We're almost home, and I'm sure Faith'll have some tea ready. Maybe even a treat or two."

"You know," Barry shifted his weight, providing more room for his left leg, "the hospital food wasn't too bad, really. Especially breakfast. I haven't had porridge in ages. But I did have a hankering for a slice of your sister's fruit cobbler. What does she call it? Berry something or other?"

Charly neatly edged the truck left across the highway's yellow centerline and then back to avoid a scattered pile of horse droppings. "Berryumptious, I think."

"That's it, berryumptious." Her father smacked his lips. "Sure doesn't sound as good as it tastes." He turned his brilliant blue eyes toward his youngest daughter. "Thank you, dear, for picking me up. I'm so glad to be coming home."

"We're all very excited," Charly said. "Wait'll the kids see you."

Barry smiled and happily drummed his fingers along the door's handle.

Charly wondered if now was a good time to ask him what he had meant by the few words he had uttered in front of the ambulance attendants. She had intended to ask a number of times, but they had either not been alone, or the timing hadn't felt right. He'd been through enough.

He'll tell me if and when he's ready.

But his shocked expression, a painful mix of anxiety and fear, haunted her. Frightened her. Her father had tried desperately to tell her something. Something so important that it was on his mind in the midst of a life-altering event. Almost as if it were a confession.

Come on, she chided herself. *You're just being a chicken. You don't really want to know, but you pretend it's for his sake that you aren't asking.*

She took a deep breath. "Dad?"

His fingers continued to tap. "Uh huh."

"After your heart attack, you…you said something…just before they put you in the ambulance. D'you remember?"

The drumming hesitated then continued more slowly.

"Not sure what you mean, dear."

Charly gripped the steering wheel tightly. "You…you tried to tell me something."

She glanced at his profile. His face was rigid, as were his fingers. "You looked, oh Dad, I don't know, scared and worried."

Her father moved in his seat. After a long moment, he said, "I'm sorry, dear…it's all such a blur."

The truck jumped, wheels hitting a stray rock. They were both jostled. Although the bouncing turned her father in her direction, he deliberately avoided her gaze.

She felt guilty for having asked. "Sure, Dad, of course," she replied quickly. "Don't worry about it."

Oh, Charly, Mom often said you push too far. Why couldn't you just leave well enough alone? If he wants to talk, he will.

She swore to herself to let him do just that.

For the next ten minutes they were both silent. Finally, the truck rounded the last corner and as she steered it up their driveway, Charly triumphantly tooted the horn.

"Welcome home, Dad," she said, leaning across to kiss his cheek. "We've really missed you."

Within seconds of the truck's wheels coming to a rest, Faith Shepherd was flying out the front door.

"Daddy," she cried, rushing up and pulling open the passenger door. Before her father could react, Faith had dived in and thrown her arms around his neck. "I'm so glad you're home." She began to sob.

Barry gently patted her and waited.

Finally, Faith pulled back, wiped at her tears and half-laughed. "I'm sorry, didn't even let you get out first." She held out her hand.

Barry took it and gingerly stepped out, mindful of the drainage sac, and onto the gravel drive.

"Oh dear, you're in pain!" Faith exclaimed. "I didn't—"

Her father flushed deeply. He reached down and tried to tug his pant leg completely over the partially exposed bag.

Faith's eyes grew wide, but before she could speak, Charly quickly jumped in. "He's fine," she said, taking her father's arm. "Wanna grab his suitcase?" At that, she threw Faith a look that clearly said, "Later!" and walked Barry into the house.

Within minutes, Barry was happily seated in his favorite spot at the head of the kitchen table, sipping a steaming cup of tea and buttering one of Faith's freshly made date scones.

His daughters quietly sat nearby, thrilled to see him almost fully recovered and safely home.

"Oh..." he said, "it's so good to be here." He held up a chunk of scone and nodded at his eldest daughter. "Mmm, dates...this's good, Faith." He munched for a couple of seconds. "Really good, but something's different?"

His middle daughter smiled. "Hoped you wouldn't notice, Daddy. I fiddled with the recipe to reduce the cholesterol...cut back the butter, added low-fat yoghurt and upped the whole wheat flour. Makes it more....uh...heart healthy."

Charly squelched a groan of dismay. She hadn't even considered changing her father's diet. Now, she would have to figure out a whole new menu. That thought pinched her with guilt and then remorse. She felt pain and looked down at her fingers. They were curled into clenched fists, nails digging into her palms. She exhaled and released her fingers.

Don't be so arrogant, Charly! Not everything's about you!

She prayed silently, asking for help and forgiveness. Of course, she'd do whatever was necessary. It'll probably be good for all of them.

Barry smiled at Faith. "Thank you, dear. Not sure that high cholesterol's the problem. The doc said it could be a number of factors. Let's worry about that later, okay?"

A sudden thought propelled Charly out of her chair and across the kitchen floor to a side counter. There, she quickly fished through an untidy pile of papers.

"What're you doing?" asked Faith, as she and Barry stared.

Charly held up a hand in a temporary reply and then continued shuffling. After a moment, she pulled a couple of sheets free and returned to her seat.

"I completely overlooked them." She handed one to her father and one to Faith. "Got these from the hospital. They're about nutrition, ideas and suggestions." She paused, before reluctantly adding, "Guess we might have to change our diets, huh, Dad?"

Faith scanned her sheet, carefully placed it on the table and gazed at her father.

Barry barely stifled a sigh. "As Scarlet O'Hara said, 'Tomorrow is another day.'" He gestured toward the pile of lumpy-looking scones sitting in front of him. "Well, aren't you all going to join your old man?"

"Of course," replied Charly, reaching for one of the roundest scones. "Can't wait."

Faith said, "Thanks, Daddy, but I've already had two…for testing purposes." Charly and her father smiled. She fingered her tea mug. "Just happy you're home."

"Me, too," Barry replied. "You know, dear, I was telling Charly on the way home how much I missed your baking." He grimaced. "And I don't care what the hospital says."

Faith beamed.

"He especially wants your berryumptious cobbler," added Charly.

Faith clapped her hands with joy and stood up. "I'm so glad. I had a little extra time." She glanced apologetically at her sister. "Hope you don't mind, Charly, I dug around your freezer and found some fruit, so," she waved in the direction of the oven, "I made a couple of cobblers and yes, they're heart healthy. They'll be ready in half an hour or so."

"Thought I smelled peaches," Barry said. "My, you've been busy." He leaned back and smiled. "My ward buddy Stan was right. You two spoil me, and I'm so grateful." He held out his arms. "Come here, both of you, let me give you each a kiss."

After embracing them, Barry flopped back in his chair and yawned.

"Oh, Dad, I'm sorry," Charly said. "You must be bushed. Come on, let's get you settled in your new digs."

"Thank you," he said, rising slowly, "I am pretty tired."

As Faith hurried ahead, Charly led her father to his room. The two women anxiously watched his face as he entered the small space. Charly felt a surge of empathy rush over her. Here stood a man who, only days before, had appeared to be in excellent shape, especially for someone in his sixties.

Sure, her father was more than a few pounds overweight and had been slowed recently by a faulty thyroid, but before the heart attack, he had been hauling manure and digging trenches on a daily basis, keeping right up with Charly. And he had been physically active his entire adult life.

Now, a dozen pounds lighter and still bearing the shadow of sickness, he was moving out of the spacious master bedroom upstairs, which he had shared with his dear wife for over forty years. His new square bedroom lacked the country charm of the master, with its broad dormer windows, sloping ceiling and full ensuite bathroom, but it was bright and cheery and there was a powder room with a shower a few steps away. Best of all, he wouldn't have to climb the eighteen steps of the wide, curved staircase.

Sure hope he doesn't feel like he's being punished or is embarrassed to be restricted to the main floor, thought Charly.

"Hey, this's terrific," Barry said, his large head turning this way and that to take in all the changes.

Gone was the vivid and chaotic sight of children's toys, furniture, pictures and rainbow-colored curtains. Barry's new quarters were dominated by a single bed and a matching chest of oak drawers and night table. The curtains, area rug and bedspread were a complementary rustic brown and the homemade family photo collages that had originally hung in the master bedroom now adorned the pale walls.

Barry moved slowly, running his eyes approvingly over everything, until he pulled up sharply in the corner near the large bay window.

"Your mom's rocker," he whispered huskily. He cleared his throat and reached out to touch its well-worn back. With a contented sigh, he dropped onto the cushioned seat—where he and his wife had rested many times while cradling one or more of their children—laid his large hands over the sculpted chair arms and closed his eyes.

Faith and Charly exchanged a look of satisfaction. Within a minute, their father was snoring lightly. The sisters crept out of the room and closed the door.

Barry Shepherd was home again.

Chapter Twenty

Plants give us oxygen for the lungs and for the soul.
Linda Solegato

As Charly and Faith tiptoed across the hardwood floor, voices floated toward them from the kitchen. A few more steps confirmed Charly's suspicions. Michael and Hope had arrived. She heard one of them say something about finding the light switch.

Ten more paces and Charly and Faith stood in the entrance to the kitchen, watching with amusement as Hope and Michael, both crouched down, peered through the glass of the oven door. Each held a half-eaten date scone in one hand.

Charly could clearly see the two bubbling fruit cobblers silhouetted against the brightly lit oven's interior.

"They've got to be ready," Michael was saying, "they smell just right." He stood and reached for the door handle.

"Wait! I don't know," Hope replied hastily, also rising to stand. "There's still six minutes on the egg timer. Faith'll kill us if we ruin 'em."

Charly moved forward, but was stopped by Faith's outstretched hand.

"Oh, what do you know, Hope? You don't even cook."

Hope turned to face her brother-in-law, bit into her scone and chewed deliberately. She was only an inch shorter than he, and could almost stare him directly in the eye. After swallowing, she replied, "And you do, Michael?"

Michael scowled. "Okay, so we're both lousy in the kitchen, but I watch Faith all the time. Forget the egg timer. Trust me, the cobblers're just the way they should be." He gripped the door's handle.

"But how do you know?"

"Faith says bubbling's the key. Well, those things're shooting like Ol' Faithful. They're gonna burn if we don't rescue 'em, and quick." He made a quick thumbs-down gesture. "*That's* when Faith'll kill us."

He yanked open the oven and the pair staggered back to avoid the swirling rush of hot fruity air.

"Come on," Michael cried, tossing the rest of his scone onto the countertop. "Oven mitts!"

With surprisingly good teamwork, the pair managed to remove both dishes and safely place them on the stovetop. For a long moment they stood proudly side-by-side as the cobblers bubbled and steamed, saturating the room with the mouth-watering scent of baked fruit, sugar and spices.

"Admiring your tasty handiwork?" Faith said softly.

Hope and Michael jumped, then whirled in unison to see the others watching from the doorway.

"Faithie!" shouted Michael happily, without a trace of reproach.

He took two quick strides, swooped down and kissed his wife affectionately on the lips. "The man's just saved the day." He stood back and waved a fat oven mitt toward Hope. "That one would've let your fruit things burn."

"Hey!" Hope shot back. "I mean, wait a minute, I was only—"

Faith held up a palm. "Don't sweat it, Hope. You guys handled it perfectly."

She slipped into the nearest kitchen chair. Charly plopped down beside her.

After a few moments, Faith said, "You don't expect me to do everything, do you?"

The others just stood still and stared at the seated women.

Charly chuckled and waited for the other shoe to drop.

"For heaven's sake," continued Faith, "which one of you sous-chefs is gonna serve?"

There was a long silence.

"Okay, Hope," Michael held out a clenched fist, "it's RPS time."

Hope grinned and followed suit. Settling disputes by playing *Rock, Paper, Scissors* was an enjoyable, albeit competitive family tradition. "On three," she thrust up her fist, "one, two, three—"

The pair pumped their fists and played. Michael went for the classic and aggressive *rock* opening by maintaining a fist, while Hope delivered the *paper* move with a deft hand flutter.

"Ha!" cried Hope. "Paper covers rock. You lose." She glanced at the others for confirmation. They nodded vehemently.

"Best of three?" Michael countered quickly.

"No way, José," Hope reached for the kettle as her sisters laughed. "I'm starving, so make mine extra large."

As Michael scooped huge portions of steaming cobbler into bowls, Charly filled the others in on Barry Shepherd's condition.

"So, he's in pretty good shape, right?" said Hope. "He'll be able to get back into the nursery fairly soon?"

"Think so." Charly cut into her cobbler. "Dr. Rogers said mild exercise's important, but nothing real strenuous. Not for a while."

"But he's still got a catheter," said Faith.

Michael hesitated, loaded spoon in mid-flight. "Ouch, poor guy."

Charly nodded. "And he's real self-conscious about it, so watch it."

Hope and Faith exchanged an uncomfortable look. "Uh," Faith laid down her spoon, "what's involved in…*caring* for the catheter?"

Charly winced slightly. "Not sure, to be honest, but a mobile nurse's scheduled to come by later to check on him."

Relief flooded all three faces.

"That's all right, then," Faith said. "What else do we need to know?"

Charly ate a couple of mouthfuls before answering. "Mmm, this's so good, Faith." She jabbed her spoon back into the bowl. "Well, I've got a fistful of prescriptions that've got to be filled—"

"We'll handle that," said Faith. "Won't we, Michael?"

Eyes down, concentrating on scraping up the last bit of fruit, her husband just nodded.

"Thanks, you two, that's a big help."

Hope asked, "Anything I can do?"

"Get that bug contract signed so we can start making some moolah," Michael said, while licking his spoon.

"Who's signing a contract without my permission?" demanded a new voice.

The foursome flinched in surprise and then swung around as one to look at the newcomer.

Barry Shepherd stood in the doorway, huge fists clenched. He was breathing heavily. There was a beat of uncomfortable silence.

"Seems a lot's changed since I've been away."

Charly jumped up and hurried to meet him. "Nothing's changed, Dad."

"Nobody's signing anything," Hope said.

Faith dragged out a chair. "Here, Daddy, have a seat. Hungry? Want some cobbler?"

"Come on, Barry," Michael extended a hand, "take a load off."

Barry held up a palm. "I'm fine, thank you."

He walked to the proffered chair and settled in, careful to make sure both legs were hidden under the table.

"Sounds like you kids've been busy in my absence." He inhaled deeply. "Well, I'm back now, so thank you for your support, but Charly and I can handle the nursery."

The Shepherd sisters stared at their father. The flat tone and blunt wording wasn't at all like him. They were speechless.

Michael saved the day. "Of course you two can handle the nursery, Barry. Nobody's saying anything different. But it never hurts to have some help now and then, does it? Especially when it might result in a little extra income."

"Yes, Daddy." Faith leaned in towards her father. "Hope's got a chance for a contract and the nursery'll benefit."

Barry fixed his eyes on his middle daughter. "What's this all about, Hope?"

Hope swallowed.

Charly, who was still standing near the doorway, moved suddenly to the table.

"Here, Dad," she reached for a bowl, "have some cobbler. Hope's gone to a lot of trouble on our behalf and we've been dying to run it by you." She looked at him. "Okay?"

Barry returned her gaze. After a moment, a shy smile crossed his lips and he said gruffly, "You really haven't made any decisions yet?"

"'Course not, Dad," Hope said. "We've all been waiting for you."

Chapter Twenty-One

To dig one's own spade into one's own earth!
Has life anything better to offer than this?
Beverley Nichols

Butterflies!" Barry exclaimed ten minutes later, after Hope, supported by the enthusiastic interjections of the other three, filled him in on the exciting new opportunity. "You mean to tell me that we could raise butterflies in one of our greenhouses?" Barry leaned back in his chair and shook his head. "Seems downright… flighty." He grinned at his own witticism.

Charly smiled, delighted to see her father's face once again filled with animation.

Hope chuckled. "Good one, Dad. Yeah, we know it sounds a little crazy, but it's not. The zoo's been doing it successfully for several years now and they're looking to expand. I mean, the grant'll cover all the costs, like buying the larval plants and housing the donor females—"

Barry held up a large palm. "Wait a second, dear. You're going way too fast. I'm sorry, but *larval, donors*. Those're words I don't understand. I'm a nursery man, Hope. I grow and sell plants. That's what I do. That's what I know. I don't know butterflies."

Charly shot Hope a fleeting look. Uh-oh. It was too soon. We shouldn't have laid it on him so quickly. "We understand, Dad.

None of us do, except for Hope. But if you'd just give her a chance to explain everything, I think you'll see it's something we could do, and it could really help us with our bottom line."

Barry continued to look doubtful.

"We'd all like to help out," said Michael.

"It'll be fun, Daddy," Faith added, beaming with enthusiasm. "I, for one, can't wait to wash their little feet."

Charly caught Michael's attention as he playfully rolled his eyes.

Barry's jaw dropped.

"Good grief, Faithie, what're you talking about?" Michael said at last.

Faith blushed right into her strawberry hairline. She turned to Hope. "Is…isn't that right, Hope? I…I read it on the zoo's website."

Hope nodded. "Good for you, Faith. You're perfectly right."

Faith smiled and affectionately jabbed Michael on the leg. "See?"

Hope looked at the others. "The butterflies're fed a sugar solution and as it dries, their feet can crack."

Barry frowned.

No one said anything for a few seconds until Charly cautiously asked, "So…why do their *feet* crack…after they've eaten?"

"Yeah, why?" Michael chimed in.

Faith's arm shot up, like an eager student.

Hope gestured to her.

"Don't you guys know anything?" chirped Faith. "Their taste buds're on their little feet." She stared at the others' blank faces. "Come on, get with the program…they step on something first to make sure it's tasty before they eat it."

Michael rubbed his jaw in amazement.

"Taste buds on their feet," Charly repeated slowly. "Wow."

Barry reached across the table and squeezed Faith's shoulder. "If that doesn't show the miraculous hand of our dear Lord, I don't know what does." He smiled at Hope. "I may not be able to tell one butterfly from another, but when something puts that kind of excitement on my Faith's sweet face, you can surely count me in."

Faith let out a *whoop* and rushed over to hug her father.

Hope looked around the table and grinned broadly. "Well, I guess this would be the right time to tell you some good news."

The others leaned toward her, waiting.

Hope nodded. "We got the contract! If Dad's willing to sign it today, we could get our first delivery of eggs in the next couple of weeks."

Charly and Michael exchanged a loud high-five.

"That's wonderful," said Faith.

"Of course," Hope added hastily, "we've got a lot to do to get the greenhouse ready."

"Oh, that'll be easy," Faith said. "Michael and Charly'll do it, won't you?"

"No sweat," the two responded as one.

"My goodness," Barry Shepherd rapped his fingers on the table, "our ancestors herded sheep and now we're going to raise, of all things, *butterflies*—" He paused, blinked and swallowed hard.

"Oh, how your Mom would've loved to be a part of this."

The rest were quiet.

"Yeah," Hope said eventually.

Faith blew her nose. "Mom would've been the first one to say yes."

"Well," Charly kissed her father lightly on the cheek, "she's watching over us, so let's do her proud."

~~~

While Hope stayed in the kitchen and went over the contract and the basic requirements for butterfly rearing with her father, the other three, itching to make a start, headed out into the nursery.

"You've sure got a lot of stuff in here," Michael said as the trio stared into the yawning entrance of the spare greenhouse.

Although currently empty of nursery stock, the big glass room appeared staged and ready to nurture young plants. Dirt-littered picnic tables ran in rows, large florescent lights hung low over plastic containers of various sizes, and the watering system's thin dark tubing snaked up and down the cavernous space. Flopped-over, half-empty bags of soil and fertilizer stood along the lower glass walls, and above everything hung three large ceiling fans.

"Looks kinda lonely," said Faith. "I loved it most when the flats

were all in and starting to bloom. It looked and smelled like heaven."
She took a deep breath and then wrinkled her brow in disappointment.

"Easter was my favorite time," Charly said, memories flowing into her mind. "Especially the egg hunt."

"Oh yeah," Faith responded enthusiastically. She turned to her husband. "We always had our hunt a couple of days early and the greenhouses would be bursting with Easter lilies and roses. Dad hid the treats everywhere." She chuckled. "Once, I found a chocolate bunny in a bag of soil. Mom was appalled. Wouldn't let me eat it."

"Sounds like Eileen," Michael said. "But what a waste."

"We'd rush about, climbing over everything, digging into plants."

"You always squealed when you found something, Charly," said Faith. "And most of the time you put it in your pocket, not your basket. Later, when we were going to bed, Mom would find all sorts of stuff in your jeans, all mushy and warm."

"Y'know, Faith?" Charly said. "Now that I think of it, we must have ruined a lot of stock." She shook her head. "Mom and Dad never complained."

"But you let Lissa and Scotty do the same," Michael said.

"Yeah, I guess so." Charly smiled. "Funny what you remember most. I loved it after the hunt—probably because I was always smaller and slower and got less." Faith grinned. "We'd sit outside at the picnic table," Charly's arms fluttered in demonstration, "all the treats jumbled up in the middle and winking in the sunlight, and Mom would divvy everything into three even piles. I loved that. All of us jammed together in the sunshine, the smell of fresh air, dirt—"

"And chocolate," added Faith. "Come on. If we reminisce any more, I'm off for lunch."

Michael kicked at some loose dirt on the concrete floor and then ran a finger lazily along a window frame. Dust spilled out and trickled down into the hazy morning light.

"I'm not really the mothering kind," he said, wiping his hand against his jeans, "but this place's gonna need a major cleanup if we're thinking of bringing in hundreds of baby bugs."

"Right," replied Charly. "That's the task of the day." She handed each of the others a pair of thick gardening gloves. "First we empty, then we clean."

Faith tugged her right glove over her fingers. "And then we disinfect!"

"Where're we going to put everything?" asked Michael.

Charly paused while tucking her neckerchief deeper into her collar. "Good question." Her eyes roamed the vast space. "Hmm, well, guess we could pile the tables outside and cover them with tarps. The lights, I'm not sure. Hope might say we need 'em, so let's put them in the other greenhouse for now." She hesitated. "The other bits and pieces, how about we bring 'em outside, and I'll go get some boxes."

"Roger that," Michael replied. "Come on, Faithie, gimme a hand."

The pair stepped over to the first picnic table and positioned themselves at opposite ends. "One, two, three…" called Faith, before hoisting up her end. As they lifted and began carrying the table toward the entrance, Faith stumbled and almost dropped the table.

"Whoa!" shouted Michael, jarred by the lurch.

"Sorry! Tripped over a bag of something."

"I'll get it," said Charly as the others managed to maneuver the table past her and outside.

Charly stared down at the concrete floor. Several sacks of fertilizer, previously hidden under the table, lay slumped against one another. That wasn't too surprising, as space was often at a premium and sometimes nursery objects got shoved in any which way. What shocked Charly was that the bags were open, and the one that Faith had bumped into was spilling its pebbled contents onto the floor.

Given the rough and tumble nature of greenhouse activities, like hauling heavy bags, carrying armfuls of full plant flats and dragging hoses, Charly and her father were meticulous about putting away or properly securing equipment and materials to avoid accidents. Neither of them would have left these bags unsealed.

She looked more closely and immediately noticed that the contents of one bag appeared to be partially filled with two very different types of fertilizer. She shuddered at the damage this combination could inflict on tender plants, and she knew her father would never have mixed the two. Then she noticed something just visible in a nearby dusting of soil.

A footprint impression.

It was very small. It took her less than a heartbeat to realize it was exactly the size of her son's foot. What on earth was Scotty doing mixing fertilizers?

She didn't have time to ponder, as her helpers were back and already heading for another table. She shoved the bags out of the way, quickly pushed the loose fertilizer against the wall and headed to the garage.

By the time Charly returned with an armful of folded cardboard, the couple had removed, swept clean and stacked half a dozen tables on the grass swath between the two greenhouses. Nearby lay a discarded hodgepodge heap of plastic flats, pots and plant identification stakes.

They worked diligently and companionably for well over an hour emptying the greenhouse. Then, each sporting a little paper facemask and armed with small whisk brooms, they tackled the ceiling, fans and walls, sweeping the stiff bristles into the crevices of the aging window frames and spider-inhabited corners.

For the most part, they worked quietly, but every now and then, Michael would explode into a loud rendition of an old hurtin' tune. The women would cheerfully join in on the chorus, all three little white masks puffing and shrinking from their intense breathing.

Finally, the trio grabbed broad push brooms, lined up at the far end and together shoved the detritus along the concrete floor, all the while performing "Tell Laura I Love Her" at the top of their lungs.

A movement caught Charly's eye and she stopped singing. At the entrance, in the brilliant sunshine, stood Hope and their father, both grinning from ear to ear.

"Tell Laura not to cry…" Faith and Michael were still bellowing when Faith spotted the two onlookers. She hesitated, but Michael's baritone continued in a grand finale, as he remained blissfully unaware that he was being watched. "My loooove for herrrrrr will neeeeeveeerrrr dieeeeeeeee."

It was only when he had finished that Michael looked up to see Hope clapping heartily. He turned crimson.

"There's nothing like getting your hands dirty to make a man feel good," Barry said, and then he quickly added, "or a woman." He stepped forward and peered into the greenhouse. "My, you've done a jim-dandy job here."

"Thanks, Dad," said Charly. "Still got to power wash and disinfect, but we're getting there."

Hope strode into the middle of the large glass building. "This's going to be perfect." Her voice echoed in the empty space. "Well done, you guys."

Faith propped her broom against a wall and yanked off her gloves. "Thanks, but if you don't mind my asking, what've you been doing for the past coupla hours?" She leveled a questioning look at her younger sister. "Can't have been going over the contract all this time."

"Hey, yeah," added Michael, leaning on his broom. "We've been workin' like dogs. What've you been up to?"

Hope took Faith by the arm. "Oh ye of little faith," she said. "Come inside. Dad and I've got a surprise."

Michael dropped his broom. It fell with a clatter. "It'd better be tasty," he replied, taking a step. "Hey!" he exclaimed, as Charly suddenly shoved him aside.

Then she was in front, sprinting for the back door. "Last one in starves," Charly called over her shoulder.

"Who said anything about food?" Hope shouted back.

Chapter Twenty-Two

Gardening is an exercise in optimism.
Sometimes, it is a triumph of hope over experience.
Marina Schinz

H ope wasn't kidding. To Charly's astonishment, there was no prepared lunch waiting on the kitchen table. As she stood staring at the blue and white tablecloth, the others filed in.

Michael said, "Boy, it's hot in here." He flopped down. "What're we eating?"

Barry shuffled past him and heavily slumped into the chair at the head of the table. His large face glistened from the effort of walking in from the greenhouse.

Faith moved to the sink, scrubbed her hands vigorously, nodded at her husband to follow suit, and then filled glasses with water. Handing them around, she said, "What have you been doing, Hope?"

But no one noticed Hope's lack of response. Instead, the hungry trio automatically went about cleaning up and scrounging for lunch. Charly headed to the fridge and began to drag out some of its contents. Michael tossed the tea towel he was using to dry his hands over his shoulder and reached to take the stream of food, condiments and drinks from Charly and put them on the table. Faith pulled out cutlery and dishes, which Barry haphazardly scattered around the table.

Just as Michael was reaching for a slab of bread, Barry raised his hand. "I'd like to say grace, if I may?"

Michael pulled his hand back. "Of course, Barry. My apologies."

Faith raised an eyebrow in Charly's direction. Their mother had always said grace before every meal, but somehow over the past year the Shepherd family had let the tradition slip.

"Dear God," Barry closed his eyes. "Bless us and keep us safe in the palm of your hand." Faith smiled at her father. "I thank you for the wonderful bounty we are about to eat—"

"Amen," Michael said and then his cheeks reddened as he realized Barry wasn't finished.

"But more importantly," Barry continued softly, "I thank you for the people who are about to eat it." He glanced at his son-in-law. "*Most* of them, at any rate. Amen."

"Amen," Charly repeated.

Hope grinned and slapped Michael on the shoulder.

Now, fingers and utensils flew rapidly as the gang impatiently made sandwiches. Everyone except Hope. She leaned against a side wall and watched with amusement.

Finally, her mouth stuffed with pastrami, cheese and pumpernickel bread, Charly looked up, noticed her sister's expression and almost choked. Gasping, she spluttered, "What're you grinning at?"

Hope pulled out an empty chair and re-joined them. Reaching for the mayonnaise, she told the others, "You remind me of my grad students. Can't shut 'em up while we're out in the field surveying, but come lunchtime, they're as silent as an empty canyon." She waved long fingers at Michael. "Pass the pickled beets, would you?"

Michael automatically reached for the tall jar, then hesitated. "Hey!" he exclaimed, brows knitted. "You said something 'bout a surprise."

"Yeah!" Faith piped in while biting into a bread and butter pickle. "Sure isn't a picnic lunch, so what is it?"

"Dessert?" said Charly.

Hope carefully laid Swiss cheese slices across two pieces of bread, added several pickles in a perfectly symmetrical pattern, and was reaching for the ham when a trio of voices hollered, "Come on, Hope. Give!"

The middle Shepherd sister calmly folded her sandwich, cut it precisely in half, took a large bite and chewed thoughtfully. After swallowing, she leaned back contentedly and replied, "Finish eating, then we'll talk."

Faith gaped at her, then turned to her father. "Daddy?"

Barry shrugged. "Sorry, dear." He sipped water. "Sworn to secrecy."

Michael said, "I could make you talk, y'know." Hope's eyes flew open, feigning fear. Michael burped and added, "Aw, just hand over the ham, will ya?"

Ten minutes later, Charly was filling the kettle as her sisters cleared the table.

Michael peered in the cookie jar and sniffed. "Mmm, peanut butter." He moved the toucan-shaped container to the table.

Barry reached out a hand.

"Uh uh," said Michael, pulling the jar out of reach. "Nobody gets dessert 'til Hope fesses up."

"All right, all right," Hope replied. "Give me a minute." Her long legs carried her into the hallway.

"This is exciting," said Faith, stuffing tea bags into the large thermos. "Can't imagine what she's got."

This time, Faith and the others didn't have to wait very long. Hope strode back in a few seconds later, gripping a flattened disc against her left side. It looked a little like a large tambourine covered by an unruly pile of netting. In her other hand she held a bunch of odd-shaped envelopes.

"What's that?" asked Charly, eyes on Hope's left hand.

Instead of answering, her sister laid the disc onto the table and then gently handed everyone an envelope. "Don't squeeze," she instructed. "And don't open them 'til I say so."

Charly stared at the small manila envelope in her hands. Curiously triangular, it had a slight bulge in the middle. Before she could examine it further, Faith shrieked, "It moved!"

Faith dropped her envelope. It flip-flopped to the floor. "Oh! I'm sorry," she said, reaching down to retrieve it.

"Careful," warned Hope. "Pick it up by the edges."

Charly felt a small rustle under her fingertips. "Hey! Mine's moving, too." Fascinated, she stared at it.

By now Michael, pushed as far back in the chair as he could go, was holding his envelope well away from his body. "Mind tellin' us what we've got here?"

"Sure," replied Hope. With a quick movement, she pulled a string from the netting on the disc. "Voila!" A tubular collapsible mesh cage, about twenty-four inches high, dangled from her finger.

"What on earth?" said Michael.

Hope tugged the bottom ring of the cage and it fell away like a trap door.

"Oh, I get it!" Faith said. Michael and Charly exchanged a puzzled look. Faith confidently held her envelope under the open cage. "Okay, Hope?"

"Go ahead."

While the others watched with their mouths open, Faith gently unfolded the edge of the envelope and pulled the sides apart.

Charly leaned forward. Inside the paper nestled a black wing with silver stripes.

"Why, it's a—" Charly began, then stopped in wonder as her sister held the opened envelope up into the open base of the cage.

The room was silent. All eyes were on the envelope's tiny, colorful occupant.

"Give it a little shake," suggested Hope.

Faith gently jiggled her hand. Suddenly, with a hurried couple of beats, a beautiful butterfly lifted up into the air. Several more strokes and the dazzling silver-streaked wings thrummed further upward. Just as Charly feared the little insect would run out of room and damage its striking wings, it twisted neatly and clung to the netting. A moment later, the wings refolded and the butterfly became still.

"Men and women of the Sweet Shepherd Nursery," Hope began, her angular face beaming with pride. "I'd like you to meet the newest member of the family. The Turner's silverspot butterfly."

"Wow," Charly said.

Faith said, "It's so beautiful!"

"And so small." Michael looked with amazement at the envelope in his hand. "You mean, I've got one of those in here?"

Barry nodded. "While I took a nap, Hope went to the zoo. In no time she was back with a small insulated box." He smiled at his middle daughter. "And inside, she had all these little butterflies, sleeping."

Hope said, "They're in a dormant state. It's safe and ideal for transporting them."

"So that's why it's so warm in here," Faith said.

"Uh huh," Hope said. "I mean, in order for butterflies to fly, the temperature's got to be over sixty-five degrees. Now, come on, you guys. Your turn."

One by one, the others opened their envelopes under the cage and released their special guests. Barry was last, and as the fourth Turner's silverspot fluttered upward, he said, "Wish we could let these little guys go outside and be free."

"We can't?" asked Michael.

"It's too cold," Hope said, shutting the trap door. "They'd die. Besides, I've got to get them back to the zoo. The Turner's an endangered species. Every one of them's precious. I really shouldn't have taken them, but I wanted you all to see exactly what we're going to be rearing."

"Guess we've got an awful lot to learn," Charly said, peering intently at one butterfly.

"It's a big responsibility," said Hope. "No question."

For a moment, the group watched as the quartet of rare insects rested comfortably, hanging inside the cage.

"Don't see why we can't succeed," Barry said finally. "The good Lord's seen fit to give us all the right people and tools."

He laid his large hand in the middle of the table. The others quickly followed suit, with Hope adding her strong hand last.

"All for one Shepherd," each one said firmly, "and one Shepherd for all."

Nicola Furlong

Chapter Twenty-Three

We can complain because rose bushes have thorns,
or rejoice because thorn bushes have roses.
Abraham Lincoln

Not fair. I'd rather go see the butterflies," said Scotty three days later as they were driving to town. "I wanna hold one."

"We've already been through this, honey," Charly said. She glanced at her son in the rear-view mirror. "We'll be getting our own butterflies soon. Now, stop squirming. You'll crease your pants."

"Don't wanna go."

"Mo-om!" Though she was sitting beside her brother, Melissa had hitched herself toward the passenger door, creating as much room as possible between her brother's sneakers and her new dress. "He's going to ruin everything."

"No, he's not," Barry replied. "It's a beautiful Saturday afternoon, it's my first outing since the hospital and I'm going to enjoy it. Isn't that right, Mr. Scott?" He turned to glare at his grandson.

Scotty sighed and gazed out the window.

"Thank you," Barry said. "Don't you worry, Lissa. Our heavenly Father saw fit to keep me on His green earth and I trust it was for many reasons. This's one of them, I'm sure. Nothing's going to stop us from attending your band recital."

"Thanks, Grampa," Melissa replied. She clutched her clarinet

121

case more tightly, but the anxiety in her young face disappeared. "I'm so glad you're coming. I've told Mr. Burgess—he's our music teacher—all about your heart attack."

"You have, have you?" Barry glanced at his daughter. Charly shrugged. "And what did Mr. Burgess say?"

"He said I should be thankful that you're okay." She leaned forward quickly and hugged her grandfather around the neck.

"Your Mr. Burgess sounds like a good man."

Charly smiled at their exchange. After a few moments watching the road and the farm fields spilling out before her, she realized something. For the first time since the hailstorm she felt relaxed. No throbbing against her forehead and no gnawing pit in her stomach. Thanks to her family, the nursery had a bright future and thanks to God, Dr. Rogers and the rest of the hospital staff, so did her beloved father.

She sneaked a glance at his figure in the passenger seat. Though he had lost weight, her father's familiar bulky profile and thick silver hair both comforted her and buoyed her spirits. He did look better, she thought, positive he was acquiring more strength and confidence every day. She had figured out his medication schedule, and he was enthusiastic about the new planting season, excited about the butterfly project, and absolutely tickled to be without the catheter.

And to think it could have been another tragedy. That at this very moment, she and her children might have been driving to town to attend his funeral. And that she would then be an orphan, and raising her children alone. She swallowed a shiver and pushed those thoughts away. Charly knew her father and her family weren't out of the woods yet, but they had hope and they had each other. What more could a person ask for?

It's going to be okay, Charly told herself. *It really is.*

Perhaps not for the first time, but now with an acute awareness, Charly wondered at how carelessly humans can lead their lives and how thoughtlessly they often take that priceless life for granted. Automatically, she peered in the rear-view mirror to absorb the images of her children's faces. She squelched a laugh. Scotty was intermittently breathing on and then kissing the side window, while Melissa focused intently on her clarinet's mouthpiece as she rapidly primed the reed with her lips.

Please God, just be with us and I'll do the rest.

~~~

Like most parents, one of Charly's greatest pleasures came from watching her children's activities. What they were doing didn't matter, so long as they were happy, safe, and not causing trouble. She found being part of her kids' lives could often be tricky and was at times impossible. Having a pre-teen girl and a young boy added to the complexity of parenting. At that moment, leaning against a wall in the school auditorium, Charly was grateful to have both children nearby.

Melissa was in clear view, seated on stage along with the thirty other members of the Silver Shores Middle School band. Charly gazed up at the stage and smiled. Some of the kids were giggling, others were peering and pointing into the audience, and all were fiddling with their instruments.

That left Scott, who upon arrival had grudgingly headed off with his grandfather to find seats, offering Charly the chance to chat with the band's director.

"I'm glad your father's recovering so quickly," Derek Burgess shouted over the din, warmly shaking Charly's hand.

His lean figure loomed over her as they stood below the raised stage in the old gymnasium. Though he was relatively new to the school, Charly had met the forty-something teacher several times. She liked his boyish, heart-shaped face with its unusual dimpled chin and serious attitude, and she appreciated his love of teaching both math and music, which was evident from her daughter's ongoing glowing comments about her teacher.

Above them, the band was still warming up, and Charly leaned closer so she could hear Derek's deep voice above the cacophony. "Melissa often talks about him." His deep blue eyes narrowed behind square black-framed glasses. "She was very upset the day after it happened."

"I know," Charly replied automatically, but inside she winced, wounded to hear of her daughter's obvious pain. "It's been tough on all of us, but he's doing well. In fact, he's here—" She glanced around the huge hall where family and friends were laughing and chatting while noisily filling the rows of hard-backed chairs. "Somewhere."

"That's wonderful," said Derek. "I look forward to meeting him after the recital." He glanced up at the large wall clock. "Well, if he's going to see his talented granddaughter in action, I'd better get this show on the road."

With that, he bounded up the steps.

Charly stepped back toward the wall and surveyed the large crowd. Her sisters had planned to come, but at the last minute, neither was able to make it. Hope had to attend an urgent budget meeting, and Faith was called into the emergency services center to cover for a dispatcher who was ill.

Within thirty seconds, Charly's old shyness resurfaced. There were a number of faces she recognized. A couple of women her age in the front row beckoned to her and she nodded hesitantly in acknowledgement. She couldn't believe it, but she felt reluctant to approach them.

Ridiculous! She told herself. This was a rare opportunity for her to make new friends and reconnect with old ones. Given that she worked out of town at the nursery and spent the majority of her free time with her kids or on some plant-related endeavor, she generally had little time to socialize.

It must be the location, she thought, anger rising in her cheeks at her reticence. Unlike her older sisters, Charly had found attending school taxing. Academically, she had held her own and had superseded most of her classmates in history and religious studies, but socially, especially at this school, she had been tongue-tied and awkward.

The gym held a special place in her album of high school horrors. It was here, on this shiny hardwood stage during her second year that the square-dancing incident had occurred. Her male Phys.Ed. teacher had picked her as his partner to demonstrate the steps. Of course, she was terrible. Slow to understand the moves and clumsy when she attempted them. She realized later that her teacher was probably trying to be kind, but her classmates' laughter echoed in her ears for months afterward. To this day, she hated dancing.

She often wondered if her teen angst came about because Faith and Hope had been so popular. Having two bright and charming sisters—the pretty and daring one, and the athletic and determined one—forging a path before you might seem ideal. The reality was much more difficult. Made even worse because Charly had carried her baby fat well into her late teens.

She feared that Melissa, so like herself in personality, would suffer in a similar way. Charly glanced up, eyes roaming across the faces of the eager young musicians, who had been shuffled into their pre-assigned spots by Burgess. She spotted her daughter on the opposite side of the stage. For a moment, Charly's heart ached for her, anticipating the inevitability of the teenage temptations and turbulence her twelve-year-old would soon experience.

Then Charly stared.

Melissa was sitting bolt upright, clarinet confidently cradled in her hands as she listened to Mr. Burgess's last-minute instructions. She didn't appear nervous. In fact, she was bending forward, an aura of excitement surrounding her as she lifted the clarinet to her lips. At Mr. Burgess's signal, the young band members launched into their opening piece.

Charly offered up a small, silent prayer, *Please let her be poised and admired, just like her aunts.*

At that moment, Melissa twisted, caught her eye and winked.

Charly's heart flipped with pride. She rested against the wall and let the opening strains of "Joy to the World" wash over her.

Chapter Twenty-Four

In all things of nature there is something of the marvelous.
Aristotle

C harly waited until the band finished Beethoven's choral symphony. During the eruption of applause that followed, she edged through the crowded aisles to take her place beside her father and Scotty.

Her father spotted her and half-waved. But to Charly's dismay, he was bookended by two empty seats. She dropped into the closest one. "Where's Scotty?"

Barry wiped sweat off his brow. "It's awfully hot in here." His cheeks flattened in consternation. "He's with you…isn't he?"

Before Charly had time to respond, a woman nearby *shushed* her as the familiar notes of the theme from *Sesame Street* began to fill the gymnasium.

Several small children raced toward the stage and began dancing to the jaunty tune.

A middle-aged man in the front row shouted, "Big Bird rocks!"

Laughter filled the gymnasium. Then Mr. Burgess joined in the fun. He turned to face the crowd and sketched a deep theatrical bow before turning back and directing his musicians to start over. Once again, the music from the popular children's TV series poured from the stage and the gaggle of small kids continued to frolic and entertain the audience.

Charly scanned the faces in the huge room in search of her dark-haired son. Her initial once-over was unsuccessful, so she turned to ask for her father's assistance. The words died on her lips.

Barry was gaping at the stage, his broad face a mask of shock. Oh no! *He's had a stroke.*

"Dad!" she whispered urgently while reaching to touch his arm. "Dad! What's wrong? You okay?"

For a dreadfully long moment, her father remained immobile and silent.

"Dad! Talk to me. Should I call 9-1-1?"

She was reaching into her pocket for her cell phone when her father released a shaky breath.

"I'm all right, Charly," he finally replied, though his uneven voice betrayed him. Beads of perspiration dotted his upper lip.

"You sure? You look terrible. Maybe we should go."

"No, no. Don't fuss. I'm okay." He offered a slight shrug. "Just a little hot and tired from the drive, I expect."

"Okay, but just to be safe, let's run through Faith's tests."

"Not *here*, Charly," her father replied, glancing around the gym. "I told you, I'm fine."

She just sat and looked at him.

"Oh, all right. I've already done the speaking part." He forced a wide smile and lifted both arms. "See?"

Charly sighed with relief. Her father had passed the impromptu health check. It didn't appear as if he had experienced a stroke. "Okay," she said, giving him a peck on the cheek and mentally reminding herself to thank Faith for making sure they all knew and could apply the simple tests.

Charly swiveled in her chair, smiling politely at her neighbors while scrutinizing the audience once more. Way at the back, beyond the chairs, she caught a glimpse of dark hair. She glanced at her father. Though slightly pale, he was smiling at the antics of the youngsters dancing up a storm near the front. "Be right back," she whispered as the band began playing another tune.

She ducked and crept across her aisle until she reached the end before striding quickly toward the back. Her son's back was turned, but his companion, a large, tow-headed boy named Alex, looked up and froze.

Charly noticed that he held a small gaming console in his hands. Loud revving sounds burst from its tiny speakers. Her pulse quickened.

Scotty swung around to face her. Guilt flashed across his freckled face. He pushed out his lower lip and made an effort to reply nonchalantly, "Hey, Mom."

Charly waited a second. This little show of defiance was new.

"Hello. If you'll excuse us, Alex?" she said, firmly grasping her son's forearm. She steered him over to an open space against the back wall. "What're you doing here?" she hissed. "You're supposed to be watching your grandfather."

Scotty scowled. "I did. Took 'im to his seat like you said." He jammed his fingers into his pockets. "It was boring. He looked okay and Alex has a new game."

"You know the rules about gaming."

Charly wasn't keen on video games, thinking them mindless and often violent, and did not allow them at home. She knew Scotty had many chances outside her control to experience them. Some of his friends had their own consoles or other devices, and even though they were not allowed, a few smuggled the smaller versions to school. Obviously, Alex had done just that. Nonetheless, her son was well aware of her position. She worried that he was deliberately challenging her authority. Something he hadn't really done...yet.

Nodding, her son rocked on his heels. "But it's the Indy 500, Mom. No violence, just cars goin' *real* fast."

She watched his face for a moment. Was this the start of behavioral problems? She prayed not. He was only nine, after all. Perhaps she was overreacting. He might have been taken aback by her sudden arrival and put on a brief show of rebelliousness for his friend's benefit. She was tempted to make her son rejoin the audience when the band began another popular children's song. Scotty's lips tightened, but he remained quiet.

Oh, what's the harm? A few minutes with a friend staring at tiny racing cars. What would I rather do as a nine-year-old? Hang out with the old folks or watch fast cars?

"Oh, go ahead," she said finally, "but don't leave the gym."

"Thanks, Mom," Scotty replied, his face flushed with pleasure. "And keep an eye out for us, 'kay?"

His arm fluttered in a half-hearted response as he rejoined his friend.

Once again, Charly leaned against one of the gym's walls and watched the recital from afar. The little children were no longer boogeying beneath the stage. She spied her father's white hair among the rows of attendees. He appeared relaxed and was watching the band. She glanced at the large clock above the stage. It was 3:17 p.m.

Just as she came to the realization that the concert was almost over, Mr. Burgess signaled to his musicians. The boys and girls lifted their instruments in readiness and waited.

The crowd hushed. After a few moments, they were rewarded with the swelling opening to "Amazing Grace". When the last notes of the famous folk hymn died away, the audience jumped to its feet and let loose with enthusiastic applause, whistles and shouts. Within seconds, the band members began breaking ranks and shedding their instruments before racing down the stairs and rushing through the milling crowd, making a beeline for their proud parents.

As Charly picked her way toward the stage, she glimpsed Melissa far ahead, already hugging her grandfather. As she turned to the back to locate Scotty and give him a sign to join them, she noticed that Derek Burgess was approaching, slowly working his way through the crowd. It took her a few moments to spy Scotty and catch his eye.

He nodded in response.

In that moment, something changed. Charly felt the atmosphere in the gymnasium tighten and a choking scream split the air. This was immediately followed by a man's voice calling out sharply, "Please, everyone, stand back! Everything's all right."

She spun. Her heart stopped.

The commotion was coming from the exact spot where she had last seen Melissa and her dad. Charly could just glimpse Melissa among the swarm of bodies, but couldn't see her father anywhere. Her eyes raked over the faces and shapes surrounding the area, but Barry's large silhouette were nowhere to be seen.

"Mom!" Melissa's voice shrieked. "Mom!"

Charly was already sprinting in her direction and rudely shoved her way into the tightly packed throng. As she burst through the tangle of arms and legs, her heart stopped again.

Barry Shepherd sat slumped in his chair. His eyes were open but glassy, his face glistened with sweat. Derek Burgess knelt at his feet, holding Melissa's hand.

Charly dove to her father's side. "Dad! Dad! Can you hear me?"

"I think he's in shock," Derek said.

Melissa flung herself at her mother, her small face marred by tears and terror.

Charly embraced her as Derek said, "Don't worry. Ambulance is on the way."

"Grampa! Grampa!" A second later, Scotty squirted through a pair of legs and scrambled over to his grandfather.

Charly grabbed her son's arm and held him along with his sister. "It's okay, Scotty, Melissa. He just needs air." She reached toward her father. "It's gonna be okay, Dad. Help's on the way. Just hang in there."

Barry didn't respond, just continued to stare ahead blankly.

Derek stood up, turned to the circle of anxious faces and raised his arms. "Please, folks, everything's all right. If you would just move back and give us a little space."

The crowd reluctantly shifted backward and began to slowly disperse. Then someone shouted and the remaining stragglers shifted quickly, allowing two ambulance attendants to march directly toward them.

Charly leaped up to meet them. "I think he's had another heart attack," she said quickly as the pair set down their gear.

"Another?" one of the paramedics replied sharply. The other moved immediately to Barry's side.

Charly nodded. "He had one almost two weeks ago." Tears flooded her eyes. "He...he uh, just came home a few days ago." Charly inhaled sharply. She knew she was babbling, but couldn't stop herself. "This's his first outing. Oh dear, maybe he shouldn't have come. It's all my fault—"

The attendant spun and deliberately held up a large hand in front of the remaining crowd. "Please, folks. Back off and let us do our work."

He beckoned to Charly.

As she attempted to calm herself in preparation for the now familiar questions, Charly couldn't really believe that they were in the same dire circumstances all over again.

Not another heart attack. Please, God. Please.

Chapter Twenty-Five

*People who love this world, people who pay attention, are
gardeners...
regardless of whether or not they have ever picked up a
trowel. Because gardening is not just about digging. Or planting,
for that matter. Gardening is about cherishing.*
Terry Hershey

Your father's fine," Dr. Rogers said.

Charly felt her chest muscles relax and she breathed deeply for the first time in over ninety minutes. She was holding her children's hands and squeezing tightly. The entire Shepherd family, including Michael, stood in the small waiting room in the hospital's emergency ward, encircling the red-haired cardiologist.

"Thank God!" the trio of sisters replied.

"What happened?" asked Michael.

Faith swallowed. "Was...was it another heart attack?"

Dr. Roger's brow wrinkled. "No. His heart function's good. I believe he—"

"I know what happened," Scotty said.

The adults stared down at the small boy.

"He's got 'Soldier's Heart'."

"Soldier's heart?" said Michael.

Faith added, "What on earth's that?"

"Scotty, honey," Charly said, "please let the doctor—"

But Dr. Rogers squatted down to face the young boy. "Where'd you find out about Soldier's Heart?"

"School. We're learning about the Civil War." He stuck out his small chin in defiance. "My Grampa fought in Vietnam and I betcha he's got that PST thing."

"That PST thing?" Hope said. "Now what're you talking about, Scotty?"

Dr. Rogers stood and gestured to the group. "Let's all sit down, okay?"

After everyone was seated, he continued, "Scotty, you believe your grandfather's suffering from PTS or post-traumatic stress disorder, is that right?"

"Oh," Hope said.

Faith and Michael exchanged a puzzled look.

Scotty nodded vehemently. "Yeah, during the Civil War they called it—"

"Soldier's Heart, I know," the cardiologist said. "It's got many names: shell shock, battle fatigue, post-Vietnam syndrome and combat psychological disorder." He leaned toward the young boy. "Why do you think he's suffering from Soldier's Heart?"

For the first time, Scotty looked doubtful. "Uhhh, my teacher said lots of vets have it. Makes 'em act weird sometimes. Grampa's always mad when I ask him about the war, so I figure he's got it." He scooted forward to direct a fierce look at the heart specialist. "Doesn't mean he's a coward or anything."

"Of course not," Dr. Rogers said. "I'm sure your grandfather served with distinction."

He paused while an orderly pushed an empty hospital bed across the room and jammed it into a corner.

"You're right, though, Scotty. Many veterans suffer all sorts of psychological damage. However, in this case, I don't think that's what happened."

"Oh," replied Scotty in a disappointed voice. He slipped deeper into his chair.

"Then what did happen?" Charly said.

Dr. Rogers cast his eyes around his audience. "We believe he experienced a panic attack."

"A panic attack!?" Faith bounced in her seat, her dangling earrings jiggled wildly. "You mean, we all thought he...he'd suffered another heart attack and he was just...panicking?" She slumped down.

"I don't understand," said Hope. "A panic attack can look like a heart attack?"

Dr. Rogers nodded. "They share many symptoms, like dizziness, sweating, shortness of breath and increased heartbeat. Exactly what your father appeared to be experiencing."

"But if it was just a simple panic attack," Hope said, "wouldn't he know the difference?"

Dr. Rogers shook his head. "Not if he hasn't had one before. And there's nothing simple about panic disorder. It can be one of the most upsetting and frightening experiences, especially for first-time sufferers like your grandfather. If not properly diagnosed and treated, the effects can be devastating."

Hope flushed. "I...I didn't mean—"

The cardiologist waved his hand. "I know. The main thing is that he's fine. His heart function's improving, he appeared to be recovering well at home—"

He hesitated and glanced at Charly.

She nodded.

"Right," he continued, "but something happened. Something so sudden, stressful and dramatic that it triggered a full-blown attack of anxiety."

He flipped up his palms. "Anybody know what that was?"

The Shepherds exchanged glances, then shook their heads.

"You were there, Charly," Faith said. "What happened?"

Charly frowned. "I don't know. Honestly. He seemed fine during the trip and when we got there." She bit her lip. "He did say it was hot, and then..."

"And then?" said Hope. "So something did happen."

Charly jumped up and started pacing. "You see, I didn't sit with him for very long. I was late joining him and then left almost immediately to look for Scotty."

Charly paused.

135

Her son dropped his eyes and fingered a magazine atop a nearby coffee table.

Now Faith leapt to her feet. "Come on, Charly. What was it?"

"Well, we listened to the band. It was playing—" Charly smiled briefly, "'Sesame Street.' And a bunch of little kids got up and started dancing. I was looking all over for Scotty and when I turned back to Dad, he was just staring ahead, like he was in shock."

"Shock?" Hope grimaced. "From what?"

Charly shook her head. "I thought he'd had another heart attack right there and then. It took him a moment to speak to me but when he did, he seemed fine. So then I thought, maybe a stroke." She glanced over at Faith. "But I made him go through the tests, which he easily passed, and he told me he was okay. Just a little hot and tired from the drive."

She slumped back down and ran a hand over her eyes. "And I didn't do anything about it. Instead, I went to find Scotty."

Hope gave Charly a quick embrace. "Don't beat yourself up, kiddo. He said he was okay. None of us would've done anything different."

Faith said, "She's right. It's not your fault."

"He might have been feeling a bit anxious," said Dr. Rogers. "It can happen when someone who's experienced a heart attack returns to normal life."

"Then what happened?" asked Michael.

"I found Scotty," Charly said, "and was about to go back to my seat when there was a commotion. I looked up and through a bunch of people I saw Melissa." Charly smiled comfortingly at her daughter. "Poor kid, you were really upset."

Melissa blinked rapidly, her eyes suddenly vivid with tears.

Charly reached out to pat the youngster's knee. "Couldn't see Dad anywhere, so I just rushed over and he had...collapsed."

"It was like he'd seen a ghost," Melissa whispered, knuckling away her tears.

The room went suddenly quiet.

A metallic voice boomed a message over the hospital's loudspeaker.

"A ghost?" Hope's tongue ran over her bottom lip. "What do

you mean, Lissa?"

The young girl shifted uneasily. "Well, I was coming to see him after we'd finished playing. At first, he was smiling and then...his face *changed*." Her own expression crumpled at the memory.

"Come here, honey," Charly said, holding out her arms.

Once Melissa was comfortably seated on her mother's lap, Dr. Rogers said, "Melissa, how did his face change? Did he seem to be in pain?"

The young girl chewed her thumbnail. "No." She swiveled toward her mother and whispered in Charly's ear.

Charly softly kissed her daughter's cheek, then turned to the others. "She said Dad had the same look on his face that he had at... Mom's funeral." She gazed directly at the cardiologist and added, "He thought he'd spotted our mother among the mourners. He was in—" her voice caught for a moment, "very bad shape, poor thing."

Hope gulped loudly, and reached to squeeze Melissa's shoulder.

Faith blew her nose and blinked rapidly.

"I understand," Dr. Rogers said gently. "So, it would seem that your father saw someone or something at the concert that shocked him. We need to know what it was so we can help him."

"What if he won't tell us?" asked Faith. "Our father can be very private, very stubborn sometimes."

"You're not kiddin'," said Scotty.

"Shhh," Hope said quickly.

"Well, he'll have to tell someone soon or there's a very good chance this will recur. And, as you know, your father doesn't need this kind of stress."

Dr. Rogers stood.

"I suggest one of you tackle this with him as discreetly and sensitively as possible. But you tackle it and *soon*. Now, I've got to go. I'll release your father. He'll be out in a minute."

He strode away.

Charly popped Melissa off her lap and hurried after him. "Dr. Rogers?"

The cardiologist turned.

Suddenly, Charly felt timid faced with his authoritative air and good looks. "Uh...thanks," she managed. "You've been very helpful and kind." She was babbling again! "I just want you to know how much we appreciate it."

The doctor didn't seem to notice her discomfort. He grinned. "All part of the service, ma'am." Another announcement blared over the loudspeakers and his expression darkened. "I'm serious about getting your father to talk. If you feel it's inappropriate for a family member, let me know. I can refer you to a specialist."

Charly anxiously ran fingers through her hair. "You think he needs professional help?"

The cardiologist took a step toward her. "Ms. Shepherd, your father's suffered two major blows in as many weeks. He may not survive a third. You and your family need to get to the bottom of this. Now, please excuse me."

With that he spun on his heel and disappeared through a pair of huge swinging doors.

Charly felt the heat of his reprimand rise in her veins. For an instant, she wanted to shout back, "Hey! We've suffered, too, you know!"

That humiliated her more. Instead of immediately returning to her family, she leaned against the wall, thankful for its cool solidity. For a minute, she stood silently and felt her heart thumping in contrast to the irregular *swish-swish swish-swish* of the heavy doors.

For the first time since her father's heart attack, Charly allowed herself to consider a terrifying truth. Her relationship with him had changed for good. He was no longer the strong provider and protector, and she no longer the vulnerable and needy child. Their roles were in flux and beginning to reverse.

Chapter Twenty-Six

When one of my plants dies, I die a little inside, too.
Linda Solegato

C harly?" a voice asked.

"Charly, you all right?" asked another.

Charly turned. Her sisters were looming over her.

"What? Oh, sorry. Yeah, I'm fine," she replied, moving from the security of the wall.

"Dad'll be out any minute," said Hope. "We need to decide who's going to talk to him."

The two women stood, their confident manner and posture eerily similar, and eyeballed their younger sister.

"No discussion needed," said Faith. "It's you, Charly. You live with him. It'll be easier for you to find the right moment."

Hope wagged a long finger as though responding to an obstinate student. "Uh-unh. I don't agree. In fact, I think that's the main reason it shouldn't be Charly. They're too close, Faith. It'll just be awkward for both of them."

The sisters began arguing and their voices rapidly rose.

Charly sighed. It was ever thus for the youngest Shepherd. All her life, she had been the unwilling and sometimes unwitting tie-breaker. It was an untenable situation, and one she detested. No matter what decision or side she chose, she automatically wounded one dear sister. And each took it personally, despite their best efforts and claims not to.

Charly understood this all too well. She also realized, to her very marrow, that it would never change. As the third sister, she was forever locked into the murky position of mediator, emissary and sometimes even referee, sandwiched between two strong women with near-opposite personalities.

She didn't know which of them their father would feel most comfortable with. How could she? There was a good chance he wouldn't unburden himself with any of them. So she decided on a strategy that had succeeded on occasion in the past: throw a dark horse into the race and see who snagged the lead.

"How 'bout Michael? You know, Dad might feel more comfortable man to man."

Her words had the desired magic effect. Charly was no longer the object of her sisters' interest.

Hope's eyes nearly popped from their sockets. "Michael! You must be kidding. I mean, Dad would never tell Mikey anything personal. And even if by some miracle he did, what on earth would our dear bro-in-law have to say to him?"

"There's absolutely no reason that Daddy wouldn't feel comfortable speaking to Michael," Faith retorted quickly. She jammed her hands on her hips before continuing to defend her man. "Michael's a lovely man, you know that. Isn't he, Charly?"

Charly suppressed a groan. This wasn't working out as well as she had hoped. But before she could answer, Hope retook the lead.

"Come on, Faith. We know you think he's lovely and all that and yeah, he's a very nice and generous guy, but—" she leaned toward Faith's ear and whispered loudly, "nobody's gonna mistake him for being sensitive. Right, Charly?"

Charly held up her hands. "Look, it was only a suggestion, okay? I've no idea who Dad would want to talk to and neither do the two of you." She paused for a moment. "Hey! Here's an original idea. Maybe we should just ask him."

"Ask him what?" another voice interjected.

The three women whirled. Their father was sitting in a wheelchair staring up at them. Immediately behind him stood Michael and the two kids.

"Uh, nothing, Dad," Hope replied quickly. She glanced up at the large clock which hung on the opposite wall. "Is that the time? Wow, sorry, guys. I'm gonna be late for a field trip." She reached down and gave her father a hug and a quick peck on the cheek. "Real relieved you're feeling better, Dad. I'll call later, 'kay?" Before he could respond, Hope's long legs had carried her to the wide doorway leading to the main entrance.

"Hope!"

Hope turned at her father's voice.

"Come for breakfast tomorrow."

It wasn't a request.

Hope glanced at her sisters and smiled hesitantly. "Sure, Dad. Be there 'round 8:30. 'Bye."

Barry looked at Faith and Charly. "Either of you in a hurry to go somewhere?"

Charly wished she was and from the sudden stiffness she sensed in her sister's body, she guessed Faith felt the same.

"No," she replied after a brief hesitation.

"'Course not, Daddy," added Faith. She linked arms with Michael and gave him a pleading look. "Not unless my lovely man here has something special planned."

Michael blinked uncertainly.

Charly nearly laughed. It was obvious from his panicked expression that the former cop knew he was being called on to rescue his wife, but had no idea from what. As a result, he remained mute, shifting uneasily on his feet. Strike him from the competition to be the father confessor, thought Charly.

"Let's go, you guys," Scotty whined, breaking the awkward moment. "Mom, can we get a burger?" He stepped over to tug on his mother's hand. "I'm starving."

"I'm up for that," Michael replied, almost shouting in his relief. "Last one to the car shares his fries."

~~~

By the time the Shepherds returned home, darkness had settled in around their big Cape Cod house like a favorite fleece jacket, tucking into the corners of the yard and softly folding over the jagged peaks of the perennial garden beds. Charly loved coming home. No matter where she had been or what she had done, she was always relieved to be within shouting distance of the family home's wide, welcoming porch.

In her youth, her parents had regularly sat side by side in their old rockers, chatting amiably while waiting for their girls to return. The porch light was always on, a light Charly could spot from a long way off, and her steps would quicken after the first glimpse. Being the youngest, she was usually back first and she cherished shouting out a greeting into the gloom and hearing her mom's affectionate reply. Best of all, she would then perch on the porch railing, enjoying having her parents all to herself, and regale them with her exploits.

Both parents were interested in every aspect of their daughters' lives, but Eileen had taken this one step further. She had known the names of all their friends, their friends' parents, their teachers and coaches, and she had understood who was mad at whom or who was in trouble. Even as the three girls matured and took on jobs and lives of their own, Eileen had kept up to date with each one and remained constantly involved, without being nosy or interfering.

Charly hadn't appreciated her mother's extra effort and attention until she had her own children. Then she was amazed and grateful at what her mother had quietly accomplished and set forth as an example, one which she tried to follow. And now, it was she and her father who often rocked the evenings away, waiting for the next generation of Shepherds to come home.

The house light, now a powerful spotlight directed up the driveway, poured a warm yellow glow onto the gravel, allowing Charly to easily navigate its slight curves. As she pulled up to the front door, she heard her father sigh.

"Yeah, it's good to be home, isn't it?" she said, pushing open her door.

As she stepped up onto the porch to open the front door, she hoped the return to his beloved property would buoy his spirits.

He hadn't eaten or spoken much since they had left the hospital. She wondered what was going through his mind, but hesitated to ask until they were alone. Now, as the kids sleepily pulled themselves from the backseat and dragged past her and through the entrance, Charly swung back to face the car, which stood in a pool of light.

The passenger door remained closed, her father still inside, staring into the inky air.

Charly didn't know what to do, so she took a moment to think. As the soft night wind caressed her hair, she asked for advice from someone she was certain would understand.

Please, Mom, help me figure this out. You know Dad. He's a proud man. And even though he's starting to falter a little, he's still my father and neither of us is too keen or able to change our relationship. I know that some change is inevitable, but it feels like crossing a minefield and every step's agonizing, so I could really use a tip or two.

Do I stay or do I go?

Her mother didn't reply. At least not directly, but Charly experienced a calmness gliding slowly over her. She took a moment to peer at her father's face and posture, partially visible behind a deep shadow. He appeared alert, though lost in thought and completely in control.

Maybe he's asking for advice, too.

She counted to twenty, but he remained in place. Then, with whispered thanks to her mother, Charly turned and walked into the house, leaving her father alone in the dark.

Chapter Twenty-Seven

There is no gardening without humility. Nature is constantly sending
even its oldest scholars to the bottom of the class for some
egregious blunder.
Alfred Austin

I've got something to tell you," Barry said at the breakfast table the next morning. He delivered the words plainly, with no hint of the emotional turmoil that must have accompanied his decision to say them. That turbulence was written all over his broad face.

Charly and her sisters exchanged quick, apprehensive glances.

"You're gettin' a Hog!" cried Scotty as he spooned up more cereal.

"What?" Michael nearly choked on his coffee and then continued to sputter, "A Harley? Barry, why didn't you ask me? I know—"

"Grampa's not talking about motorbikes," Melissa said sharply. "Can't you see? This is something important. Isn't it, Gramps?"

Barry smiled warmly at his granddaughter. "Thank you, dear. You're right." His gaze swept over Michael and Scotty. "Sorry to disappoint you, guys, but it's not a bike."

Melissa inched forward on her chair. "You're not moving away, are you, Gramps?"

"Moving?" Faith exclaimed. She glared at her sisters. "You two in on this? Why am I always the last to kno—"

"Hold your horses!" Barry bellowed. His family jumped, startled by his tone. "What is it with this family that a man can't make a simple statement and not have everyone runnin' off half-cocked without listening to the rest?"

The kitchen was suddenly silent, save for the soft ticking of the old grandfather clock in the hall.

"Thank you," Barry rubbed his palms together, "I'd like to finish what I started."

"Of course, Daddy, go ahead," Faith said hurriedly.

"Sorry, Dad," said Hope.

Charly began, "Maybe the kids should—"

Barry held up a palm. "They stay."

Six pairs of eyes watched him expectantly.

Barry exhaled heavily. "What I'm going to tell you isn't easy. It's something I should've told you years ago." He looked down. "I'm ashamed to say I never even mentioned it to your mother."

"What, Dad?" Hope said.

"You can tell us anything, Daddy. You know that."

Barry nodded at Faith. "I appreciate the offer, dear. It's not that I couldn't tell anyone. It's that I didn't want to."

Scotty kicked at a table leg, jarring a couple of glasses. "You do something...bad, Grampa?"

Barry's cheeks pinked.

More glasses rattled until Charly reached out to touch her son's knee.

"Yes, son. I wish with all my might that I hadn't, but..." He opened and closed his eyes. "Actually, that's why I wanted you and your sister here. So you might learn from my mistake. So you all might learn."

"Okay, Dad," Charlie said softly. "We're listening."

"I'm sorry I scared you all yesterday. I...I had a shock." He smiled faintly. "And no, Mr. Scott, before you say it, it wasn't the music." The little boy grinned. "The music was lovely, Lissa. As were you." Melissa beamed with pleasure. "It was something else, something so unexpected that it shocked me for a few seconds...to the core."

"Come on, Gramps, give!" said Scotty. "What was it?"

Barry slowly looked each and every one of them in the eye and then he sighed and said softly, "For a moment there, I believed I saw a ghost. Now, I think it was just my imagination."

No one said anything for several heartbeats, and then Melissa cried out, "Told you! I said he'd seen a ghost, didn't I, Mom?"

"You did, dear," Charly replied. She carefully observed her father before asking, "Whose ghost, Dad?"

Instead of answering directly, Barry removed a piece of yellowed newsprint from his shirt pocket and reverently unfolded it on the table in front of him.

Charly leaned forward to get a better look. It was a sheet torn from a foreign newspaper, but Charly immediately recognized that someone had used it to hand-print a musical score and lyrics.

"It's a complete song!" Michael said, reaching for the paper. "Hmm, called "Battlefield". Strong title." The others watched as he scanned the page. A moment later, he started humming a tune with a strong military beat and then softly singing lyrics, "This old jargon's tasting stale. Is morale the Holy Grail, and glory just a nail in the chest?"

He hesitated then looked at Barry, his expression one of deep curiosity.

"It's a war song, isn't it?" asked Charly.

Barry nodded.

Hope leaned forward. "Anti-war?"

"No!" Barry said.

Hope flushed slightly and shifted back.

"I didn't know you wrote music, Daddy," Faith said.

Her father grimaced. "I don't. It was written many years ago by my best friend, Graeme Walker." He looked at Melissa. "Your band leader looks a little like him."

Hope said, "So this Graeme Walker's the ghost?"

"Yes. It's been a long time since I last saw Grae. You see, he died in the Vietnam War."

Faith eyed her father. "Why were you so shocked at seeing someone who resembled a guy who died so long ago?"

Barry's expression darkened.

"Anybody want a drink? Tea, coffee, juice?" Charly asked,

wanting to give her father a breather.

But her offer went unheeded. They were all too focused on Barry's story.

"Been dreading this day for years," said Barry. "I've asked our dear Lord for advice and I know what I have to do." He sighed. "Still doesn't make it easy."

"Mom always tells me if I've done something wrong, to just spit it out and get it over with," offered Melissa. "Right, Mom?"

Charly smiled. "That's what your grandfather used to tell me."

It was Barry's turn to smile, temporarily banishing his expression of fear and anxiety. "Good advice, child. Okay, here goes."

The others' concentration was so finely tuned, it was as though they were collectively holding their breath.

"Graeme asked me to give the song to his child if I survived the war and he didn't."

"That's it?" breathed Faith.

"A pal's last need," Michael began quoting, "is a thing to heed, so I swore I would not fail..." He smiled self-consciously. "Sam McGee sure understood that."

Barry nodded. He sat back and became still. After a moment, he closed his eyes and spoke softly, "We were dug in, under heavy fire. It was wet—monsoon season—and dark, no stars...no light anywhere except from the nearby bursts of gunfire. One minute Grae was at my shoulder, firing...the next...he...he was...lying in my arms, coughing, semi-conscious."

He inhaled deeply and suddenly his blue eyes opened, staring fiercely as though he were reliving the scene.

"We both knew he'd been shot bad. Could feel his blood through my field jacket. Warm. Medic couldn't get to us."

He grimaced. "Tried to stop him from talking to save his strength but..." He moaned as a tear etched down his cheek. "He wriggled, face contorted with pain, and managed to pull something out of one of his cargo pockets."

"This?" said Michael, holding up the yellowed paper.

Barry looked at the paper. "He begged me to take it home for him. First I refused, told him he'd do it himself...but his eyes...changed, darkened." He drew a large hand across his wet cheek. "And then

I...gave him my word," he said finally, voice cracking with emotion.

After a lengthy silence while they processed Barry's heartrending story, Hope said, "So you didn't fulfill your promise?"

Barry shook his head. "I wanted to, but...it was complicated." He watched his grandchildren for a moment. "You see, Grae's baby hadn't been born yet and he and the baby's mother weren't...married." Again, he looked at the children. "They planned to, they just didn't get the chance."

"That was wrong, wasn't it, Grampa?" said Scott.

Barry nodded.

Melissa said, "But...but my friend Amy's parents aren't married." She frowned. "They don't think it's bad."

Scotty jumped up. "They're living in sin!"

"Don't say that!"

Barry held up a hand. "Hold on, you two. Now, Melissa, you know full well we believe people should marry before starting a family."

Melissa nodded.

"And that's exactly how most folks felt back then."

"Come on, Daddy. What happened when you returned from Vietnam?" Faith said.

"Well...I tried to find Grae's girlfriend, but couldn't. I knew her name, but that was about it."

"What about Graeme's family?" Charly said. "Surely, they knew her?"

"No. I gather she came from a modest background and Grae was afraid his parents wouldn't approve, so they kept their relationship a secret."

"A secret," Scotty said softly.

Barry nodded. "His family's very rich and his father—"

Michael's low whistle cut him off. "It's General Derek Walker!" he exclaimed. "Wow. No wonder Graeme kept it a secret." Michael glanced at the others. "Y'know, the Walkers?"

The three siblings all nodded in agreement.

"One of the richest families in Silver Shores. Now, that old man didn't suffer fools gladly, lemme tell you." He arched back, his chair rising off the floor. "And that I know from personal experience."

Faith jabbed him with her elbow. Michael grimaced. "Sorry, Barry. Your show."

"Thank you." Barry dropped his eyes and fidgeted with his coffee mug. "And this's where I really let Graeme down." He glanced up, eyes now bright with tears. "I always thought I'd lived my life with enthusiasm, intelligence and integrity."

"You have, Dad," Charly replied quickly. She cringed to see the pain etched across his broad face. "You have."

Scotty punched his grandfather's mug. It shot forward a few inches. "What's integrity, Grampa?"

"It's about keeping your word, son. I've always tried to do that, but this time...I failed myself and my friend." His large fingers moved from the mug to the music sheet, but he didn't touch it. "You're right, Hope. The song's sort of an anti-war statement and I didn't want Graeme's father to think less of him. He was so proud that his son died for his country."

"You really think his father would've been disappointed in him?" said Charly.

"Because of a song, Daddy?" added Faith.

Barry looked round the table. "It sounds a little foolish now, but times were different then. The Vietnam War wasn't popular. Those of us returning home didn't feel that our efforts were appreciated. There was, well, let's just call it...heated discussion."

"No kidding," Michael said. "Lots of anti-war protests and politicking, big-time."

Barry gave him a look of gratitude. "I just didn't have the courage to tell General Walker that Graeme was really against fighting, against war in general. That he'd only signed up to please his father. I wanted the General to be proud of him, to honor him. After all, he'd made the supreme sacrifice."

"So," Faith said, "you never found Graeme's girlfriend?"

Barry slowly shook his head.

"And you never told his family about her or the baby?" Hope said.

Barry studied his hands for a long time. "No. To my everlasting regret. I wanted to put the war behind me, to move forward." Without raising his head, he added softly, "I'm ashamed to say that I didn't keep my promise and...I failed my best friend."

Faith reached across and gently laid a hand over her father's.

Scotty jumped up and down. "All right, already. Would y'all stop talking? I just wanna hear the song."

"Yeah, me, too," said Melissa. "Sing it, Uncle Michael."

Michael gestured toward the piano and asked quietly, "May I?"

Barry closed his eyes. When he reopened them a few seconds later, his whole demeanor had changed.

"Yes, thank you, Michael," he replied in a strong, clear voice. "I would dearly love to hear it."

"Let's all go," suggested Faith, rising with her husband. "Okay, Daddy?"

The family trooped into the living room. Michael dropped onto the piano bench. While Melissa and Scotty bookended him on the narrow seat, the adults gathered round.

Michael held his hands suspended over the piano and hesitated. "You haven't heard it before, Barry?"

"Sadly, no," the older man replied. "I can't read music, and I... couldn't ask anyone to help."

"Until now," Hope said.

Michael's fingers moved. He started playing slowly, feeling his way into the haunting melody. Even though the notes were played on piano keys, Charly immediately felt the rhythmic beat and could almost hear an accompanying military trumpet and snare drum.

The words from a lonely and disheartened soldier were incredibly romantic and sad. Almost in the form of a letter home to a loved one. Charly was so caught up in their raw emotion that she forgot her surroundings and her family. For a minute, she was one with the story, feeling the soldier's pride and his shame.

When Michael reached the middle of the chorus, singing, "You're my lifeline, compass and shield," Barry stepped forward and touched his shoulder. Michael stopped playing immediately and turned.

"I'm sorry," Barry said, his voice thick with emotion. He reached for the sheet music, folded it carefully and slipped it back into his pocket. "I...I can't listen anymore. You'll have to excuse me."

With that, he turned and walked out, so quickly that the others were caught off guard. They stood silently, close together, and stared after him.

"Now a promise made is a debt unpaid," Michael finally recited softly, "and the trail has its own stern code."

Chapter Twenty-Eight

*Through gardening, we feel whole
as we make our personal work of art upon our land.*
Julie Moir Messervy

About fifteen minutes later, Charly joined Michael and her siblings outside. She found the trio working in the second greenhouse. All three were stooped over a tableful of flats, busily thinning out weak bee balm seedlings.

Hope stood and wiped her gloved hands on her jeans. "Kids okay?"

"Yeah, thanks. Scotty's biking with a couple of friends, and Melissa's upstairs working on her scrapbook."

"And Dad?"

Charly lifted her shoulders. "In his room with the door closed."

Hope exhaled heavily and then gestured to the others. "Thought we'd get some of these guys picked out for you."

"Great," Charly said. "I'll take the back table."

They toiled for over an hour without another word, each lost in thought. Charly wondered how the others felt about their father's stunning revelation. She wanted to ask, but needed time to reflect and decide on her own reaction first. She felt sorry for her father. He was so obviously distressed. She was also concerned about what this added trauma might do to his already precarious health.

These emotions were to be expected. What caused her the most apprehension was how she felt toward her father, having just learned how he had neglected a pledge to a dying man. She knew immediately that something had altered irrevocably between them. The others might be feeling the same way. She shoved the prickling anxiety to the back of her mind and focused on plucking out the weaker plants.

This didn't help much, because each spindly, floppy seedling that she removed reminded her of weakness. That led to thoughts of her father's failing, which took her back to being uncomfortable. In the end, she let her mind's eye roam and was surprised when it finally landed on a very pleasing image, that of the red-headed cardiologist, Dr. Rogers.

Finally, Michael groaned and stretched. "My back can't take much more of this. Any chance for a coffee, Charly?"

"Charly?" Hope said. "Hey, you back there! Penny for your thoughts?"

"What?" exclaimed Charly, jolted from her schoolgirl reverie.

Hope called again, "Penny for your thoughts."

This time, Charly felt her cheeks flush. "Uh, nothing." Feeling foolish, as though Hope had read her mind, she swiveled to shift a couple of flats.

"Hey! You're blushing!" said Faith, who was working at the next table.

She stepped nimbly toward her younger sister.

"What's going on? What or whom are you thinking of?"

But Charly was also on the move, beetling to exit the greenhouse.

"Nothing," she replied quickly. "Coffee's a great idea, Michael." She stopped momentarily. "You guys keep on going, I'll be back in a flash."

"But—"

Charly cut short Faith's reply with a curt wave and then she spun on her heel and hot-footed it to the house.

She hustled up the steps and stood in the doorway for a moment, half in and half out.

Don't be so foolish! she told herself. *You don't even know if he's available, much less interested. Besides, don't you have enough going on as it is?*

154

She heard Michael's voice rumbling from the greenhouse and hurried into the kitchen. "Dad?" She paused, waiting for his reply. Nothing. She called out again. Still nothing. "Coffee'll be ready in a few minutes, if you want it," she finally said while filling the percolator.

The work crew was hunched around the family's picnic table when she returned outside with a tray of steaming mugs and some oatmeal pecan cookies she had found in the freezer and quickly defrosted.

"Thanks!" Michael said, stuffing a cookie into his mouth before grabbing a mug.

"Mmm, good coffee, Charly," Hope said, sipping contently. "I mean, we get such junk at the university."

Faith sat quietly, her round face looking thoughtful.

Michael placed a mug in front of her. "You okay, Faithie?"

She started. "What? Oh, yeah. Guess so." Her fingers fiddled with a cookie. "Isn't anyone gonna bring up that whole—" she frowned, "business of Daddy's?"

Charly and Hope exchanged a questioning look.

Charly replied first. "We're all thinking about it, Faith."

"I figure we're in as much shock as Dad," said Hope. "Honestly, I don't know what to say."

She sipped coffee for a moment.

"I mean, this happened ages ago, yet did you see the look on his face when he first pulled out the sheet music?"

She looked at her siblings with a mixture of astonishment and embarrassment.

"He was *afraid*." She blinked away tears. "I've never seen Dad afraid before."

"He wasn't afraid," Faith said.

Hope's eyebrows shot up. "Okay, Faith. What was he feeling?"

Faith's back straightened. "Not sure. But it wasn't *fear*. Not Daddy."

The two locked eyes momentarily.

"Come on, you two," Charly said in a calm voice. "We don't have a clue what Dad's feeling. Right, Michael?"

Michael lowered his eyes and gulped his coffee. "Uh, sure,

Charly."

Hope shrugged and took another cookie. "So, what're we going to do?"

"Why do we have to do anything?" said Faith.

"Oh, for heaven's sake!" Hope said. "You've gotta get Dad off that pedestal of yours, Faith. He's obviously very troubled, been worried about this all our lives. Y'know how he'd never talk about the war, how touchy he got if we ever asked."

Michael nodded. "Exactly what Scotty said."

"Well, the boy's right! Something's been bugging Dad for years and now we know what it is."

Hope stood and started pacing along the muddy ruts near the picnic table.

"He's been through an awful lot lately. I just think we've got to step up to the plate a little more. Help him out."

"Ha!" Faith said. "As if he'll let us."

Charly felt a familiar faint rustling deep inside her. It was never uncomfortable, but it was intriguing. Today, though it was somehow different. What did it mean? She observed Hope for a few seconds.

She said, "Help him...how?"

Hope threw her long arms up toward the billowing clouds above. "How do I know?"

"Daddy wouldn't like us prying into his affairs," said Faith. "I think we should leave him be."

Hope scowled, but held her tongue.

Michael tapped a spoon against his mug. "What do you think, Charly? You're closest to him."

The three sisters stared at him in amazement. Charly felt a surge of admiration flow through her. "I'm not sure, Michael. I do think he wants to talk, to get it off his chest once and for all."

She paused, taking in the lovely view of their old homestead. Her father was inside. She hoped that his being in his own home was a balm to his agitated emotions.

"Maybe he just needs a little more time, huh? After all, he confessed a lot this afternoon. It can't have been easy."

She wanted to ask if her sisters now felt differently toward their father, but she couldn't bring herself to do it. That would be to acknowledge her own rogue feelings, not to mention probably pitting one sibling against the other.

Charly knew that in any emotional family situation, Faith would blow hot and Hope cold, and she would be, as usual, floundering in the middle. When they were little, their mother had nicknamed them her three baby bears, directly as a result of their distinct personalities. Charly believed that her sisters were comfortable with the allusion to the children's story, but for Charly, being thought of as just right never *felt* just right.

"Why don't you let Charly handle it?" Michael said, tossing the dregs of his coffee into the soil. "Barry's been through the hard part, the admission of guilt. If he's like any of the guys I've taken in, he'll want to talk."

"Michael!" Faith slapped the tabletop. "Daddy's no criminal."

Her husband regarded her affectionately. "I know, sweetie. I'm not suggesting he is. I just mean, I've seen a lot of guys with guilty consciences, and when they finally let loose, they really *let loose*."

He leveled what the family called "The Look" straight into Charly's eyes.

Despite herself, Charly froze. No matter what, Michael's relentless cop-in-pursuit stare always made her feel like she had been caught red-handed, doing something terribly wrong.

"It's better one on one," Michael said. He stood and stretched. "Just be there, Charly. It'll happen."

Charly wasn't at all sure she wanted it to happen, especially to her.

Michael was oblivious to her inner struggle. He took his wife's hand and tugged.

"Let's go, Faithie. A man's got important things to do."

"Don't push him, Charly," Faith said, pulling her legs out from under the picnic table. "He's stressed enough already. We don't want—"

"She knows, Faith," Hope said, her tone peevish. "Why don't we just back off a little and see what happens, 'kay?"

"Back off? You saying I'm pushy—"

"She saying nothin' of the kind," Michael said quickly. He pulled Faith toward the motorbike. "Come on. See ya, girls."

The others waved them off and waited quietly until the roar of the motorcycle was swallowed up by the late-morning wind.

Hope started piling the mugs onto the tray. "You okay, kiddo?"

Charly exhaled heavily.

"Don't let her get to you," Hope said. "You know how she is 'bout Dad. She wouldn't admit he had a fault if his name was San Andreas."

Charly stared at her in disbelief.

Hope stopped, her angular cheeks reddening slightly.

Then, Charly let loose a loud *whoop!*

"San Andreas fault!" She laughed heartily. "That's a good one, Hopeful." She smiled for several seconds before her expression turned serious. "Thanks for the support, though. Appreciate it."

Hope brushed bits of cookies onto the ground. "I think Michael's right, believe it or not." She popped an errant pecan in her mouth and crunched. "Just wait, see what happens."

Charly nodded, picked up the tray and started toward the house.

Hope hurried to catch up.

"Not so fast. You still haven't answered my question."

"What question?" Charly said, faking innocence.

Hope pulled open the back door, stepped aside and waved her younger sister in.

"Who were you thinking about back there, before you went for coffee?"

Charly edged past. "Nobody."

Hope grabbed Charly's shoulder, halting her progress.

"Uh-unh. You were blushing, kiddo."

She tugged harder, spinning Charly around.

"Someone I know?" Hope stared at her, narrow-eyed, for a long moment.

Charly steeled herself, met Hope's gaze and kept her expression neutral. How could she admit anything to her sister when she hadn't had time to process her surprising thoughts herself? Besides, she had learned years ago that when she was ready to reveal anything serious, especially matters of the heart, she must do so to both sisters at the same time. Though more cumbersome, it was the best strategy in the long run.

Charly moved, breaking free and heading into the kitchen.

"Haven't a clue what you're going on about, Hope," she called out while filling the sink with hot water and soap. "Sun must've been in your eyes."

"Maybe, maybe not," Hope said, trotting in after her. "One thing's certain, I'm gonna find out."

Charly knew her sister was right. She dumped a couple of mugs into the water and swirled the soap bubbles around. Just like she felt.

Like some little puff of air getting spun around every which way.

Chapter Twenty-Nine

Gardening is about enjoying the smell of things growing in the soil,
getting dirty without feeling guilty, and
generally taking the time to soak up a little peace and serenity.
Lindley Karstens

Charly actually enjoyed the next few days, as the entire Shepherd family returned to its routine. The kids trotted back and forth to school, Faith helped save more lives dispatching emergency services, Hope continued to teach and to finalize the requirements for their butterfly experiment, and Charly, Michael and her father spent many happy hours watering, thinning and transplanting, despite a spate of stormy weather.

And no one mentioned Barry Shepherd's revelation.

Though Charly felt a bit awkward with her father and occasionally almost avoided his gaze, she was determined to let him initiate the conversation. Fortunately, they were very busy. The first day of spring was a week away and their phone had already started ringing with clients clamoring for plants.

"Beware the Ides of March, missy," Michael said one overcast morning, as he hauled another flat of *aquilegia* seedlings off the back of the half-ton pickup.

"*Et tu, Brute,*" Charly said from inside the cargo box.

She playfully jabbed him with her foot before shoving another flat in his direction.

"You're not the only one who knows Shakespeare."

Michael grinned and reached for the plants.

The driver's door slammed and Barry stepped down onto the gravel.

"Who's reading Shakespeare?" His large boots crunched toward them. "Always been a sucker for *Romeo and Juliet.*"

He paused, thrust up a gloved hand to the sky and whispered solemnly, "See, how she leans her cheek upon her hand! O that I were a glove upon that hand, That I might touch that cheek!"

He nodded at Michael. "How's that for a suitable quote?"

Michael tossed Charly an amused grin and replied, "Wouldn't have taken you for such a romantic, Barry."

Barry jammed his hand into his overalls. "Don't see why not. You're not ashamed to show your sensitive side, are you, Michael?"

It was Charly's turn to grin, though she turned toward Michael before expressing it. She didn't, however, move quickly enough to miss the flash of pain that crossed her father's face.

Michael feigned embarrassment. He plucked an orange *aquilegia* blossom and sniffed it dramatically.

"'Course not. I'm just as sensitive as the next guy, aren't I, Charly?"

"Don't drag me into it," Charly said. "This's obviously a man's issue. I'll just finish checking off the inventory, okay?"

As the men continued to unload and wheel the flats into the second greenhouse, Charly ticked off everything, careful to make sure they had received the exact numbers and types of plants they had ordered. She was pleased. Though they were stuck paying a premium, they now had a healthy supply of young *crocosmia, aquilegia and agastache* plants to cover off the losses from the previous month's hailstorm.

Perched on the side of the pickup's cargo box, Charly took a moment to examine the nursery. She was surrounded by thousands of plants of varying sizes, heights and leaf shapes. A scattered few even bore early blossoms. She had heard that one could spot endless hues of green in Ireland's landscapes, but at that moment, she believed she could see just as many in her own backyard.

Though spring was her favorite time in the nursery, most of their customers preferred seeing the Shepherd family's landscape in early to late summer, when the front and back garden beds and the greenhouses were exploding with colors, scents and shapes. Charly appreciated the nursery's stunning mid-summer palette and perfume, but personally preferred the soft greens of the young plants with their hint of something to come.

Or maybe, she thought as she gazed about, she just preferred having the area to herself and her immediate family. Once the gardening bug bit the locals, there would be little time for reflection or privacy. With all that was happening, she felt the family needed a few more weeks of breathing space to get things sorted out.

Michael's voice pulled her from her reverie. "Hey, Charly! Sorry, but I've got to go."

Charly blinked.

"Dentist, remember?"

"Oh, yeah. 'Course." She stood. "See you tomorrow?"

"Roger that," her lanky brother-in-law said before lumbering over to his bike. As he smacked down his helmet's visor, he flipped them a thumbs-up and rocketed out to the main road.

Charly and her father stood silently while the engine din faded, then Charly walked quickly toward the second greenhouse. Her father's slow footsteps followed. She was plucking off dead leaves at the first table when he stepped up beside her.

"Charly? You angry with me? I...I know my...secret was a bit of a shock."

A desiccated leaf slipped from Charly's fingers, but she didn't turn around.

"'Course not, Dad." She paused, pinched off a couple of buds and then said, "I'm not angry."

She heard him sigh. "Okay. Not angry, but you're *something*. What is it?"

Charly busied herself with another plant. "It's nothing, Dad."

She felt his heavy hand on her shoulder almost before she realized he was again standing beside her.

"Please, honey. Tell me."

His hand remained, but he didn't pressure her to move.

Charly turned and looked deeply into her father's brilliant blue eyes. She glimpsed fear, anxiety and bewilderment, and her breath caught in her throat.

He waited. After a couple of moments, he let his hand slip from her shoulder. He dropped heavily onto an upturned plastic crate and gazed up at her.

He looked so forlorn, so vulnerable that Charly almost hugged him.

After an eternity, her father said, "You're crushing that plant, hon."

She glanced down in amazement to see that her fingers were squeezing the life out of a plump *agastache*. She released the pressure and just stared at her hand.

"Just tell me, Charly. Please. We can't go on like this."

Charly pinched back tears and leaned against the table.

"I'm not angry, Dad. I'm...disappointed."

As she said the almost-whispered word, she noticed the light fade in his eyes. She keenly wished she could take it back.

Her father passed a hand across his mouth.

"That's a...tough one to hear from your daughter."

For an instant, Charly attempted to imagine how she would feel if she were having this conversation with Melissa. And found she couldn't, really. She forced a quarter smile.

"It wasn't easy to say."

"I know and I'm very grateful." Barry stared at the roughened skin on his hands. "Is that how your sisters feel?"

Charly shook her head. "We...we really haven't talked about it. Nobody really knows what to say or do."

"How about the kids?" He hesitated, and added in a voice deepened by emotion, "I'd hate for them to be disappointed in me, too."

"I think they're okay, Dad. I think they're proud of you for telling the truth."

"And you?"

Her answer was a quick movement and then she was holding him with all her might.

"I'm so sorry, Dad," she whispered, tears streaking down her cheeks.

He squeezed her hard.

"No, honey. I'm the one who's sorry. I fooled myself all these years, thinking it didn't matter anymore, that I could avoid telling your mother, even that I could forget..."

They held each other for over a minute and then Barry gently pushed Charly back.

"What can I do?" he asked as she kneeled at his shoulder. "I can't forget...and yet I...I can't forgive myself."

He reached out to squeeze her hand.

"I want to do something before it's too late, Charly. I've asked God for forgiveness, but I don't want to die without trying to make amends."

At that moment, something fluttered then curled open inside Charly's soul. The knowledge was so profound, so sudden, it was as though someone had ripped open a soundproofed door and let fly the stirring notes of an opera.

Charly was astonished.

She *knew* that she was destined to assist her father. She realized this mission, this calling, had always been there, deeply hidden. Perhaps only her mother had been aware of it before, but since Eileen's death, Charly had felt cracks begin to open, hinting at her pre-ordained path.

Without thinking it through or understanding what she was promising, Charly stood.

"Let me help, Dad. I want to help you find...redemption. I think I'm *meant* to."

Barry watched her for a few seconds, then got up slowly. "Thank you, Charly." His broad face widened with a genuine smile. "You mother would've been so proud. She always said you and your sisters had more to offer. Plans to prosper you and not to harm you, plans to give you hope and a future."

"Oh, Dad. I know she always rattled on about that quote and about us having some sort of special destiny, but I just thought that stuff was her way of being proud of us. Never really thought she truly believed it."

"Well, she did, my girl."

They stood for a moment, thinking.

Charly would have liked more time to contemplate what was happening, to enjoy the idea that she had something more to offer, but Barry suddenly interrupted her inner deliberations.

"So what do we do now?"

Uncertain, Charly looked at her father. She could see by the brightness of his eyes that he was eager and that fuelled her own exhilaration. She was about to respond when she noticed something else that sickened her. A grayish cast dulled his skin.

He's exhausted!

She immediately scolded herself for over-exciting her father. Like a child giddy with the night-before-Christmas fever, he doesn't know that any second, he may just collapse. She laid a hand on her father's shoulder, almost wincing at a new hollowness near his collarbone. Her father needed rest, first and foremost.

"First, you gotta lie down for an hour or so—" Barry frowned, his lips parted to speak, but Charly pressed on. "Come on, Dad, you need it. Look at you...you're dead on your feet."

Barry grimaced, but after a moment admitted slowly, "Well, I am a little weary."

"'Course you are, Dad. You've been through a lot. Come on," said Charly, gently turning him towards the house. "We'll have a quick lunch then you take a nap. When you wake, we'll go to the church and you can make peace with Mom."

Barry blinked furiously for a few seconds and then just nodded.

"Good. Tonight, we'll talk some more. You tell us everything you know and remember about Graeme Walker. We'll do the rest."

"You said 'we.' You're sure your sisters will want to help?"

Charly really hadn't a clue, but as clearly as she now saw the path of her new calling, she knew that Faith and Hope would be walking it with her. She hugged her father enthusiastically.

"Of course, Dad. We're not Shepherds for nothing."

~~~

Charly zipped up her wind jacket and slipped out the back door. She paused briefly, eyes unfocused. She began to walk, not down to the nursery to tend the thousands of seedlings, but to her surprise, she realized she was headed towards the family's double garage.

Without thinking, she opened the side door and went in. She cruised past the tools she might normally have reached for—lawn mower, hedge trimmer, weed whacker—straight to her old bicycle, which hung from a couple of large hooks on one wall.

As her eyes took in the familiar midnight blue frame and upright handlebars, she smiled and ran a finger through the thick dust, which blanketed the wide black saddle. Her children's bikes hung off racks on either side. With a quick stab, she tweaked her son's balloon-shaped bell and laughed as it chirped.

At that very moment, she knew what drew her here. A chance for fresh air, the feeling of movement, and the liberty of self-propulsion. A combination conducive to freewheeling thought.

Whenever she had a bit of free time, she had always cherished jumping on her bike and sailing by the farm fields, stony outcrops and thatches of firs that defined her nearby surroundings. She loved and enjoyed her family's company. However, an hour or so every week of solitary exercise improved her health, her attitude and allowed her mind to roam and to dream.

Charly hauled the old bike down, then scrounged around until she found the hand pump. Within a few minutes, both tires were hard with air, the seat was brushed clean and the chain glistened with oil. The bike was ready to rocket.

She jammed on an old helmet, maneuvered her wheeled steed out to the drive and hopped on, pedaling with ease. A bit of the lyrics from one of her father's favorite tunes, "Hotrod Lincoln" floated into her mind—the brakes are good, tires fair. She thought they summed up the state of her bike and began humming Charlie Ryan's classic fifties hit while rolling forward.

As the bicycle curved out onto the main road, Charly embraced the soft moist air sliding over her cheeks, filling her lungs and energizing her body. She hadn't been riding for months. She pedaled hard, enjoying the pumping of her legs and the feeling of flying alongside the fence posts which flickered by.

As she rounded a shallow bend, a scattered herd of Holstein cows swung their bulky salt and pepper heads to stare. In response,

Charly yodeled out a greeting, startling several young heifers into lurching sideways and galloping off.

"Sorry!" she sang at the top of her lungs, her knees thrusting vigorously, spinning her wheels along the pitted asphalt.

She exerted herself and the telephone poles streaked by until her lungs and legs burned. She slowed twenty minutes later, exhausted much earlier than she would have expected. Charly turned around and walked her bike back leisurely along the grass-tufted edge of the highway, regaining her strength and breath.

She had thought her daily chores in the nursery would keep her in decent physical condition, but she realized to her dismay that she was out of shape! And now in her thirties, getting and staying fit was crucial to her and her family's financial future. She just had to think about her father as an example. He had toiled physically as a nurseryman his whole life yet still suffered a dangerous heart attack, the physical and emotional ramifications of which would affect him and his loved ones the rest of his days.

Possibly even shortening his time on earth.

She didn't want that scenario for herself or for her children. "Enough walking, Charly Shepherd!" she hollered, before climbing back onto the saddle. "Today's the day you start lengthy cardio workouts!"

Inhaling heavily, she drove down her knees. At first, her calf muscles shrieked, her forearms grumbled and her breath hissed irregularly. Over time, each piston-like leg movement generated speed and gradually her body relaxed, stopped griping and labored smoothly. With her focus on her physical condition relaxed, her thoughts swirled freely about her experiences on two wheels.

As a child, she often road to and from school, as a teen she explored neighboring country roads, and as a mother, she accompanied her children, directing them along the safest back lanes and rural paths. Her husband, Matt, had always refused to join them, citing a need to golf instead, insisting that it was an essential way to meet and entertain clients for his real estate business. At the time, though disappointed, Charly had reluctantly acquiesced—at all times wanting to be supportive—but both she and their children had missed his companionship, energy and humor on their outings.

Now, when she gazed at the countryside pockmarked by the yellowing stubble of last year's crops, she realized that her last excursion had been with her kids in the heat and blazing light of mid-summer.

She grinned quickly to herself, initially enjoying the vision of Scott pedaling furiously up their drive and of Melissa rolling along a couple of yards behind, fiddling with her hair so it flowed just right behind her helmet.

But then, the image flickered and froze at a single frame. Of Charly...her torso twisting backwards, right index finger to her lips.

Charly stopped pedaling, her heart thumping high in her throat. Not from exertion this time, but from the devastating memory. That dazzling day in late July wasn't just the last instance the family had biked together. It was also the first and only occasion that year.

After her mother's death in May, the family had struggled with re-establishing some traditional routines, like Friday pizza and movie nights and doughnuts after Sunday services. Although her parents no longer rode bicycles, they had loved relaxing on the front porch to watch the trio suit up and mount and to offer energetic waves of goodbye.

And as she followed her children, steering her bike off home property, Charly would swivel, snap a jaunty salute to her father and then air kiss her mother a goodbye. An everyday gesture of love. Something she had offered automatically just a few months ago, but today...today she had...*forgotten*.

Her tires wobbled to a jarring stop, forcing Charly to lurch off her seat and awkwardly balance herself and her bicycle. She slammed her left shin against a pedal, exhaling sharply at the pain. Arching back, she squeezed away tears.

Oh Mom! I'm so sorry! For the first time, her mother hadn't been instinctively in her thoughts. *You really are gone. Gone forever. And I'm already beginning to...oh!...forget you. To move on with life without you. Oh, Mom, please forgive me...I won't forget. I won't. I promise.*

After a moment, she moaned, dropped her head and let both her shoulders and tears drop. For a long time, she leaned over the handlebars, gasping for air and for solace.

Chapter Thirty

The man who has planted a garden feels
that he has done something for the good of the world.
Charles Dudley Warner

I t's very peaceful here," Barry said a couple of hours later as
he carried a terra cotta planter exploding with grape hyacinth
blossoms.

Charly's eyes roamed over the old cemetery flanking the large
side and backyards of the church of St. Peter's-by-the-Sea. "Yes."
How could it not be? She admired the charming scene as they
approached a misshapen oak tree.

It had rained as they drove the few miles to the church. Now, a
fresh wind blew softly, shaking drops from the trees and glistening
on the expanse of wet grass. The little wooden building stood atop
a knoll overlooking the sea and beyond to the small town of Silver
Shores. Tucked away at the top of a winding lane, the location was
both lovely and isolated, surrounded by a rolling green landscape
dotted with bright stony outcroppings and smudges of towering
stands of Douglas fir.

It was an ideal spot to commune with nature and with God.
The church was a brown rectangle highlighted by gothic stained-
glass windows and crowned with a gleaming cross. Nothing special

architecturally. However, Charly appreciated its simple dignity. She treasured the well-tended cemetery, with its chipped headstones, pebbled paths and tufts of wildflowers. It used to be a favorite place to play when she was a child, a spooky haunt when she was a teen and now sacred ground as her mother's final resting place.

Though she currently found it difficult to visit the cemetery, she had never confided this to her father. She accompanied him whenever he wanted to go, and she brought her children every month, but she never came to the cemetery by herself. She was afraid to be alone in front of the black headstone that marked her mother's grave. She didn't know how she would react, nor did she want to know. After her earlier realization while bicycling, now she was not only frightened of her feelings, but also ashamed.

Charly held a pair of pots, each topped by a mass of yellow daffodils, and stood beside the tombstone. At its base stood a Faith original. A battered tin watering can sprouting colorful poppies, crafted from a tangle of wires and bent pieces of cutlery. The artwork provided a whimsical contrast to the stone's austere surface.

Her father kneeled and placed his offering next to the jug. While Charly nestled her pots on the opposite side, Barry twirled an index finger through the carved lettering that read: EILEEN (MACKINNON) SHEPHERD, BELOVED WIFE AND MOTHER. CALLED TO GOD BUT GREATLY MISSED.

"After your mother died," Barry said, standing up slowly, "I didn't think I'd want to come out here anymore." He surveyed the weathered headstones nearby, most of which carried the names of members of his and his wife's families. "But now, it's comforting to see her name along with those of her mother and father and her other relatives." He brushed a couple of twigs off the top of the headstone. "Tradition's important, Charly."

She nodded, now deadheading the little pots and thinking how ill at ease she felt at seeing the deeply cut lettering.

"Maybe not so much when you're young, or at least you don't recognize it as such, but family rituals, histories—they're what life's made of."

"I know, Dad," Charly said. "Both you and Mom taught us that. I'm trying to do the same with Lissa and Scotty."

"They like to come here, don't they?" He smiled. "Just like you girls did when you were young." Again, he gazed at the bucolic scene. "It's a great place for kids to roam."

He reached down and fiddled with the fake poppies.

"Faithie's been here. She's very conscientious about bringing her art." He sighed. "Just wish she'd be the same about attending services. She was always so dependable, sometimes, I thought, even devoted."

"She'll come back, Dad. She's...angry. We're all angry." Charly was surprised to find her voice wavering. "She just needs...a little time."

"And Hope?"

Charly shrugged slightly. "She's often busy with field work, you know that. She comes when she can."

This last statement wasn't completely true. Of the three sisters, Hope was the least spiritual. She visited the church more to please her parents than to benefit herself and often used work as an excuse. Her attendance had become more erratic since her mother's death, and Charly knew that she hadn't visited the grave since the funeral. She didn't think her father was aware of that detail.

"Hallloooo!" A deep voice called out, interrupting her thoughts. The Shepherds looked up.

A small man wearing a dark suit crunched quickly along the pebbles in their direction.

"T'isn't it a fine day for young ducks?"

"Hello, Pastor Joe!" Charly said. She took a few steps and embraced the diminutive clergyman warmly.

"I've come to see how our Barry's making out."

He reached up and shook Barry's hand and then pulled the larger man into a brief hug. His grey eyes sparkled. "Sure, you're looking well." He playfully punched Barry's stomach. Though an octogenarian, Pastor Joe Ritchie's movements were quick and efficient. He even skipped slightly, still showing the grace and hustle learned from the boxing training of his youth.

"Lost a few pounds, but that's for the good."

"Feeling much better, Pastor," Barry said. "Thank you."

"Tis'a fine day to visit your dear wife's grave. And such *beeeuutiful* flowers."

173

"May I speak to you for a minute?" Charly said, wanting to give her father some privacy. "Got some ideas for your perennial beds to make them more drought tolerant."

Pastor Joe grinned lopsidedly. Part of his face was frozen from a childhood bout of Bell's palsy. Charly often wondered if it was the reason he took up boxing, or was it because he was so small? Possibly both, was her usual conclusion.

"Tolerance is something we're always puttin' our shoulder into, Charly. Onward."

For a couple of minutes, Charly chatted as she and the pastor paced along the large garden beds which swept up to church steps. Charly found the conversation lacking. Pastor Joe's replies showed only polite interest. He seemed somewhat distracted.

Finally as they neared the yard on the opposite side of the church, far from the cemetery, he whispered, "I'm so glad you came today, Charly. I'm a wee bit on me toes about your Da. I see he's back on his feet from the heart attack but..." he paused, glancing around. "This might be a bit of a flyer, considering our location."

He rubbed at some wisps of his flyaway white hair.

"You're going to think I'm a daft old man, child, but I fear your Da's haunted by something."

Charly blinked in surprise. How on earth did he know?

"Ahh, so *that's* how it t'is, is it?" He nodded thoughtfully. "He wouldn't confide at the hospital, but I'm thinking maybe I'll visit sometime."

He spun, peered up at her and took her further by surprise.

"So what're you and your *luvly* sisters' doing about it?"

Charly was speechless. Not only had Pastor Joe shrewdly observed her father's angst, he expected the Shepherd sisters to help.

"Charly?" The pair turned as Barry Shepherd came round the back of the church. "Oh, there you are. Just wanted to let you know that I'm ready when you are."

Distracted by her whirling thoughts, Charly didn't respond.

"And I must be away," Pastor Joe said, offering Charly a slight nod. He shook each of their hands and scooted across the grass towards the church's back door.

"Charly?" her father said. "You all right?"

"What? Oh, sorry, Dad."

"You were miles away. What did Pastor Joe say to you?"

She studied his face, took a deep breath and said, "Earlier, you said that Mom thought Faith, Hope and I had more to offer. D'you mean we've got some sort of...special destiny?"

"Oh *that*," said her father. He made the sign of the cross. "Your dear mother and I wondered if it would ever come to pass." He looked at Charly with a puzzled expression. "Are you saying you think...you know what it is?"

Charly cocked her head in surprise. "You mean you don't?"

"It was your mother's idea." Barry smiled ruefully. "Gotta admit, I thought it was just a lovely bit of fanciful thinking. After all, most parents believe their children are special and might do something extraordinary."

Charly nodded, understanding that sentiment completely. After all, she expected Melissa to discover the cure for ovarian cancer and for Scotty to help end Third World poverty.

"So what did she foresee for us?"

Her father took her arm and steered her in the direction of the parking lot.

"She didn't tell me all the details—she was a little superstitious about that. All she'd ever say was 'The Good Lord's given our girls a particular calling, something that'll bring people closer to heaven.'"

"Calling," Charly softly repeated. The same word that had come into her mind when she realized she had to help her father find redemption.

That can't be a coincidence.

Chapter Thirty-One

*To see a World in a Grain of Sand, and a heaven in a Wild
Flower,
Hold Infinity in the palm of your hand, and Eternity in an
hour.*
William Blake

H old it!" said Hope as she shifted position.

Charly stopped pushing the yellow dolly and stood, leaning on the small refrigerator that was strapped to it.

"Helping Dad's one thing." Hope dragged aside a couple of boxes to clear the path to the back of the large greenhouse. "But as to a special destiny? Come on. That's just one of Mom's weird ideas."

"You mean like the one that convinced her Charly was gonna be a girl?" Faith said as she appeared in the entrance, wheeling another compact fridge. "Or that you'd get your doctorate on the first go-round?"

Hope threw up her hands. "Okay, so some of Mom's little ideas came true. Doesn't mean this one will."

Faith shoved her dolly toward the back, aiming directly at Hope. The taller woman stepped hastily aside as the fat wheels churned past her feet.

"I, for one," said Faith, "adore the idea of being *special*."

Charly had to smile because she thought Faith always appeared special. Today, her oldest sister had pulled her hair into a loose bun and sported a soft pink sweater, newish jeans—stylishly patched—beaded red tear-drop earrings and scarlet biker's boots. Quite a contrast from Hope, who was dressed as usual in torn khakis and a paint-smattered sweatshirt, or from her own regular wardrobe of carpenter pants and a man's quilted shirt. She self-consciously adjusted her neckerchief, pleased with its charming mauve and gold swirl pattern.

Faith stopped against the back wall and released the dolly. The fridge *thumped* onto the concrete.

"Hey!" said Hope. "That's university property. Careful." Faith slid her eyes sideways toward her sister but remained silent. "And anyway, your idea of being special isn't what Charly's talking about. Is it, Charly?"

Charly sighed and wheeled her dolly to the back before gently depositing her fridge beside the other one. She pulled the dolly free, turned and faced her siblings.

"I'm not really sure what I'm talking about, okay? I mean...it's just that Dad needs our help and..."

"And what, kiddo? Hope said.

"Can't you see she's thinking?" Faith said quickly. "Give 'er a second, will you?" She spun, her earrings flashing, and nodded encouragingly at Charly.

"Go ahead, Charly."

"But...but," Hope said, "you just said 'Give 'er a second!'"

Faith continued looking at Charly, deliberately avoiding Hope's gaze.

Charly dropped the dolly and it fell onto the floor with a loud *clank*.

"Outside," Charly said and walked briskly past her stunned sisters and plunked down on the picnic table.

The spring air was thick with humidity. Overhead, gloomy purple clouds swirled. Charly buttoned up her shirt and hoped the rain would hold off for a few more hours. She had been thinking, planning and fretting about this conversation for over twenty-four hours, and though she had yet to solidify her thoughts, she prayed she was capable of initiating a positive discussion with her siblings.

A couple of moment later, the others arrived. Faith slipped in beside Charly while Hope clambered onto the opposite bench.

Charly spread her hands out on the wooden tabletop. "Okay, what I said earlier, about a special destiny, I know it sounds a little, out there."

"You think?" Hope said.

Faith glared across at her and she shrugged.

"But you need to know that it's something that's been on my mind, been building ever since Mom died. It was probably there long before, but I just didn't listen."

"Uh huh," Hope said, her angular face now shadowed by doubt.

Faith nodded and squeezed Charly's forearm in encouragement. "I think—"

Charly stopped as a sudden surge of confidence energized her body.

"Check that. I *know* that I've got something more to give than working here in the nursery." She swallowed, then said quickly, "A divine destiny to help people...a spiritual calling."

Charly Shepherd was almost giddy with relief, the words sounded so true. She reached across and grabbed each of her sister's hands.

"We all do. Mom knew it, she prayed for it."

"Mom?" Faith said.

Hope cocked her head. "Spiritual calling? I mean, what're you talking about, Charly? It sounds crazy...like you...I mean, I don't know, but like you've had some sort of—"

"Epiphany." Faith's voice was below a whisper.

"Yes," Charly said. "That's exactly what I've had. An epiphany."

~~~

Hope put her lips to the steaming mug of tea and tentatively sipped. "Ahhh, that's what I needed." She smiled at her sisters, who now faced her across the kitchen table. "Real sorry to cut you off out there, Charly—"

Charly stopped in mid-pour. "It's okay. Know it's a lot to take in." She topped up Faith's mug and then filled her own before adding, "You ready for the rest?"

Hope swallowed and nodded.

"Always have been," said Faith as she reached for a chocolate chip cookie.

Charly cupped her fingers around the hot ceramic mug and gathered her thoughts.

"I'm not sure for how long, but I've had something niggling deep inside me. Maybe dissatisfaction? Maybe fear?" She shook her head. "Not sure. I kinda just ignored it. You know? Life's so busy, there's really no time for what Mom called 'contemplative thought.'"

Both sisters smiled at hearing the familiar phrase.

"But every now and then—especially since Mom died," Charly said, words coming easily now, "I'd find myself thinking, is this all there is? And somehow, I knew it wasn't."

"I've felt that," Faith said softly.

The others stared.

Faith fussed with her hair for a moment, but stammered on. "I, I always thought it was because we..." her gaze dropped, "...we weren't blessed with children. But like you said, Charly, something would happen. Usually after a tough emergency call and I'd just be blank and then..."

She looked up and gazed directly into her youngest sister's eyes.

"I'd want more. I felt, oh I don't know how to put it, other than I felt *I could do more*."

For the second time in as many days, a shiver whirled up Charly's spine.

"Oh, Faithie," she said. "You understand."

Faith's eyes flashed with tears.

"Wait a second, here," Hope said. "I feel like a kid sister on a hot date. Things're sparking between you guys and I'm totally confused. You're both saying *what* exactly?"

Charly and Faith exchanged a long look and then Charly said, "What we're saying, Hopeful, is that we three have been put on earth for more than what we've been doing so far."

"We three?" Hope said. "Where'd you get the idea that I'm involved?"

"Trust us," Faith and Charly said instinctively.

The two looked at one another and laughed.

Hope chomped down on a cookie, swallowed and said, "And

what special divinely conceived job are we supposed to be doing?"

"Well," Charly said. "We start by helping Dad with Project Heartsong."

"Project Heartsong," said Faith. "I like that."

Hope nodded. "And then?"

"And then, dear sister," Faith said. "We go forward on faith."

Chapter Thirty-Two

*There is a little plant called reverence in the corner of my
soul's garden,
which I love to have watered once a week.*
Oliver Wendell Holmes

S omebody having a party?"

The Shepherd sisters looked up as their father strolled
into the kitchen.

"Any tea left?" he said, grabbing a mug from a nearby cupboard
and sinking down onto an empty chair.

Though his white hair was flattened from sleep, Charly noticed
that his blue eyes were bright and he appeared relaxed.

"Sure," said Charly, unscrewing the cap on the large thermos.
"Have a good rest?"

Her father grunted and stirred milk into his mug. "Pass me those
cookies, please, Faith." He reached for the proffered plate and took
two. "You're not having some kinda surprise 'welcome home party'
for me, are you?"

Charly blinked. "Uh, no."

But maybe we should, she thought with a sudden wrench of guilt.

Faith glanced at her, eyebrows raised.

She's thinking the same thing. Since her father's heart attack three weeks earlier, no visitors had been invited to the house. In fact, Charly realized, she had turned down both dragon ladies and several other offers, believing she was doing her father a favor.

"You...you want a party, Dad?" said Hope.

Barry stopped in mid-chew. "No. Not much for socializing. That was your dear mother's domain."

The three women were speechless, confused and uncertain what to say. Finally, Hope tried again, "I mean, you...you mentioned a party?"

Barry sat back, hooked a finger into one of his suspenders and stared at his daughters.

"You're the ones hauling fridges. What else do you need 'em for, if not for food and drink?"

There was a brief silence and then Hope chuckled. "They're for the butterfly larvae, Dad."

"Butterfly larvae? You keep 'em in a refrigerator?"

"Uh huh," Faith said quickly. "They're in winter diapause, uh, hibernation—" She glanced over to Hope.

"Yup. Sort of sleeping, Dad. Soon they'll break their dormancy and then we'll start feeding them, big-time."

He finished off his second cookie. "And what do we feed the little rascals?"

"*Viola blanca pacifica*."

Barry nodded. "Pacific white violet. Easy enough to grow, but..." He looked at Charly. "We don't have any germinating, do we?"

"No, Dad. Not enough time."

Hope said, "The university's going to supply us this time, and if we rear our test sample of butterflies successfully, we can start producing our own food supply for next year."

Barry leaned back. "My word. Still not used to the idea of growing butterflies."

"Don't worry, Dad," Charly said. "It's a new concept for all of us, except Hope."

There was another momentary pause and then Faith said, "Speaking of new concepts, Daddy..."

He looked at her quizzically.

She swallowed and glanced at the others for support.

Charly didn't know what to say and Hope bit her lip.

"Well, uh, you seeee," Faith yanked at her right earring, "Charly told us about wanting to..."

Charly was about to chime in when Hope's voice startled her.

"Oh for heaven's sake, Faith! It's dead simple, Dad. We'd like to help you find Graeme's son and give him the song." Hope paused. Her sisters stared at her in wonder. "What? You're the only ones interested? You don't think I'd also do just about anything to help Dad out?"

Words tumbled incoherently out of her sisters' mouths as they rushed to respond.

Hope raised a palm to quiet them. "Dad, if you're willing to let us try, we want to help. Charly's even got a name for out little venture: Project Heartsong. Right, ladies?"

The others nodded vehemently.

"Good." Hope snatched the second-last cookie off the plate and swallowed it in two bites. "What?" she said finally as the others continued to stare at her. "I've got to do everything?"

Faith gasped. Charly chuckled and soon everyone was laughing.

This's good, thought Charly. *We've made the first move as a team. Thanks, dear Lord. We're on our way.*

"Sorry to break up the fun," she said, "but now's the time, Dad, to tell us everything you know about Graeme Walker."

Her father's expression slipped from one of comfortable enjoyment to rigid uneasiness, and Charly immediate regretted her question. But then her father nodded his appreciation. Her chest muscles relaxed slightly, then tightened again as she realized that this was just the beginning of their new journey. She feared there would be more heartache ahead for her father and the rest of her family, and prayed it would be leavened by the joy of redemption.

Her father sat back and laced his fingers across his broad chest. "As I said, Graeme was a Walker. Until his father's death about ten years ago, they were one of the richest families in the county. Possibly in Oregon."

"Where'd they get their money?" Hope said.

Barry shrugged. "Not sure. They were rich when I was still a farm boy. Sad thing, they pretty well lost it all during the Eighties.

Stock market crash. Anyways, Graeme was an only child and the last of the Walker line. His mom died in childbirth and his father, Derek, was a famous general—"

"Michael mentioned that," said Faith. "World War Two, right?"

Barry nodded. "Being a soldier meant everything to the old man. Real hard case, all spit and polish. Very strict, very arrogant. Not much of a father, really. More like a distant figurehead. I'm sure he blamed Graeme for his mother's death." He paused for a moment. "Think Graeme was afraid of him. I sure felt sorry for him."

"Why?" Charly said.

"Well, that's kinda the key question, isn't it?"

His daughters waited, holding their breath.

"It defined his relationship with his father, and *that* defined who Graeme was as a man."

Faith knitted her brow. "Not sure I understand, Daddy."

Barry leaned forward. "It meant he had a love-hate relationship with the old man, and *that*—as you'd probably say—screwed him up. He had a real hard time trusting people and making friends. He and his father were never close. Graeme hardly spoke to him, but..." He sighed. "Graeme still loved him. After all, he was his Dad and Graeme desperately wanted to make him proud. Which is why a peacenik like him signed on to fight the Vietnam War."

Hope said, "That where you met him?"

"On the bus to basic training." Her father smiled, obviously remembering the day. "He was a big guy, but real shy."

"You didn't know him from school?"

He shook his head. "Heard of him. He was a few years older and lived in town."

"But you went to the same school," said Faith.

"Uh huh. There was only one in those days, but we went back and forth on the school bus, never had any extra time in town. Anyways, we became buddies at basic." He closed his eyes for a moment. "And in 'Nam, best friends. And let me tell you, when you're patrollin' out in the open, along some mucky rice paddy dike, and think, *really* think that someone could shoot you that instant and it would all be over...." He swallowed and then whispered, "You really depend on your buddy to protect your back. And I let my buddy, my best friend down."

Faith squeezed his shoulder. "Don't worry, Dad. We're gonna help."

"So there're no other Walkers in Silver Shores?" said Hope.

Her father fingered the rim of his mug. "Don't believe so. As I said, Graeme was the last." His expression brightened. "But he wasn't, was he? He had a child."

"What about his girlfriend?" Charly said.

"Only know her first name. Sophie. Sounds strange now, but back then, we were just kids, scared to death, tryin' to survive each day. Never thought to ask her last name."

"He must've told you something about her, Daddy," said Faith. "What'd she look like? Where'd they meet? What was their favorite song? What perfume did she wear? Was she in school? Working? Anything about her parents? Siblings?"

"Whoa, Faithie," said Charly. "Give him a break. This isn't a 9-1-1 call."

Faith sighed impatiently.

Barry chewed the side of his mouth, trying to remember. "Don't remember any of that stuff. She was pretty, at least that's what he said, but doesn't every guy?"

The women exchanged amused glances.

Hope grinned. "Maybe at the beginning."

Her father smiled briefly, then frowned. "Wait a second... something you just said, Faith. One of your questions..."

Faith responded quickly, "What'd she look like? Where'd they meet? Her family?"

Excited, Hope jumped in. "What was her perfume? Was she working or in school?"

Their father shook his head.

"Their song!" said Charly. "Is that it?"

Barry's eyes lit up. He reached across and poked Charly's shoulder. "That's it!"

"Yesss!" Faith shouted.

"What was it?" said Hope.

"Beats me."

"What?" Faith almost levitated from her seat. "I thought you sa—"

"Music," Barry said triumphantly. "They both loved music."

Everyone cheered and Hope high-fived her father.

"Way to go, Daddy," Faith said.

He kissed her noisily. "It was your question, honey. Thank you."

"This's great," Hope said. "Now we're cookin' with gas."

"Speaking of cooking, anybody for a sandwich?" Faith looked around. "I'm so hungry I could eat one of those little fridges."

"Me, too," said Hope. "I missed breakfast."

The pair jumped up and began pulling jars and leftovers from the refrigerator. Barry contributed by grabbing cutlery and glasses and setting them on the table. It was only after a couple of minutes of excited activity that Hope noticed that her younger sister wasn't helping out.

"Why the long face, Charly?"

Charly grimaced. "Don't want to be a downer, but..."

"But what, honey?" said her father.

"Please don't take this the wrong way, Dad, but...I don't see how us knowing that they both loved music is much of a lead."

Her father unscrewed the jar of pickled beets. "Aw, you're thinking like somebody in the twenty-first century. You girls get music from all over the ying-yang." He jabbed a fork into the jar and plopped a wine-colored beet onto his plate. "In my day, there was only one place to go in Silver Shores."

Charly reached for the rye bread and began slicing.

"Where was that?" asked Faith, helping herself to a couple of slices of bologna.

"The Vinyl Peel."

"The what?" said Hope.

Her father looked affronted. "The Vinyl Peel. You know, records're made of vinyl. Family who owned the store's name was Peel."

His daughters looked at him blankly.

"We thought it was very hip. I'll tell you for nothing. It was the hangout back then." His expression lightened at a new thought. "And old man Peel loved taking Polaroids and sticking 'em on the store windows." He slouched back and chuckled. "Bet you my Felco pruners that's where they met. Maybe they're even in one of his pictures."

"Never heard of the Vinyl Peel," Faith finally said.

"Not surprising," said her father. "Went out of business when old man Peel passed."

Charly stopped making her sandwich. "Uh...any relation to Millie Peel?"

Her father nodded while chewing. "She was married to his son, Jake," he said after swallowing. "He passed, too. Come to think of it...from a heart attack."

In the silence that followed, Charly thought, wouldn't you know it? Our first lead and it was one of the dragon ladies.

"This seems so roundabout, Dad," Hope said eventually. "Why don't we just go to Lissa's teacher and ask him?"

Her father started coughing. Faith thumped him rapidly between the shoulder blades. After a couple of moments, he took a long wheezing breath.

"Don't want anyone disturbing that young man. More I think of him, less I think he looks like Graeme. Just a passing resemblance."

"Enough to put you in a state of panic when you first saw him," Hope said.

Her father stared at her.

An awkward silence dampened the cheery kitchen.

"Maybe so, but it was just a momentary likeness. I'm asking you to leave him alone, least for now. What I want is to find Sophie."

Hope nodded, eyes widened in surprise.

"Right," Faith said with forced cheerfulness. "First step, someone's got to talk to Millie Peel." She turned to her sisters. "I'm working tomorrow."

"I'm teaching," said Hope.

Charly stood up and started clearing the table. "No problem. Like my little Mr. Scott would say, 'I'm on it like ketchup on fries.'"

Chapter Thirty-Three

Some keep the Sabbath going to church, I keep it staying at home
With a bobolink for a chorister, and an orchard for a dome.
Emily Dickinson

W hy on earth do you want to know about the Vinyl Peel?"
The librarian's head popped up from behind her computer
screen. "It closed ages ago."

Charly swallowed the urge to push the unruly grey kinks of hair
away from the thin woman's eyes.

"Just doing a little personal research, Mrs. Peel. Was hoping
you could help."

During the half-hour it had taken Charly to drive into Silver
Shores and steer the truck into the gravel parking lot of the library,
she had devised a plan of action. She wanted to find out as much as
she could from the chatty library manager without giving much back.
Getting Millie to talk was one thing, but Charly knew that making
sure her inquiries stayed private was another.

Having deliberately hit two of Millie's pet passions—research
and being a fount of knowledge—Charly waited. She wasn't
disappointed. The older woman's thin lips pursed automatically,
then softened.

"You want my help in researching something?"

Charly nodded. "Yes." She pushed aside an untidy pile of returned books and DVDs and leaned over the front countertop. "D'you think we could talk somewhere privately?"

Millie glanced around the small one-story building. It was a quiet afternoon. An elderly couple sat together in the central readers' corner, sharing a newspaper. Only three users rattled the keyboards on the free Internet terminals. And a half dozen people milled about the stacks.

She thrust her narrow chin toward Charly, nodded and lifted up a hinged section of the counter. Charly slipped through and followed Millie into her tiny inner sanctum. Charly glanced around as Millie pulled out and offered her a battered wooden chair. The room was windowless but still bright, the result of cheery lemon paint, colorful floral art and a gleaming fish tank in which several goldfish flashed about.

"Sorry, my dear," Millie said breezily, patting the chair. "It's older than Grant's Tomb, but I rarely have company back here."

She quickly settled herself into a plush office chair and stared at Charly from behind her immaculate desk. And waited.

Charly shifted on the hard seat and began, "Well, I'm doing a little research for my father—"

"Oh, I'm sooo relieved Barry's doing well," Millie said. She leaned forward to brusquely add, "Just wish you girls would let folks visit."

Charly was expecting this complaint and offered a genuine smile. "We will, Mrs. Peel, don't worry, and you'll be first on our list. It's all just been a bit hairy, I'm sure you can understand, what with Dad's health and us gearing up for gardening season."

Millie relaxed back into her chair, mollified by Charly's response.

"So," Charly started again, picking her way carefully, "as I said, I'm helping out my father. The heart attack really affected him, all of us actually, but it's spurred him on to do one particular thing. He wants to find a friend from the past. From the Sixties, just before he enlisted for the Vietnam War."

Millie nodded. "What's my father-in-law's old record store got to do with it?"

"Well," said Charly again, "he's completely lost touch with this person, and there's no other family that he knows of in town, but the one thing he remembers is...she liked music."

Millie's hazel eyes blinked rapidly. "She? He's looking for a woman?"

The tone of her response said it all. She suspected a love affair gone wrong. "Oh, not anything like that!" Charly rushed in, eager to correct Mrs. Peel's hasty conclusion. "They...they were just casual friends."

"Casual?" Millie observed Charly for a long moment. "Yet Barry's need to see her comes after a brush with death."

"Well, I'm not sure I'd put it quite that dramatically," said Charly, knowing that the librarian's quick insight was correct. This wasn't going at all the way she had hoped. She felt trapped, like the goldfish, and found herself hard-pressed to keep ahead of the astute woman.

"Let's just say he'd...well, he'd just like to see her again, and we figure she must've visited your father-in-law's store."

"Perhaps she did, but that was decades ago and my father-in law has been dead for years." Millie swept the curls off her face in exasperation. "Really, my dear, I don't see how I can help."

It was Charly's turn to lean forward. "I know it's an imposition, Mrs. Peel, and a heck of a long shot, but Dad says your father-in-law loved taking photos."

"He surely did." Millie smiled.

Charly was taken aback at how much younger she suddenly looked.

"He was a bit of a shutterbug. Why, I remember he bought one of the first instant cameras in Silver Shores. You know, the Polaroid?"

Charly nodded, remembering the funny whir and click the boxy camera made as it ejected a developing picture.

"He drove us crazy, taking photos all the time." Millie paused, her bony brow wrinkling. "And he took shots of people in the store. Candids, he used to call them. He got the idea from a crazy TV show at the time. *Candid Camera*. You remember?"

"It's a little before my time, Mrs. Peel." Charly tried hard not to show her excitement. Uh...d'you still have any of those pictures, by any chance?"

Millie tapped her long fingernails on the top of her clean desk.

"We packed up all his things and stored them in the attic, ages ago. No idea what's there." She looked doubtful.

"I'd be happy to...well, if you'd consider letting me," Charly said, "I'd be happy to whip through the boxes, and—" She pulled up short in response to the look of astonishment flooding Millie's narrow face.

Charly flushed. "I'm sorry, Mrs. Peel. How rude of me. Of course you wouldn't want just anybody going through your family things. Please forgive me. I...I prob—"

She started to rise.

But Millie flipped up a thin wrist and Charly slid back down. "You're not just anybody, Charly. My goodness, you're Eileen and Barry's daughter. No, my indecision isn't because of that." She whiffed at an errant curl. "It just struck me that my father-in-law never asked anyone if he could take their picture. He just clicked away, but nowadays..."

Her eyes widened. "We have to be so careful, what with copyrights and what's in and out of public domain. You wouldn't believe the problems I've seen and..." she bent forward conspiratorially, "from some of my colleagues, I've heard worse." She whipped back abruptly. "I wouldn't want to be put in a position of risk."

"Of course not, Mrs. Peel," Charly said, thinking quickly. "Don't see how you'd be exposed in any way. We're not planning on using the photos, if there are any. We're just hoping we might find one or two with Dad's friend and then..."

She stopped, suddenly aware she was about to contradict what she had just promised the librarian. She felt her cheeks burn.

"Uh, um, guess we might need 'em to show to others, but we wouldn't be posting them on the Net or anything like that." She paused again, knowing she was treading on dangerous ground, and fearful of what her next step or misstep might bring.

Millie's slender fingers rattled off a tattoo on the table and then she spoke, "Well, this could all be moot if we don't find anything." She rose. "Why don't you come to my house, say tomorrow morning, eight sharp? I have to be in here before nine."

Charly jumped up. "Thank you, Mrs. Peel." She reached out to shake the older woman's hand. "I'm grateful to you. My whole family is."

"Quite all right, my dear," Millie said. "Anything for the Shepherds."

Charly headed for the door.

"Oh, one last question," Millie called out.

Charly turned. "Yes?"

"What's the woman's name? The one your father's trying to get in touch with."

Charly hesitated for a moment before replying, "Sophie. Her name's Sophie."

"Sophie?" Millie stuck out her chin. "Not uncommon, but it rings no bells. The family name?"

Charly shrugged. "No idea."

"Really?" Millie's attitude was one of disbelief.

"Yeah. Like I said, my father only knew her casually. Oh, and would you please keep this just between us?" She looked directly into Millie's eyes. "My Dad would greatly appreciate it."

The librarian observed Charly quietly and then nodded slowly.

"Odd bit of doings, Charly. Very odd."

~~~

"Hello? Helloooo? said Charlie as she poked her head past the open heavy door. "Hello? Father Joe?"

She took another step into the vestibule, let the door shut with a soft sigh and walked into the still coolness of the nave. She loved the simple cross-shaped layout of St. Peter's-by-the-Sea. Except for the entrance vestibule, the interior of the small church had only two architectural lines. A long vertical stretch with pews flanking either side of the sole aisle, and a shorter, perpendicular rectangle crossing at the axis. In the center, stood the raised alter with its twin anterooms, one off each side.

Constructed both inside and out with old-growth Douglas fir and yellow Cedar, the Church's dark wooden walls were ringed by gothic-shaped stained-glass windows, depicting the Stations of the Cross. The soft sounds of singing drifted towards her. Charly knelt and crossed herself before stepping along the thick carpet to follow the music. As she reached the first step of the altar, she recognized both the song and the voice.

A moment later, Paster Joe almost danced into view, singing, "...In the lilt of Irish laughter, you can hear the angels sing—oh, Charly!" he said, obviously startled by her presence. His wrinkled cheeks pinked slightly as he spun to face her.

"Didn't realize t'wasn't only meself and the Lord listening." He held out both hands and clasped hers in greeting. "Is anything wrong? Your Da?"

"Everything's fine, Pastor Joe," Charly said quickly. "Dad's doing real well. I'm sorry, didn't mean to surprise you."

The little man smiled and flipped up a palm. "Not to worry, was just foostering about."

Used to his odd Irish expressions, Charly nodded. She didn't need to know the exact meaning of 'foostering about' to understand that he probably meant something like 'putzing about'.

"Have you got a few minutes? I...I'd like to talk to you about something."

"Of course, child."

Pastor Joe gestured to a nearby pew. He waited for Charly to sit then slipped down beside her, angling his thin body so that he could look directly at her face. He didn't speak, just waited, eyes warm with interest.

Charly appreciated his silence and patience. Pastor Joe certainly had the Irish gift of gab, but he knew when to turn it on and when not to. One of the many reasons he was so popular with his congregation. Charly took a deep breath, opened her mouth and hesitated.

"Uh...," she hunched forward, "I'm not sure how to begin." She stopped, looked down at her hands. *Maybe I'm crazy. Thinking my sisters and I were special. That I had some sort of mission in life...*

"Don't worry your head with the thoughts, Charly. Why don't you just tell me what's in your heart?"

Charly looked up, and buoyed by the older man's earnest attention, she half-smiled. "Okay, but it's a little...uh...vain." His white eyebrows flickered, but Pastor Joe remained silent, intently watching her face. "You remember saying you thought my Dad was...haunted by something?"

His gray eyes narrowed and then he nodded. "'T'is a strong

word, I know."

"And you asked what my sisters and I were doing about it."

Another nod.

"Well, something's haunting him—that *is* the right word— and... oh, this's where I'm afraid I'm being vain."

He frowned.

Charly rushed on, "I know, Pastor Joe. I know. I should be humble and not vainglorious but..." She paused and shrugged helplessly. "If I listen, really listen to hear our Lord's wishes, as you often remind us to do, well, what I'm hearing will seem...arrogant."

"Why not let me be the judge?"

Charly cocked her head, mulling over his suggestion.

"Okay," she finally said. "You asked for it so here goes. I think... no Pastor Joe, I *believe* that I have a calling. A calling to help others find...oh, I'm not sure what. Peace, maybe? Forgiveness? Possibly even redemption?"

She stopped, feeling the flush of embarrassment burn her cheeks. She had so much to say, had even practiced by saying some of it aloud to herself. Yet now, the words sounded inadequate and hollow.

"It's crazy and conceited, I know. And it gets even wilder. You see, I think my mother knew all along. I've told myself that it's nonsense over and over, and if my Dad wasn't so desperate for help, I'm not sure I'd listen."

"You believe you can help your Da?"

"Oh, yes! My sisters and I—and I really feel that all three of us have this calling—we're already helping. He's trying to—" She stopped. "Uh, I'm sorry, Pastor, but I think my Dad should tell you himself."

"That is only right and proper," he said. "And I'm ever so thankful you and your sisters are pitchin' in to help." Pastor Joe hesitated for a long moment, worrying a gnarled hand over his half-frozen cheek.

"T'is a funny thing, Charly, now that I'm puzzling on it. Your dear mam, God rest her soul, told me she had designs on you girls."

"Designs?"

"To be sure she was proud of you all. Faith with her 9-1-1 work, Hope and her teaching and you with your plants but..." he paused, rubbing his chin.

"Yes, Pastor? But what?"

"Your mother was a true believer, very connected, shall we say, to her spiritual being. As you well know."

He stood and began walking down the aisle so Charly stepped along with him. A shard of light spilled through one window, casting a multi-colored display at their feet.

"One gloomy December day about three years ago, your mother was here early, as she always was, helping to set up the board room for another council meeting. We were alone and quite suddenly she stopped arranging chairs, looked straight at me and asked, "'Pastor Joe, do you believe in destiny?'"

He smiled self-consciously. "Now, I admit that put me back on my heels for a wee bit, but then I replied that I did and offered her a quote from Saint Jeremiah." He smiled genuinely now. "Always liked ol' Jerry. It goes something like this, 'For I know the plans I have for you, declares the Lord, plans to prosper you and not to harm you, plans to give you hope and a future.'"

"Plans to give you hope and a future." Charly whispered. "She often quoted that. I've always liked it."

"So did your dear mam. And it seemed to give her confidence because then she said, 'I believe God has plans for my girls. Special plans not yet known, but they're destined for more. I'm not sure what, but I feel it in my bones.'" His eyes widened at the memory. "I'm not afraid to admit, child that I was gobsmacked by her confidence."

A shiver moved through Charly's body like a lightning bolt. Mom really did believe! But why didn't she say anything specific? And what did she know?

She had little time to contemplate because Pastor Joe answered as though reading her mind. "Somehow she understood that all would be revealed in its own good time." He cocked his head. "The good Lord works in mysterious ways, Charly."

They stood companionably, each with a hand resting on the back of a nearby pew. Neither saying anything for a couple of minutes. Charly's mind whirled at the implications and ideas Pastor Joe's words stirred in her. She found it hard to concentrate and even harder to form her next sentence.

Finally, she asked softly, "D'you really think He's working through me?"

The old man's face lit up with a crooked smile. "To be sure. Through each and every blessed one of us, child. But do I think He's got special plans for you and your sisters?" He shrugged. "I wouldn't put it past Him. You're all crackers to be sure, Charly. Fine, intelligent women. Who better to do His work?"

Chapter Thirty-Four

If you have a garden and a library, you have everything you need.
Cicero

Barry hurried out of the house as Charly opened the truck's door. In a heartbeat, her pleasant drive home, during which she had stopped off for a tea, a sour cream glazed doughnut, and a little precious time alone to contemplate her conversation with Pastor Joe, vanished instantly.

"What's wrong, Dad?" she called out, jumping from the truck.

"It...it's Scotty." Barry stood wheezing and squinting in the noon sunlight. He touched the hood of the truck to steady himself and pulled in oxygen.

Charly's stomach flip-flopped. She didn't know what she'd been expecting to hear, but certainly not her son's name. Oh dear Lord, no!

"Scotty? What's happened? Is he hurt?"

It took her father several seconds of gasping to find enough air to reply. In those micro moments, Charly's mind raced through the worst possible scenarios. School bus crash? A crazy man wielding a gun? Accident in the playground?

"Why didn't you call me on my cell?"

"Did," her father finally sputtered.

"What?" Charly's hand fell to her cell phone, which was clipped to her jeans. One quick look and she realized she hadn't turned it on. Oh no! She grabbed her father by his broad shoulders.

"Come on, Dad! What happened?"

"It's all right, Charly," said her father, his breathing now under control. "He's all right."

She didn't comprehend immediately and began shaking her father. He laid a firm hand on her arm, stopping her.

"He's okay, dear. He's just in...a spot of trouble."

The wave of relief was so profound that when Charly let her arms fall, her knees almost buckled. This time, her father gripped and supported her.

"What sort of trouble?" she heard herself ask.

"He's been in a fight."

"A fight! Scotty?" Charly took a breath. "But...but he's never been in a fight in his life!"

Her father nodded. "Until today." His mouth twitched as he squelched a smile. "Seems like it was a doozey. Least, that's what the vice-principal says."

The telephone rang inside the house.

"I'll get that," Barry said, starting for the house. "You go deal with our little Floyd Patterson."

"Huh?"

"Heavyweight champ in the Sixties," he called out over his shoulder.

"Scotty's no champ, and don't you dare smile when I bring him home."

She climbed back into the truck and backed out. As she yanked the wheel, she glanced back. Her father stood on the porch steps, hands in fists and posed like a boxer. The phone kept ringing.

She couldn't help herself. She laughed heartily and tooted the horn before kicking the accelerator.

~~~

"I really appreciate your talking to the boys to find out what happened," Charly said, "but it doesn't really matter."

They were seated in the vice-principal's cramped office. It was sparsely furnished and the walls were decorated simply, with large framed photographs of the school's graduating classes. Charly enjoyed seeing these posed moments in the school's history. She was amused by the changing hairstyles and hemlines and appreciated the stark contrast between the black-and-white and color shots. Her favorite, however, was the photograph of the Class of 2007, which featured Melissa standing proudly in the middle row.

"Of course my son'll apologize to Alex," Charly continued. "He knows fighting's unacceptable no matter what." She nodded encouragingly at her sullen-looking son, who was slouched in a chair next to her.

They both faced the seated figure of Mr. Bedford, the popular VP. Opposite them sat Alex and his mother, Jean Davoren. Eyes downcast, Mrs. Davoren was anxiously picking at the clasp of her purse. She looked weak and lost. Her son, who was almost taller and already heavier than his mother, ignored her. Charly felt sorry for the slender woman with the anxious expression.

Scotty jumped up. "I'm not apologizing!" he said, jabbing a finger at the larger boy. "He started it."

"Did not!" roared Alex, rising quickly.

There was a sharp squeak as Mr. Bedford shoved back his chair and stood. He didn't say a word, but his tall figure loomed over the boys and they both flopped back down. For the first time, Charly clearly saw the reddening under Alex's eye, identical to the bruise forming on her son's face.

"There'll be no shouting in my office," Bedford said in a low but firm voice. "Unless it's me." Four pairs of eyes snapped up, looking into his long face. He smiled tightly and returned to his seat. "Now, let's just go over this one more time—"

"Alex wouldn't cause any trouble," said his mother.

Surprised by the strength of her voice, Charly was further taken aback when Mrs. Davoren flashed her a hard look. She might be bullied by him, but she'll still protect him, thought Charly. Like any mother.

"He's a good boy. He wouldn't hurt anybody."

"That's not true!" Scotty blurted. "He hit me first."

Alex shouted back, "It's your fault!"

"Whoa!" Mr. Bedford's bass voice silenced both boys. "Enough."

He stood and walked around to the front of his desk and looked from one mother to another.

"This isn't getting us anywhere. I suggest that you take these boys home and see what you can get out of them. It's a first offence for both, so there'll be no further punishment."

His gaze bounced between the two boys. "Not this time, anyway." He hesitated, eyeing each child and then he clapped his hands.

"Come on, guys. On your feet. You know what to do."

Neither child moved. Charly turned sharply and hissed at Scotty. Reluctantly, he rose.

Bedford glared at Alex and the boy stood as though pulled up by the VP's dark eyes.

"Right," Bedford said. "Let's go. I don't have all day. Shake hands."

The two boys glowered at one another and then Scotty stepped forward, right arm outstretched. "I'm sorry," he muttered.

"Me, too," replied Alex. He shoved his arm out and the two shook hands.

Neither Charly nor her son said a word as they walked out into the cool, bright afternoon and headed to the truck. Charly clambered into her seat and sneaked a glance at Scotty as he threw his knapsack into the backseat. His small face was taut with anxiety, and she had to steel herself from expressing concern over the angry bruise above his right cheek.

Got to wait him out. Let him want to speak to me.

It was a parenting strategy her mother had used to particular effect with Faith and Charly. Both girls were openly emotional and chatty, and found that silence intensified their feelings of guilt. Once caught in a transgression, neither could last very long without confessing. Hope was different. Her feelings ran deeper and she gained strength from holding back, much like their father. Fortunately, Scotty took after Charly and she was confident that if she gave him time to stew, he would open up.

She started the truck, waited quietly while he buckled up, then steered onto the road. Within a few minutes, she knew her nine-year-old would break before they reached home. Usually, he bounced contentedly in his seat, pushing and kicking at the panel, all the while chattering happily.

Now though, he was shifting and couldn't meet her gaze. It was just too unbearably quiet and oppressive in the confines of the truck's small cab. Again, Charly almost caved in and told him it was okay.

But she didn't. She was very worried and desperately wanted to know what was going on in his head. For the most part, her son was a happy, easy-going boy and she couldn't imagine what could cause him to hit another child. That kind of violent physical reaction was completely out of character. Although he wasn't even a pre-teen, she worried about the changes and challenges ahead of him, and about problems arising from not having his father intimately involved in his life. She had hoped and prayed that his grandfather's influence would be sufficient, but how could she know? What issues might be simmering, or worse, coming to a boil? She understood about being a girl and becoming a woman, but what did she know about being a boy and becoming a man?

Her patience was finally rewarded as they travelled along a secondary highway, about fifteen minutes from the house.

Scotty's loud outburst, at first so sudden and incomprehensible, that Charly nearly lost control rounding a steep curve, quickly gave way to whimpering sobs. She pulled the truck over to the side of the road, quickly switched off the engine and unbuckled her seat belt. In one swift movement she cradled her little boy in her arms and was whispering softly to him.

"Grampa's gonna die," Scotty bawled, shoving his head under her chin. "Alex said so. Said he'd drop any minute."

Charly was taken aback by his anxiety and by the cruelty of his friend's words. "Alex is wrong, honey. And he's just being mean. Your Grampa's fine," she said, running her fingers through his spiky hair. "We've been all through this. Yes, his heart failed him, but it's better now. They've fixed it."

Scotty gulped for air. "You're sure he's...he's not gonna d...d... die?"

Charly gently pulled her son's face into the light and rubbed the tears away from his eyes. "Of course not. That why you punched him?"

Scotty dropped his head and nodded.

Charly could hardly suppress the swell of pride that rose in her body.

"Well, you shouldn't have hit him, right?"

Her son nodded again.

"And you won't do it again?"

Scotty's body tensed and he said, "Yes, I would."

Charly sighed. It was exactly the answer she had secretly hoped for. Now what? She knew she couldn't condone fighting. After all, didn't the Son of God turn the other cheek? But she also wanted her son to stand up for himself and for his family. It was one of those impossible parental conundrums.

Not for the first time, she fervently wished she were not parenting alone. She used to talk to her mother about how to bring up her children, and together they would strategize. Since her death, Charly had occasionally discussed a couple of issues with her father. It was more awkward with him, but she appreciated his experience and input. This time, given the circumstances, she wasn't sure she was comfortable asking for her father's advice. So Charly did what she always did. She followed her instincts and prayed they were right.

"Well, young man. On one hand I'm proud you defended your grandfather." Scotty looked up, surprise brightening his face. "On the other, we've got to talk about coping mechanisms. There're other ways to handle disagreements."

The boy grimaced.

Charly locked eyes with her son. "You're grounded for a week. No friends over and no TV."

Scotty's mouth opened in protest but he remained silent.

Charly shifted back behind the steering wheel and twisted the ignition key.

"Good. Now, let's go home and have some cookies."

Chapter Thirty-Five

What is a weed? I have heard it said that there are sixty
definitions.
For me, a weed is a plant out of place.
Donald Culross Peattie

In here!" Hope's voice rang out as Charly and Scotty walked through the front door a little after one o'clock.

The pair trooped down the hall and turned into the kitchen to find Hope, Michael and Barry gathered around the table.

Hope grinned up at them, a half-eaten cookie in her hand. "How's our little bruiser?" Her eyes widened as she dropped the cookie and jumped up, taking Scotty by the shoulders. "Wow! That's quite the shiner."

Michael whistled his approval.

"Hey," said Charly. "We're not happy about this, all right? Scotty knows what he did was—" She paused in mid-sentence as her son slipped beneath Hope's hands and rushed over to his grandfather. The little boy flung his arms round the old man's neck and hugged him tightly.

Stunned, Barry looked up at Charly. She shook her head and he focused on the now-sobbing boy in his arms. "Hey, hey, now, Mr. Scott. Everything's okay. It's all right," he murmured soothingly. "Come on, now. Tell your old Grampa all about it."

Scotty's reply was a garbled mixture of mumbling and crying.

"Shhh, can't understand you, boy," Barry said. "What on earth happened?"

"Yeah," Hope said. "Inquiring minds wanna know."

Charly reached for a peanut butter cookie and flopped into the nearest empty chair. "Seems our young man felt he had to defend his family's honor."

"Good for him," Michael said. "Way to go, kid."

"Michael!" said Charly.

Her brother-in-law shrugged.

Scotty jumped off his grandfather's lap and turned to face them. "Alex said Grampa's gonna die." He swung back to his grandfather. "But you're not, are you?"

"Of course not," Barry said heartily. He pounded his chest. "See? Right as rain."

Hope asked, "You got into a fight 'cause another kid told you your Grampa's going to die?"

Scotty hesitated, then nodded slowly.

Hope reached across and rubbed the boy's cheek. "Michael's right. Well done, Mr. Scott." Charly started to protest, but Hope's voice rolled on, "Of course, you know you shouldn't fight, right?"

Before the child could answer, Michael said, "Sometimes a man's got to do what a man's got to do."

"All right, all right," Charly said. "Thank you all for your unsolicited advice."

An uncomfortable silence settled over the kitchen. After a couple of seconds, Scotty approached his mother.

"I'm sorry, Mom."

Charly smiled thinly. "I know." She reached out and he dropped onto her knee. Everyone relaxed. "Have a cookie, hon. You must be starving."

"Milk?" said Hope, already rising.

"So what've you guys been up to?" Charly said.

"Nothing as exciting as—" Michael stopped and flushed.

Hope stepped in. "Building shelves. Real thrilling work."

"For the butterflies?" asked Scotty taking a glass of milk from her.

"For all kinds of junk, kid," Michael said. "Instruments,

equipment, stuff you've never heard of."

"Sweet."

"Scotty'll be helping out big-time over the next week," said Charly. "Won't you, honey?"

Scotty's cheeks turned as red as the half-moon bruise gleaming under his eye.

Michael grinned. "Grounded, eh, kid? Well, don't let it worry you. We've all been there."

Scotty frowned. "You have?"

Hope chuckled. "Some of us more than others, that's for sure." She glanced at her father. "Your aunt Faith was always running late."

Barry grinned broadly.

"She'd always have some weird excuse, like she'd set her watch in the wrong time zone or the bus got lost."

"Best one I remember," Charly leaned in close to her son, "was when she said she thought she'd been abducted by aliens!" She hooted with laughter. "Hope and I followed her for days, whispering, "Woo, woo, woo."

"Woo, woo, woo!" Scotty shouted, dashing around the table. "Woo, woo, woo!"

Michael reached out and snared the boy. "Faith's gonna kill you two," he said as he play-wrestled with Scotty.

"I'll risk it," Hope said. She turned to Charly. "So, how'd it go with Mrs. Peel?"

Charly glanced at Scotty and Michael and then looked at her father. "Well..."

Michael took the hint. He jumped up and scooped the nine-year-old under his arm. "Hey, kid, let's go do some man's work."

Charly shot him a grateful look.

Michael nodded and staggered out of the kitchen, his fifty-pound burden giggling and squirming. Moments later, the back door slammed.

"Well?" said Hope.

Barry edged closer to his youngest daughter.

"First, Dad, don't worry. Mrs. Peel doesn't know why we're asking."

Barry hooked his fingers into the straps of his overalls and shrugged. "That's not going to last. Millie's more curious than Lot's wife."

"She was, but she didn't push. Good news is that she's still got her father-in-law's old photographs from the record store. I'm going over tomorrow to go through them."

Her father tugged something from his front bib pocket and handed it to Charly. "This's Graeme. Only good one I can find. From a train station en route to base camp. We took it in one of those booths you duck into."

Hope scooted her chair closer.

Charly held up a short strip consisting of four small black and white photographs. All were headshots of two laughing young men, both sporting longish hair. She immediately recognized her father from his thick hair, wide face and confident grin.

It was the other man that drew her attention. In three of the photos, his attractive face was partially hidden by dark unruly bangs barely held in check by a star-spangled bandana, but the last photo caught him straight on. Even features, strong nose and large clear eyes shining out from a man in the prime of his life.

"So that's Graeme Walker," said Hope, peering over her sister's shoulder at the tiny picture. "Good-looking, despite the hippie hair."

"Guys all called him Pretty Boy." Barry shook his head. "His looks gave him no end of grief."

"I can understand why you were taken aback by seeing Derek Burgess," said Charly. "He's got that attractive heart-shaped face going on." She leaned back and handed the photo strip to Hope. "This'll really help tomorrow."

"So, I mean, you're going to plow through Mr. Peel's old pics and pull out the ones with Graeme in them, right?"

Charly nodded at her sister.

"Then what?"

"Then I ask Mrs. Peel if I can borrow them so that Dad can have a look. Hopefully, he'll recognize Sophie in at least one of them."

"And then what?"

Charly frowned. "What is this, Hope? Twenty questions? I don't have all the answers. Not yet, anyway."

Hope shifted and laid the photo strip on the table.

"Sorry, kiddo, didn't mean to criticize. It's just that your approach is more organic than mine. I think we should have a plan of action, be thinking a couple of steps ahead." She looked at their father. "What's your opinion, Dad?"

Barry was staring at the photos. After a long moment, he said, "As usual, you're both right. Every discovery needs both strategy and intuition. In you two, I've got both." He held out a hand to each of his daughters, clasped theirs and then looked up. "Don't worry. Anything else we're missing, He'll provide."

Chapter Thirty-Six

*The comfortable and comforting people are those who look
upon the bright side of life; gathering its roses and sunshine, and
making the most that happens seem the best.*
Dorothy Dix

After Hope and Michael left and Scotty trudged off to his room to read, Charly and her father headed outside to check their plants. The nursery beds burgeoned with thick growth. She could hardly see any patches of dark soil. Both their plants and those recently purchased were performing extremely well, and she felt that the nursery was on schedule and would be ready for spring buying.

So as she went through the familiar and comfortable routine of weeding, pinching and watering the seedlings in the soft afternoon air, she took her sister's suggestion to heart, turning her thoughts to finding Sophie and what subsequent steps might be needed to help her father achieve his goal. She had decided earlier not to think of it as a problem. A goal was better, more upbeat, more worthy. It helped her prepare herself for the challenging road ahead.

It didn't take more than a couple of minutes of musing for her to realize she needed her father's input. Why didn't she ask him outright? She glanced over at the adjacent *Asclepias speciosa* plot. Her father's large figure was bent over one of hundreds of the milkweed plants, fingering the underside of a leaf.

Still, she hesitated. It was hard. She was keenly aware that a subtle divide now existed between them. That she, her sisters and her children were privy to something embarrassing and shameful. A part of Barry Shepherd's past that had plagued him and now both haunted and inspired her.

She wished her mother were here. She would have known just what to say and do to help bridge this thorny gap between the two of them.

But you're not here and I am. And so is he. And so is the problem...the goal...the issue *that pricks at us like the spiny bracts on a Scotch thistle's flower head.*

She looked at her father again, drawing courage from the set of his broad shoulders and the quiet diligence of his efforts. She picked her way over rows of spiky fuchsias, stiff-leafed fairy wands, and thick-stemmed milkweeds until she reached him.

"Aphids?" she said, fearing an infestation of the tiny yellow insects that sucked the juices of the milkweed plant.

"Nope," he said, plucking at another leaf.

"That's a relief," she said. "Don't think I could handle another crisis at the moment."

Her father continued to fiddle with milkweed plants, and then without turning, he said softly, "I'm real sorry, Charly, about the song, about Graeme—"

He stood and turned slowly to face her. His blue eyes brimmed with tears and Charly's heart twisted.

"About disappointing you and your sisters. I know things're different between us and...I...well, the only consolation I can offer is that I'm more disappointed in myself than you could ever be."

Charly stepped forward and wrapped him in a fierce hug.

~~~

"You've *got* to be kidding," said Faith as she watched her sister enter the kitchen the next morning.

Charly dumped a medium-sized box onto the table. Several Polaroid photographs spun out and slipped onto the floor. "I'll be back," she said before walking back down the hall.

"This is gonna be a long morning," Faith called after her as she plucked up the photos. "I'll put the kettle on."

Charly lugged the second box out of the truck and into the kitchen before dropping it on the floor near the door. She sat across from her eldest sister.

Faith grinned and shoved a plate loaded with muffins towards her. "Banana pecan."

Charly took one and bit into the still-warm, moist middle. "Mmm, this's tasty, Faithie. Thanks. You'll have to help me modify my cooking so that we all eat healthier, okay?"

"Love to," said Faith. "It's not real hard, just takes a bit of fiddling."

Charly nodded her appreciation while swallowing and then added, "Mrs. Peel wanted me there at eight sharp, so no time for breakfast."

"She let you take all this?"

Charlie nodded while swallowing. "Long as I return it all by day's end."

Faith's carefully plucked eyebrows shot up. "There must be a thousand photographs." She fiddled with her earrings, a set of dangling emeralds. "Guess Dad doesn't want to help, huh?"

Charly nodded. "Gone to check out some new stock."

"Are you sure he's okay about us doing this? It's...it's a little intrusive."

"Uh huh. Know it's awkward, but he's ready, Faith. He wants closure."

For a moment, Faith avoided her gaze. "Sometimes I wish we'd never found out."

Charly reached across and touched her sister's arm. "I know. Me, too."

Faith's face widened with surprise. "Really? I thought you felt this to be some sort of destiny."

"I do...doesn't make it any easier."

Faith sat for a moment, deep in thought. Then she fluffed up her hair and said, "Okey-dokey, better get crackin'. My shift starts at three." She shoved a freckled arm into the box and pulled out a handful of old Polaroids.

"How d'you want to handle this?"

Charly reached over to the countertop for the strip of photos of Graeme and her father. This she put in the center of the table between them. "This's the only shot we have of Graeme."

Faith picked up the small photos and grinned. "Dad in a Beatles' haircut, too much." She scrutinized the last picture. "Umm, that Graeme's a real cutie."

Charly said, "I say we rip through the pics, chunking everything except for those we think are of Graeme. Then we go back and see what we have."

Faith's fingers were already flipping through the white-framed squares of plastic.

Charly quickly became disappointed. The quality of the photographs was very poor. Most had faded and in some the subject matter was invisible. This was going to be harder than she thought. She jumped up and turned on the little radio that sat on the window-sill. Music from the Eighties blared out of its tiny speaker. Faith immediately began rocking and singing, oblivious to the fact that she had inherited the Shepherds' infamous inability to carry a tune... even in a bucket.

"This's like hitting the books in high school," she shouted.

"Didn't know you did."

As far as Charly could remember, Faith had rarely cracked open a book, whereas Hope had studied endlessly. Both had performed reasonably well in school, though Faith's marks were dramatically higher in English and art, courses that Hope had dismissed as 'girlie.' Hope had excelled at the sciences and hadn't cared how she fared in anything else. Whenever the two sisters' reports cards arrived throughout the years, their mother would sigh and sadly remark that neither was anything to write home about, but their father would chuckle and suggest that they would be a whiz-bang student if they just joined forces. As if.

Charly joined in and the pair hummed, sang and screeched for over an hour as they waded through the shiny glimpses of the Sixties. Every now and then, one of them would hoot and flash a particularly amusing Polaroid. They would both laugh at whatever groovy fashion had been captured, be it a psychedelic mini-skirt, mop-top haircut or pair of thigh-length plastic boots. Finally, Charly reached into the second box and came up empty. First round finished, she thought. Thank heavens.

Faith scooped up the last of the discarded photos and shoved them back into the boxes. Then the two sisters looked at the thin pile of shots they had set aside.

"Okay," said Faith, picking up their comparison photos and examining each closely. "Your turn to make tea. I'll have a look."

Charly was stuffing two tea bags into the thermos when Faith squealed.

"Here's one!"

Charly hurried back to the table. The photograph depicted a full-length side shot of Graeme, wearing what Charly now appreciated was his trademark bandana, holding up a record album.

"That's him, all right, but he's alone."

Faith rolled her eyes and sifted through more. "Here! How 'bout this one? There's someone else beside him and she's got her fingers on his arm."

Charly examined the photograph. Graeme was wearing different clothes, but the same bandana. Another person was in the shot, but only a bare arm and shoulder were visible. "It's a girl, all right. Looks like she's wearing a sleeveless mini-dress."

Faith shivered. "Can you imagine? Like, totally ugly."

"Wish we could see her face."

Faith continued through the rest of the Polaroids, handing each to Charly as she went along. In the end, they found one more with Graeme, but it was a blurry shot of him with two other young men.

Faith sat back in her chair. "Now what?"

Charly shrugged. "I admit, I don't know." She leaned forward, fingering the three photographs of Graeme Walker. "Really thought we'd luck in."

Faith stood and stretched. "Well, think on it. I'll call later." She stepped to the hall entrance and turned back.

"Don't worry. We're on the hunt now. We'll find something."

"Yeah," Charly said, wishing she felt the same conviction.

"As the Man says, 'Get outta the car!'"

Charly cocked her head. "What's that supposed to mean?"

"Say it."

"What?"

"Come on, humor me. Say it."

"Get out of the car."

"Again, but real loud and real fast."

"Ookaay." Charly took a deep breath and shouted, "Getouttathecar!"

Faith tossed her a thumbs-up. "Now how do you feel?"

"Strong," Charly said without thinking. "In control."

And she did, much to her own amazement. She looked up at the doorway, but Faith was gone.

"That's the spirit!" her voice floated back from the hallway. In a second, the front door slammed shut.

"Crazy," Charly said to herself, still feeling uplifted. "Wonderfully crazy."

Chapter Thirty-Seven

My idea of gardening is to discover something wild in my
wood
and weed around it with the utmost care until it has a chance
to grow and spread.
Margaret Bourke-White

Charly took some time to catch up on invoices, bills and orders, and then gratefully headed out into the mid-afternoon sunshine to join her father in the never-ending jobs of deadheading, thinning and watering.

Though slightly surprised that he didn't ask about the photo search, Charly was grateful, given the little progress they had made. She was pondering her next move while shifting bags of fertilizer in the smaller greenhouse when her cell phone rang.

"The ring!" Faith's excited voice blasted her ear.

"What?"

"The woman's arm in the photo. There's a silver ring on her hand. On the thumb."

Charly hesitated, trying to recall the picture that showed Graeme along with a woman's bare arm and hand.

"Sorry, didn't notice."

"Of course, you didn't, Charly. You never would, but I did." Faith's tone was triumphant. "Not only that, little sister, it's a special kind of ring and I know all about it."

Charly glanced up to find her father. He wasn't visible. "Okay,

Faith. Impress me."

"That's easy." Faith chuckled. "The ring's Irish. It's called...oh, I'll remember in a minute...'something dah'."

"Something dah. That's great, Faith."

Faith continued, unfazed, "It's usually given as a token of love." She paused and then continued, "You haven't taken the boxes back?" '

"Taken the—oh! I'd forgotten all about it." Charly glanced at her phone to check the time, 4:28. The kids would be home soon from their after-school activities and she still had to get supper ready and return the photos before six.

She started for the back door and realized Faith was talking again, "...go and check. You'll see."

"Okay," said Charly. "I'm at the back door, now in the kitchen." She reached down with her free hand and sifted through several photographs before pulling one up. "Got it." She examined the woman's left hand closely. On a nicely-shaped thumb sat a man's thick ring.

"Well?"

"You're right! She's got a ring, uh, hang on, lemme see." She reached up and grabbed the small magnifying glass kept for her father's convenience on top of the microwave. "Just a sec...got Dad's mag glass...hmm, looks like it has a crown over a heart?"

"That's it! Means something about love and loyalty. It's a...a...gimme a second. On the tip of my tongue...something dah... something...addah. Claddagh! That's what it's called, a Claddagh ring."

"Way to go, Faithie! How on earth do you know?"

"Remember Martha Jean O'Brien?"

Charly thought for a moment. A glimmer of an image floated into her mind. "From high school? Round face, smiling eyes?"

"That's her," Faith said, nearly shouting with pride. "She had one of those rings."

By now, Charly had flopped into a chair and continued to run the magnifying glass over the woman's bare arm and hand, but there was nothing else to see. "Well, this's fascinating," she said finally, "but I'm not sure how it'll help."

"For goodness sake, Charly! Use your imagination. What if

there's another photograph with that ring showing? That might lead us—"

"Bye!" Charly said as she shut off the phone. Within minutes, she had scoured the piles of photographs, her eye rapidly scanning for any signs of women's bare arms. After fifteen minutes, she had a couple of dozen and was wishing sleeveless mini-dresses hadn't been so popular. After seventeen minutes, she sat back and stared at one particular Polaroid.

It was a two-shot in which a tousle-haired boy was handing a record album to a young woman. Her face was in profile, her outstretched arms were bare and on her left hand, Charly could just see the outline of the thumb ring. She looked at the woman's profile through the magnifying glass. Even from that angle, she could see that the tall, fair-haired young woman was extremely attractive.

Charly stroked the small image for a moment. *Well, hello, Sophie. We finally meet.* Then her eye focused on the young man and she almost levitated off her chair. She jumped up, spilling Polaroids onto the kitchen floor as she reached for another photograph. It was the one where Graeme stood along with two other young men.

Charly held this picture in her left hand and the shot of Sophie in her right. The youth with disheveled hair was in both. She had found a connection! If she could identify the young man, he might be able to tell her Sophie's last name.

"Yes!" Charlie shouted, leaping into the air. "Yes, yes, *yes!*"

~~~

Charly stood on the back steps and scanned the nursery grounds. The light was fading, but the last arcs of watery sunlight curved right into the large greenhouse. How strange it looked. Should be a thicket of green, bursting with flats of young plants. But on this late spring afternoon, it was almost colorless, save for the soft glints reflecting off the stainless steel, wood and plastic equipment and furniture intended for butterfly production. In fits and starts during the past few afternoons, Hope and Michael had pretty well finished installing everything. Now, the Sweet Shepherd Nursery waited. Its tiny new inhabitants weren't due for another week to ten days.

As she hesitated, seeking her father's figure in the elliptical shadows blanketing the planting beds, she was amazed to find that her feet weren't automatically stepping into the dark soil. Nor were her fingers itching to grab a pair of secateurs or to start pinching off new growth.

She leaned against the heavy door and considered this surprising reaction for a full minute. For the first time in decades, she wasn't eager to get down and dirty with her beloved plants. And amazingly enough, her thoughts were focused on neither money nor children.

They were front and center on her new mission and her whole body jangled with excitement. "Dad?" she called into the growing darkness. "Dad, where are you?"

After a short delay came his distant barked reply. "Over here."

It was now almost too dark to see. "Can't see you. Can you come here? Got something to show you."

"Hang on a sec." She heard some banging and then his voice said, "Okay. Be right there."

Charly turned, opened the door and reached inside. She flicked the switch and a wide yellow beam leaped out into the nursery. After a couple of seconds, the beam became partially blocked and her father's silhouette grew steadily until he was at the bottom of the steps, peering up at her.

Barry tugged off a dirty pair of gardening gloves. He ran a thick palm over his hair, partially flattening his silver curls. "What's up?"

"Sorry, but could you come in? Like you to see something." She stepped inside and held the door for him. After he entered, she said, "I'll make tea."

He joined her in the kitchen five minutes later, face and hands scrubbed clean. She handed him a steaming mug and he took a careful sip.

"Found something?"

Charly slid the Polaroid across the table. "It's a little blurry, but—"

"As the Lord's my witness," Barry interrupted in surprise, jerking forward. Tea slopped out of his mug and narrowly missed splashing the candid photo of Graeme and the two other youths.

"That's Red James." He tapped James' head. "Don't know the

other guy."

He pulled the picture up close to his eyes. "My word, were we ever that young?" He looked over at his daughter. "What's Red got to do with Sophie?"

"That's the sixty-four-thousand-dollar question, Dad." Charly paused, collecting her thoughts. "You see, that photo links Graeme to the guy with the messy hair, the one you call Red James. That a nickname, by the way?"

"You can't see from the photo, but he was a carrot-top. Christian name's Keith."

Charly nodded. "That's our first connection. Then, we found this photo of Graeme."

She passed it to her father. "Now, have a look. There's a woman's arm in the shot, she's touching him."

She held out his magnifying glass. "Here. She's got a ring on her thumb. See? Faith twigged to that and gave us our way to find another link."

"She did, did she? Good for her." Barry peered through the glass.

"Okay, so it's obvious that Graeme and this girl knew each other." She slouched back on her kitchen chair. "More than that, 'cause she's got her fingers on his forearm." She reached for her mug and gulped.

"That's our second connection."

Barry observed her with admiring eyes. "This's kinda like a detective story. And you're Miss Marple."

Charly smiled. "She'd have solved this already, Dad. Anyway, we also found our third connection, the one that ties Graeme and this girl together." She slipped another Polaroid across to her father.

He fingered the plastic square while eyeing the image carefully. "I'll be a monkey's uncle. The girl with the ring and the boy who needs a haircut." He grinned widely. "Sounds like a really bad movie. So, you think this girl's Sophie and Red knew her?"

Charly chewed her lip and then said simply, "Yes." She reached across and touched his large hand. "And you know Red."

"Knew. A long time ago." Barry frowned. "He was some sort of administrator. Hospital, I think. Our paths never crossed much after high school."

"He still lives in Silver Shores?"

Barry nodded. "Probably retired and out to pasture somewhere." He played with his suspender straps and thought for a few seconds. "Veronica might know. Think she did the hospital's books."

Charly glanced at the kitchen clock, stood up and stared out the window. The path and much of the drive glittered in the golden spill from the front porch lights. She desperately wanted to duck her family responsibilities and race over to talk to Veronica Bergeron that very instant. Can't believe she was looking forward to seeing another dragon lady! But she was. Her father's sigh caught her attention and she swung back to face him.

He was intently eyeing the three photographs. After a moment, his large index finger gently touched each as though it were a talisman. "We really might do this, Charly," he finally said, in a voice just above a whisper. "Make the call."

Nicola Furlong

Chapter Thirty-Eight

Anyone who keeps the ability to see beauty never grows old.
Franz Kafka

Although Veronica Bergeron immediately admitted to Charly over the phone that she knew Red James, the retired accountant had refused to say any more until she had seen Barry in person. So, after feeding her family a quick salad and pizza from the freezer along with molasses cookies for dessert, Charly dropped off the remaining photographs at Mrs. Peel's. As the librarian wasn't home, Charly carefully placed the boxes in the garage and wedged a note into the front screen door, offhandedly mentioning that she was temporarily keeping three Polaroids.

Then she hurried back home, flying along the busy strip of highway under a corona of glittering stars. As she turned up their long drive, she almost ran over Scotty's bike and skittered to a halt. After taking a moment to catch her breath, she climbed out, dragged the bike to the side and got back in.

She sat for a moment, contemplating. *What's going on in my nine-year-old's head?* Of course, she had just grounded him—for only the third time in his life—so he was miffed, but something more was up. She couldn't swear to it, but the sporty two-wheeler seemed to have been placed deliberately in her path. It wasn't like her happy-go-lucky son to be spiteful—

225

Charly gasped, her worries yanked in a new direction. Up ahead, she spied the outline of another car against the house and knew that Mrs. Bergeron had arrived early.

Her father, never one for prevarication, was alone with one of nosiest women in Silver Shores! This was exactly the situation that Charly had hoped and raced to avoid. She stamped on the accelerator and roared up the drive. Seconds later, she sprinted up the front steps and down the hall without shucking her jacket.

Just as she reached the living room, she realized she was hearing music. Entering, she saw her father and Mrs. Bergeron on the old leather couch, watching Melissa. Scotty was jammed in between the two adults.

At least the rarely used room was tidy. Charly glanced quickly around, eyes skimming the denim-blue leather furniture and matching armchairs to land on the polished surfaces of the oak coffee and end tables. Great, she realized shamefacedly, there was a thin layer of dust winking under the scattered light from the old chandelier.

Her daughter stood in the center of the large rectangular space, confidently playing her clarinet, and the rounded tones of *When the Saints Go Marching In* filled the air.

Charly's heart rose. Mrs. Bergeron, a large bespectacled woman with colorless hair, was leaning forward, listening intently. Maybe the old bat hadn't had time to bully Dad for answers. Still wondering, she waved at Melissa to continue and, nodding a hello, slid onto an over-stuffed Lay-Z-Boy recliner at Mrs. Bergeron's elbow.

But as she caught her breath, something extraordinary happened. Scotty carefully peered from behind Mrs. Bergeron's blunt pageboy haircut and deliberately winked at her. A half second later, her father followed suit.

Charly was still processing what these astonishing twin gestures might mean when Melissa, cool as a cat burglar, slid her eyes round in her direction and flicked an eyelid. Unable to contain her shock, Charly gasped audibly and then began coughing, trying to cover her impulsive need to laugh. Obviously, her children had stepped in to prevent Mrs. Bergeron from having free access to their grandfather.

"You all right, dear?" Mrs. Bergeron said, raising her apple-crisp voice above the clarinet notes.

Charly felt the heat of embarrassment flood her face and swallowed hard. "Yes, just a tickle," she managed to croak. "Excuse me." She turned deliberately to watch as her daughter triumphantly blew out the old spiritual's last notes. Everyone applauded and Melissa curtsied and grinned, then slipped onto her mother's lap.

"Wonderful!" Barry said. "Thank you, honey." He swiveled to face Mrs. Bergeron and asked innocently, "Would you like to hear another song, Veronica?"

Again, Charly swallowed hard, stifling a chuckle. She felt a tremor in Melissa's body and squeezed her tightly. Somehow, the young girl managed to limit her reaction to a broad smile.

"Thank you, Barry. No." Mrs. Bergeron patted her bangs. "It was lovely, but I'd like to find out how you're feeling. Better? Fully recovered?"

"He wasn't sick," Scotty said, staring up at her defiantly. "He had a heart attack."

She glared down at him through round red frames. "I am well aware of your grandfather's condition, child."

"I'm feeling much better, thank you," Barry said quickly. He gently shook his grandson's shoulders. "In the pink. Right, Mr. Scott?"

Scotty giggled in reply.

"How 'bout you two go and make us some tea?" Charly suggested to her children.

After a brief hesitation, the pair dutifully trooped out to the kitchen. Moments later, sounds of running water and rattling dishware filtered into the living room.

For the next few minutes, Mrs. Bergeron and Barry discussed Barry's heart attack and recovery. Mostly, Veronica asked brusque questions, which Barry attempted to answer. He never got far, as he was quickly cut off by the woman's authoritative voice. She sounded like an expert on everything. As a result, Charly couldn't help thinking of long hours watching television medical dramas.

Charly waited awkwardly, uncertain whether she should interrupt. Her father didn't appear to be in any distress. After observing his reaction for a couple of minutes, Charly realized that he was just letting Veronica have her way, thus saving himself from too much talking and perhaps revealing more than he wished to.

And the retired accountant loved to talk.

"I am so careful what I eat," she said. "Only whole grains, organic vegetables and free-range eggs, of course." She smiled coyly. "One of the doctors—he's been on my favorite show for years—swears by free-range eggs. It's all about Omega three's, you know." She carefully smoothed the folds of her floral skirt before adding, "Of course, you're going to change your diet and exercise more, aren't you? That's what all the doctors recommend."

Charly was so surprised by the woman's coquettish expression when she mentioned her fantasy doctor that she thought she had misheard her last comment. But from her father's grimace, she hadn't. Why you old...thought Charly. She may be careful about what she ate, but not about how much she ate.

"I believe my dear wife tried hard to give her family the best nutrition possible," Barry said, his tone mild but slightly reproachful.

Mrs. Bergeron's dark eyes bulged from behind their red frames. "Oh, of course I never meant to suggest anything different! Eileen lived for all of you."

"She did, thank you," said Charly. "And as to exercise, I don't think there are many men my father's age who're half as active. He's out in the nursery every day, digging, hauling and moving things about."

Again, Mrs. Bergeron appeared a little taken aback. "Yes, well, I'm sure I meant no harm. Your mother would've understood. They were only suggestions, of course." Eyes and bangs downcast, she picked at her skirt. "Merely suggestions."

Charly began to feel sorry for her. She realized that in the past, she never really gave the sixty-something woman due respect. Dismissing her as one of the dragon ladies was where her interest and involvement had begun and ended. But now that she was really listening, it was obvious that Mrs. Bergeron was lonely, and like every other human being, just wanted to be needed and respected. Of course, that's just what her mother would have told her.

"It's very thoughtful of you," Charly said, "to think about Dad's health." She avoided her father's eye—his surprised expression would have thrown her—as she continued, "We do appreciate it."

Mrs. Bergeron rewarded her with an upturned fleshy face and

grateful smile. "Thank you, dear. It was a terrible shock to lose your mother last year." She reached across and patted Barry on the knee. "I'd hate to lose you, too."

Barry reached out and took her hand. "Very kind of you, Veronica."

Everyone sat still for a few seconds. Charly was wondering how to casually steer the conversation to Red James when Mrs. Bergeron politely inquired of Barry, "You wanted to ask me something?"

Barry shifted uncomfortably.

"Yes," Charly stepped in. "Um, well, after Dad's heart attack he realized there were some people—you know, from the past—that he wanted to see again. Didn't you, Dad?"

Her father nodded.

Charly leaned forward, focusing on the large brown eyes behind Mrs. Bergeron's circular glass lenses. "I'm sure you can understand."

"Of course," the older woman said, "there was a patient last week who—"

"Well, anyway," Charly bulldozed on, "it's not surprising that some of the people are hard to find. They've moved, maybe even died." Charly shrugged. "We just don't know."

"And you think I might?"

"Yes. At least, we hope so."

There was a cough and all three looked to the entrance. There stood Melissa, holding a loaded tray.

"Tea and cookies! Tea and cookies," shouted Scotty, as he rushed in past his sister and dropped another large platter onto the coffee table. Several oatmeal raisin cookies escaped onto the wooden tabletop. From beneath his arm, he pulled out and threw down a short pile of napkins. Then he whirled to face them, ducked his head in a comical bow and sprinted past his infuriated sister.

"Scotty!" Melissa whined after him. "Told you to wait!" Then she took a deliberate breath and carefully walked toward the coffee table.

Charly leaped up and helped her to settle the tray, heavily laden with mugs, tea thermos, cream and sugar, on the coffee table. Mrs. Bergeron's eyebrows shot above her corrective lenses at seeing the battered old thermos, and Charly swallowed another wave of embarrassment. Melissa had forgotten to use her grandmother's beautiful ceramic teapot and matching cups and saucers, which waited beside the microwave for just these sorts of occasions.

"Please excuse my fingers," Charly said, delicately placing the errant cookies back onto the platter. After she poured and offered the platter to her guest and her father, Charly bit into a cookie, chewed and swallowed.

"D'you know a man called Red James?"

Mrs. Bergeron's hand, which was holding a full mug of sweet tea, stopped in mid-flight toward her thick red lips.

"You mean Keith James? I do believe he was called Red in his youth. Well, of course. He ran the hospital while I was in accounting." She turned to Barry. "I didn't realize you were close to him." She paused, patting her bangs. "And anyway, he's been in town all his life."

"Uh, yes, well," Charly wiped her mouth with a napkin, "you see, Mr. James isn't really who we're looking for." She glanced at her father. He swallowed heavily, but remained silent.

Mrs. Bergeron placed her mug on the coffee table and observed Charly expectantly.

"We think that he might know someone who'll be able to help us find...a woman."

Her guest's bangs lurched. "A woman? Who?"

"I'm pretty sure you don't know her. She left town decades ago."

Mrs. Bergeron didn't reply. She just stared at Charly through her thick glasses.

Barry Shepherd stirred slightly. "Show her the photo, Charly."

Charly hesitated and then rose to take an envelope off the sculpted fireplace mantle. She withdrew the Polaroid and handed it to Mrs. Bergeron.

Mrs. Bergeron looked at the photograph for a long time without speaking. She took off her glasses and held the plastic square up to the tip of her nose. She turned to Charly, squinting myopically. "That's Keith, all right. My, he's young!"

She laughed and Charly was taken aback because the hard voice was replaced by a girlish giggle.

"But the blonde girl..." she sighed with real disappointment. "You're right, Charly. I don't know her. What's her name?"

Barry replied, "Sophie. Don't know her last name."

She shook her head slowly, handed the picture back to Barry.

"She's the woman you're trying to find?"

"Yes."

"Well, I'm very sorry I can't help you with her, but now, as to Keith, well, that's easy." She swiveled her bulk towards Charly.

"Why didn't you just ask his nephew?"

Charly blinked. She shot a look at her father and he stared blankly back.

"What?" Charly said. "Sorry, his...nephew? How do I—"

Mrs. Bergeron slid back and collapsed in large heaving giggles against the couch. Finally, she gasped and managed to wheeze, "Why, he just saved your father's life, didn't he?"

It took Charly a few seconds to process the last statement. She cocked her head in surprise.

"But the last nam—"

"His sister's child."

Everything clicked. "Of course, the red hair!"

"Hold on a minute!" thundered her father. "Who in tarnation are we talking about?"

"Dr. Rogers!" the two women exclaimed together.

"Doctor Rog—oh!" Barry shook his head in amazement. "Well, I'll be." He chuckled heartily. "My carrot-topped cardiologist." He looked at Mrs. Bergeron.

"His uncle's really Red James?"

"The very same. In fact, Calvin lives with him in the old family home on Baker Avenue." She took another cookie, bit into it and chewed. She was enjoying being in the limelight. "Fine men, both of them. The last of their family."

Charly wasn't really listening. She couldn't hear over the roaring in her head. She jumped up.

"I'll just get the phone number," she said, walking swiftly toward the kitchen. She could hardly feel her legs and wondered if her exhilaration was due to finding the next clue to solving Project Heartsong, or to having an excuse to see Dr. Rogers again.

She laughed to herself as she breezed into the kitchen and opened a drawer. Mom would have had a field day with this one. As she pulled out the small telephone book, she realized that the clear image of her mother that had been front and center in her mind was now slightly distorted. Usually, her mom's smiling face popped up as if she had double-clicked her photograph on a computer screen.

She paused. The phone book slipped from her hand and thumped onto the countertop. It was as though she were seeing her mother's face through swirling water. The lovely green eyes were crystal clear, but her high cheekbones and one ear were magnified, while the left side of her head was fuzzy.

Charly lurched and grabbed at the countertop. For the first time since her mother's death, she couldn't perfectly recall her mother's strong, angular features. With a moan, Charly dropped her head, leaned on the hard surface and let the tears tumble down.

Oh Mom, I'm so sorry.

After a few minutes, she arched and straightened her shoulders, then wiped her face. It didn't take her long to find the listing for Rogers on Baker Avenue and she pressed the digits on the kitchen phone before she could talk herself out of calling.

"Rogers' residence," a business-like voice said.

Charly hesitated, taken aback by the female voice. "Uh, I'm sorry." She stopped again, realizing her voice was uneven, and cleared her throat. "Sorry. I'm looking for Dr. Rogers."

"Yes, this is the doctor's residence. Mrs. Epco speaking."

"Oh hello, Mrs. Epco. May I speak to him?"

"He's just come in from the hospital. I'm his father's caregiver. Who's calling, please?"

"My name's Charly Shepherd. Dr. Rogers is my father's cardiologist."

"Well, I'm sorry, Ms. Shepherd, but the doctor doesn't do house calls. I'll give you his office number and you can make an appointme—"

"No! Uh, sorry, you misunderstand. We don't need an appointment. I need to speak to him...on a personal issue."

"Personal issue?" Mrs. Epco paused. "Well, if you'd just wait a moment."

Charly heard her put down the phone. There was the sound of fading footsteps and distant voices.

Suddenly, a familiar baritone filled her ear. "Ms. Shepherd, is your father feeling unwell?"

"No, no, quite the opposite. Sorry to call you at home, Dr. Rogers, but it's not about my Dad."

"Mrs. Epco said it was *personal*?"

Charly flushed at his teasing tone. "Uh, yes. Is your uncle Red James?"

"Yes, but not many people call him that anymore. Why?"

Charly swallowed. "Well, my father—"

"Thought you said this wasn't about your father?" Rogers sounded disappointed.

"It isn't about his heart, at least, not directly. It's about what happened to him after his heart attack."

"You intrigue me, Ms. Shepherd. Go on."

Charly felt a lift in her spirits and let her words rush out, "There's someone my Dad would like to see again, someone from his past. We think your uncle knew her and might be able to help us find her."

Dr. Rogers didn't answer.

"Dr. Rogers? Did you hear me?"

"Oh, yes, Ms. Shepherd. I'm sorry, I was just thinking. You see, my uncle suffers from Alzheimer's and I'm not too sure how much he could tell you."

"Oh." Charly felt crushed and wanted to hang up.

"Now, hold on a minute. Uncle Keith's best in the mornings, so if he's going to tell you anything, that would be the time. It's worth a shot, anyway. Can you come over tomorrow? Say just after nine?"

"Of course I can. Thank you, Dr. Rogers. Thank you."

"On two conditions."

Charly's diaphragm jumped. "Yes?"

"First, you call me Cal, and second, you let me buy you a coffee afterwards. I don't have to be in my office 'til the afternoon."

Charly smiled broadly and it brightened her voice. "Why, Cal, thank you. I'd be delighted, and by the way, my name's Charly."

Cal chuckled. "Oh, I already know that. First non-medical question I asked your father."

"You what?"

But the line was already dead.

Heartsong

Charly just stood there, listening to the dial tone and grinning.

Chapter Thirty-Nine

Opportunity is missed by most people because
it is dressed in overalls and looks like work.
Thomas A. Edison

Think it's best if I go alone, and Dad agrees," said Charly, as she waved from the kitchen window at her two children. The pair, backpacks loaded, trooped off to catch the morning school bus. She hadn't had time to discuss the bike incident with Scotty, but as he trudged past his still-intact two-wheeler, he threw a look back in his mother's direction. Charly was heartened to see his shamed expression. She turned round and fiddled with the phone cord.

"Told Faith the same thing five minutes ago."

"But you and Faith're having all the fun," Hope's voice said. "You got the photos, Faith twigged to the Red James connection and now you're off to interview him."

Charly and her sisters generally exchanged phone calls roughly every other day, but since their new mission, Charly had been calling each with a daily update, which Michael insisted on calling the 'Shepherd sit-rep.' The first time she'd heard it, it had taken Charly a couple of seconds to translate this new bit of cop-speak to 'situation report.'

Charly heard her sister sigh. "All I'm doing is getting yet another lecture ready for my first-year students...and they're only interested in sex, drugs and Facebook."

"Well," Charly said, eyeing her father, who was spooning cereal into his mouth, "if it's any consolation, I don't think Mr. James's gonna be any help. He's got Alzheimer's."

"Oh. That's too bad." Hope paused for a moment. "At least tell me the set-up. I'm dying for a distraction. Where's the old dude live? Some sort of old folks' home?"

Charly felt her pulse quicken. "He lives with his nephew," she said, with forced nonchalance. Hope was notoriously adept at ferreting out any inkling of passionate emotions. She had known before anyone else when Charly's marriage was collapsing, could spot when Faith and Michael were having a tiff from fifty yards off, and had earlier suspected Charly's budding interest in the attractive cardiologist.

"Oh, yeah? That's different. Nephew a stay-at-home kinda guy, or is there some professional help?"

"There's home care, I believe."

"So that's who's going to be on hand today?"

"Gee, Hope, I'm not exactly sure. Is it important?"

"No. I'm sorry. I mean, it's just I'm a little bored. The butterflies aren't due for several days and there's not much else happening in my world."

In the past, Charly had often envied her single sister's freedom to do what she wanted, her lack of family responsibilities, and her ongoing opportunities for travel and learning, but these feelings quickly vanished when she recalled all the good fortune in her own life.

Feeling badly for Hope, Charly unconsciously let down her guard. "Sorry about that, Hopeful. 'Course it'd be great to have you along." Her father grinned and plopped a slice of whole wheat bread into the toaster. "It's just that since Mr. James isn't all there, his nephew thinks it's better that I speak to him alone. Not as threatening or confusing."

"I guess that's reasonable. What's this nephew like?" She laughed. "Got red hair?"

Charly almost choked and couldn't reply for several seconds. Her father glanced up, eyes alarmed, but Charly waved him off.

"Charly? Charly, you okay?"

"Y-yes," Charly finally managed to sputter. "Sorry. Tickle in my throat."

"Well, take a deep breath and gimme on the nephew."

"Love to, but I've gotta go. Tell you about it, tonight, okay?" She hung up before her sister could respond.

Barry observed his youngest daughter for a moment. "'Hope's radar's buzzing, isn't it?"

Charly blushed.

The toaster dinged and her father's bread popped into view.

"Ah," he said with a knowing smile, "saved by the bell."

~~~

The James' brick home on leafy Baker Street was a large two-story that had been charming once, but now seemed slightly disheveled. Though more austere Georgian than fancy Victorian, it was blessed with a few unique features, including a copper-topped portico, curving S-shaped shutters, and a double-wide front door.

Charly's stomach fluttered as she mounted the three steps, and she reproached herself.

For heaven's sake, Charly! This's an interview, not a date!

She paused for a moment, fingertip on the doorbell, and breathed deeply to slow her heart rate. After a moment, she pressed the button, and as it chimed, peered through the stained glass. The low morning light cast an array of colors onto the foyer's dark hardwood floors and then the door swung open. Calvin Rogers stood, ginger hair glinting in the harlequin light.

Charly just stared, entranced.

"Hello, Charly. Right on time. Come in, come in."

He stepped aside as Charly entered and she noted how trim and professional he looked in his dark pin-striped suit and olive-green tie. She felt a little underdressed in her jeans, white blouse and shaggy fleece vest, and self-consciously fiddled with her fringed gold scarf.

"Who's there?" a reedy man's voice floated in from somewhere. "Calvie?" The voice became louder, rising with concern. "Who's there?"

"It's all right, Uncle Keith," Cal called over his shoulder. "We've got a lovely surprise."

Pleased by the expression, Charly glanced swiftly at his face, but it was turned away.

"What's that?" Keith James shouted.

Cal looked at Charly and grinned.

"A SURPRISE!" he bellowed, then dropping his voice, he added, "Come on. He'll get agitated."

Charly followed him down a dim corridor all the way to the back of the house, where they turned right into a large room lined with glass on two adjoining walls. A river-rock fireplace dominated the wall across the room, and Charly noted the array of greeting cards that littered the broad mantle.

Adorned simply with comfortable leather chairs and large-screen TV on the left, along with a wealth of bookshelves, it was an ideal sitting room, decorated with a masculine touch. Through the huge windows on her right, she could see a swath of overgrown grass encircled by mature fir trees. Someone had made the effort to rig up and fill a number of bird feeders—some tubular, some platform—and a variety of winged creatures were flitting about.

An extremely frail elderly man, wrapped in a bright red tartan blanket, sat hunched in a wheelchair facing the backyard. A middle-aged woman, likely the caregiver, sat engrossed in her knitting in a large rocking chair nearby. She looked up and nodded.

Keith James turned at the sound of their footsteps and smiled shyly. He had a full head of white hair, a mouth empty of teeth and sea-green eyes, identical to those of his nephew.

"Calvie?" he said anxiously.

Cal stepped over to him and gently took his hand.

Charly confirmed a conclusion she had formed at the hospital. Cal wasn't wearing a wedding ring.

"This is Ms. Charly Shepherd, Uncle Keith. She's come for a visit."

Charly walked around behind the wheelchair and reached out for James's other hand. "Hello, Mr. James. Pleased to meet you."

James's eyes blinked up at her. "Charly?" The folds of flesh on his face contorted. "No name for a lady."

Cal flushed slightly and opened his mouth, but Charly beat him to it.

"Well, Mr. James, you're almost right. I've got two older sisters and my parents were really hoping for a boy." She knelt beside him and looked straight at him. "When I arrived, they decided the name suited me and that was that."

"I'm hungry," James said.

"Now, Mr. James," the caregiver said, "we've just had our breakfast."

He turned and looked at her blankly. "Hungry."

"Hey, Uncle Keith, Charly's come to talk to you about the old times, when you were young. Didn't you, Charly?" Cal pulled close a hard-backed chair and gestured for Charly to sit.

"Yes, Mr. James." Charly sat and leaned toward the wheelchair. "I've got a photo of you. Back when you were a teenager."

She held up the Polaroid and James's expression showed interest.

"You were very handsome," she said as the old man's swollen fingers gripped the plastic. He stared at the photograph, but his face showed no recognition.

"That's you, Uncle Keith," Cal said, touching the picture. "You and a very attractive young woman." He playfully prodded the old man's chest. "You devil, you. Who is she?"

"Her name's Sophie," Charly said. "Do you remember her?"

Unfortunately, James' eyes had roamed from the photo back to the birds and he didn't answer. Charly exhaled and felt her spirits fall with her breath.

Cal sighed. "My apologies, Charly. Guess you're not going to get anything from him today." He glanced over at the caregiver. "What d'you think, Mrs. Epco?"

She shook her head. "I'm sorry, Doctor, but Mr. James has been more confused than ever the last few days."

"Regrettably, his disease is progressing rapidly." Cal hesitated and then continued, "A lot of the time now, he doesn't even recognize me."

"I'm so sorry. I...I shouldn't have come." Charly stood. "Goodbye, Mr. James," she said softly, but he gave no reply or sign of having heard. "Thank you, anyway, Cal. I'd better go."

She turned toward the doorway. As she moved, a couple of greeting cards trembled in the disturbed air and one flapped to the floor.

As she reached down to pick it up, Cal called out, "Wait a second!"

He stepped toward her. She handed him the greeting card, but couldn't help noticing that it was a Christmas card.

"You promised to join me for a coffee." He took the proffered card and shoved it back onto the mantle. Several others flopped down like falling dominoes.

He smiled ruefully. "Guess we really ought to tidy up now and then."

He stood a couple of the cards upright and then he stopped, fingers in mid-air. Cal spun and nearly struck Charly.

"What'd you say her name was?"

It took Charly a second to control her tongue. "Uh...Sophie."

"That's what I thought," he said, eyes lighting up. "Just a second here."

He whirled and began grabbing the greeting cards, giving each a quick look and then dropping it without further thought. "Aha! Being tidy's not what it's cracked up to be," he said finally, holding up one small card festooned with a large red heart.

"Check this out."

Charly glanced inside the stiff colored paper. Written in elaborate gold scroll were the words, "To my sweet Valentine", and below that, someone had scrawled a name in large looping black letters: Sophie du Pont.

"It can't be," she whispered.

"I don't see why not," Cal said. "I've never paid much attention, but my uncle always gets a Valentine's Day card from this woman, every year. He said she was his first love." He hesitated before shrugging self-consciously.

"In fact, it wouldn't surprise me if last year's card was still here. He likes seeing them, so I just let 'em pile up. You think it's from your Sophie?"

Charly stared at the signature and felt a tingle rise in her blood. "Don't know, but at least I've got a last name to go on."

"You've got more than that." Charly stared up at him. Cal nodded. "She lives in Bridgewater."

"Bridgewater? But that's only fifteen miles away." She scanned the back of the card, but there was no address written on it. "How on earth d'you know the name of her town?"

Cal grinned broadly. "Simple, really. I open his mail. Last name's du Pont, return address Bridgewater. Struck me as funny, y'know? Du Pont's French for bridge."

"Of course! Well done," Charly said, instinctively stretching up to kiss him quickly on the cheek. "Thank you, Cal. I'm getting closer."

"If that's the sort of thanks I'm going to get," he said, "I'll try even harder."

To avoid letting him seeing the slight flush rising in her cheeks, Charly bent to examine the Valentine's card for the last time. Sophie du Pont of Bridgewater, Oregon, she thought. Was she Graeme Walker's girl?

Chapter Forty

The simple act of stopping and looking at the beauty around us can be prayer.
Patricia R. Barrett

C harly's a very cool name for a woman," Cal said, reaching across the little outdoor table to offer Charly a small teapot and cup. "'Y' or 'ie'?"

"Thank you," Charly said, taking the pot and then the cup. "We spell it with a 'y', but I can tell you, as a first name, it's had its challenges."

The little coffee shop, FullaBeans, was only two blocks from the James' home. It was small but quaint, and offered an excellent corner view of two main streets. While Cal fetched their drinks, Charly had settled in at a small table near the entrance. Within seconds, her eyes and thoughts were roaming, warmed by the glow of his obvious interest in her and by having added another piece to the Project Heartsong puzzle. It was nice to be having coffee with someone. It had been a long time since her last social outing, much less date.

Having served her, Cal slipped into a seat beside her, placed his mug of coffee in front of him and set the tray on a nearby chair.

"Get teased a lot?"

Charly nodded. "Bad enough having sisters named Faith and Hope and everybody automatically expecting me to be called Charity, but to have a boy's name..." She shook her head and poured tea.

Cal stopped stirring in his dollop of cream. "So why aren't you called Charity?" He grinned suddenly. "Not that I'm saying you should've been."

Charly leaned back, greatly enjoying their easy conversation and the delicate frisson of mutual attraction.

"It was close. My parents had decided if I was a girl, I'd be Charity, and if a boy, I'd be Charlie, with an 'ie'."

Cal gave her a look of genuine approval. "Well, you're obviously all girl, so what happened?"

Charly took a sip. The late morning air was damp and the tea heated her right down to her stomach.

"I was born real chubby with a whack of black, unruly hair, which ended up falling out the next week. But my sisters were both slim and fair newborns and I believe my Dad was—" she took another drink and then chuckled, "truly horrified. Anyway, that's how my Mom says he looked the first time he saw me. Supposedly, he shouted to her, 'Heavens to Betsy, Eileen, she's no Charity!'"

Cal's body reared back and he let loose with a deep infectious laugh. A couple of passersby turned and smiled at them.

Charly watched and enjoyed, and then finally said, "So that's how I became Charly with a 'y'."

"With kids of your own," Cal said, turning serious. "Your father often spoke of them." He fiddled with a spoon while eyeing an approaching car.

"He didn't mention their father."

Charly shot him a quick look of curiosity. "He's been out of the picture for years. He, he left me and the kids for someone else. Since then, we've been living with my parents." She looked directly into his eyes.

"And you?"

Cal blushed slightly, darkening the sprinkling of freckles across his nose. "Similar outcome. I got married in med school in Portland. It lasted about three years. No children, unfortunately. We both specialized, me in cardio-thoracic and her in obstetrics, so we hardly ever saw one another. We're still—" he smiled ruefully, "no, we're *not* friends, I hate it when people say that, but we're still in touch."

"How'd you come to be in Silver Shores?"

Cal drained the last drops of his coffee before saying. "I used to visit Uncle Keith sometimes as a kid. When my parents were killed—"

"Killed! Oh, my goodness, Cal, I'm so sorry."

Cal nodded. "It's all right, but thanks. It happened a long time ago. Anyway, what with my failed marriage and losing my parents, I had nothing holding me in Portland. A job came up here and I took it. And at this very moment, Charly Shepherd, I'm really glad I did."

Charly was tongue-tied, struggling to answer when Cal's cell phone rang, startling them both.

He excused himself, stood and held the phone to his ear. His sudden grave expression told Charly everything she needed to know.

"Sorry," he said, turning back to her. "I've got to go."

Charly stood. "That's okay. I understand."

Cal turned and took a couple of steps toward his car. He paused, whirled and said, "May I see you again? I'd really like to know how it all works out, and—" His phone jangled again. He shook his head in frustration. "Sorry!"

"Bye!" Charly called after him but he had already broken into a trot and didn't hear her over the din of traffic.

~~~

"Du Pont?" said Faith. "But isn't Melissa's teacher called Burgess?"

Charly shrugged. "Maybe she remarried."

"I'm coming to Bridgeport with you," Hope said with her hands on her hips.

"Me too," Faith said.

Charly shot Michael a glance and then observed her sisters across the kitchen table. The trio had arrived together after dinner, which was unusual in itself, but her siblings acting as a united front was making Shepherd history. Moments before, she had sent her reluctant kids off to complete their homework, their grandfather having assured the pair that he would discuss everything with them later. Then, Charly filled her siblings in on her trip to the James' home. Now the adults were mulling over their next move in Project Heartsong.

"Not sure that's the best approach," Charly said finally. "I think we'd overwhelm her." She turned to her father, who was finishing off a bowl of chocolate fudge ice cream. "What d'you say, Dad? Should you go it alone, go with me, or with all of us?"

"Hey!" Faith said. "Why is going with just you an option? Why not with Michael and me, or with Hope?"

Hope nodded.

"Okay, okay." Charly raised her palms in submission. "Dad?"

Barry licked his spoon thoughtfully. "Have to admit, I'm not sure, having never met the woman." He leaned back and observed his three daughters. "What if just one or more of you went?"

Charly frowned. "You want us to go without you?"

Her father's broad cheeks turned slightly pink. He pushed his bowl around and dropped his eyes.

Hope stepped in. "Sure, Dad, we could do that. It might be the best approach. Huh girls?" She turned and gave her sisters an encouraging look.

"Yeah," Faith added. "Could be. Sort of like a little reconnaissance. Introduce Sophie to the whole thing gradually."

The foursome looked at Charly.

"Uh, well," she began, "I can understand your being a little worried about seeing her, Dad, but..." She hesitated.

Okay, Mom. Here's where I need your strength. I think this's what I'm supposed to do. Isn't it?

She took a deep breath. "Meeting her, your personally meeting Sophie du Pont and telling her about Graeme, isn't that what this's been all about?"

The kitchen was suddenly quiet and Michael stopped spooning out more ice cream. No one moved for nearly a minute and then Faith let loose.

"What difference does it make if we meet her first?"

Charly didn't know. She just instinctively understood, deep in her heart, that the next step was her father's and that his daughters could not make it for him. So she remained silent and waited.

Finally, Barry said, "Thank you, girls and Michael, for your stalwart support. You don't know how much it means to me." He placed his large hands on the table and stood.

Charly realized that he looked extremely fatigued, and she was about to suggest they either pack it all in or delay their next action, when a loud clattering crash resounded from the backyard.

"What was that!?" said Faith.

"The nursery!" Charly was racing for the back door before the others could take another breath.

Charly flew out the door and down the steps into the dark, shouting, "Hello! Who's there?" She raced along the grass, darting between garden beds, toward the greenhouses.

"What's going on?" Faith called out as the back light flooded the area in a dazzling glow. "Anybody hurt?"

By now, Charly was at the side of the large greenhouse and almost slipped as her sneakers skated over a patchy carpet of glass fragments. She stood, mouth gaping, staring into a large jagged hole slashed into the wall of glass. Moving quickly inside, she looked up in horror as slices of glass glittered like teeth in the moonlight, and almost tripped over a fist-sized stone. She reached down, picked it up and turned it over. It was one of the thousands of rust-stained rocks on the property.

She held it for a moment, the weight heavy in her hand and in her heart, for she thought she knew who had thrown it.

"Oh no!" Hope whispered beside her. She was holding a flashlight and its narrow beam shot upward, glinting against the glass shards. Her sisters, her daughter, Michael and her father were now standing by Charly, their necks bent upward, eyes staring through the ragged hole into the inky night sky.

"That the culprit?" said Hope, flicking the beam down at Charly's fist.

Charly said, "Everybody out. Now!"

She turned and urgently shooed them out. As they reached the entrance, another crinkling collision of glass and concrete floor made them all jump.

From a safer distance, Hope played the flashlight's beam around the damaged area.

"I think we got lucky," she said, holding the light steady. "The rock went through one of the smaller side panes. See?"

But Charly wasn't feeling lucky. She shouted, "Scott Alexander

Shepherd, you hear me? Come out wherever you are. Right now!"

"Scotty?" her father whispered. "Can't be. No."

Charly held up her hand for silence. After a couple of moments, they heard a soft crunching sound and then Scotty's face, whiter than the full moon above, peered at them from several feet away.

"What? I didn't do anything," he whined.

Melissa took a breath, about to speak, but stopped when she saw her mother's expression in the dim light.

"Come here, son," Charly said, in a voice as hard and smooth as the glass littering the floor.

After another hesitation, the little boy took a couple of slow steps toward them.

"You didn't break the window, did you, Scotty?" Hope said.

"No way," Faith added. "You wouldn't."

Scotty's face crumbled and he began to cry.

Charly moved toward him and her son burst forward and rammed himself into her body.

"I didn't do it!" he shouted. "Didn't do it!"

Charly stroked his hair and led him through the yard and the house to the kitchen. The others silently followed. As they gathered at the entrance, Charly took her boy and tenderly pushed him into a chair and then sat down facing him.

"Do you want to try telling me the truth?"

But he shook his head and buried his face in his hands.

Charly reached across and gently pulled one of his arms free. She opened her own hand and then his much smaller fist.

"Look, honey," she said. "Look."

Scotty peered through his fingers. Both their palms were marred by identical orange-brown stains.

"The rock that went through the greenhouse has rust on it. I picked it up. See?" She held up her hand. "Your hand has the same stain. Now, if you didn't throw the rock, how did the stain get there?"

"You and Grampa don't love me anymore!" he said suddenly, before jumping off his chair, running and latching onto Hope.

Chapter Forty-One

In search of my mother's garden, I found my own.
Alice Walker

W hat?" Charly spun and stared at her son, who was now bawling into Hope's waist.

The others were speechless.

"What are you talking about, Scotty? Of course, your Grampa and I love you. We're not too happy about your smashing the greenhouse, but that doesn't mean we don't love you."

Barry reached out and ruffled Scotty's hair. "What's all this stuff and nonsense, boy? You're my Mr. Scott."

"Come here, baby," Charly said softly. "Come. Come to Mommy."

The dark-haired boy sniffled and then whirled. A second later, he was on his mother's lap, clinging tightly while she rocked him. He cried and mumbled incoherently for several minutes while the others slowly sat at the table to wait out the boy's tears.

Finally, he began to take long ragged breaths and Charly titled his face up. Wiping away his tears, she softly said, "Tell me what's going on, little man."

Scotty's small face twisted. "You don't love me anymore," he said in a whisper.

Charly tightened her grip on his thin shoulders. "Of course I love you, my dear sweet Scotty." She kissed him on the forehead. "You and your sister are the most important people in my life. What've I done to make you think I don't love you anymore?"

"It's my fault," he said, jabbing a finger toward his grandfather. "You almost died and it's all my fault."

Barry stared at him from across the kitchen table. He stood quickly and moved to the boy.

"What d'you mean, son? I had a heart attack. It wasn't your fault."

Scotty stuck a thumb in his mouth and remained silent.

Charly looked around the table. "Anybody know what he's talking about? Lissa?"

The young girl twirled her hair and shrugged.

"Okay," said Charly, looking back at her youngest child. "You're not going to get into any real trouble. Just tell us what's bothering you, okay? We can't help you unless we know."

Scotty blinked at her.

Barry ruffled the boy's hair. "Nobody's blaming you for anything, Mr. Scott."

"You will," he whispered.

Barry and Charly exchanged a knowing glance. Barry pulled his chair around and sat opposite the boy. "Okay. Maybe you've done something you shouldn't have."

"Duh, yeah," Melissa said, folding her arms.

Charly reached across and touched her hand to silence her. "We all do that, sometimes. Don't we?"

"Sure," Hope said enthusiastically. "Everybody makes mistakes. Right, Michael?"

Michael grinned and pointed at Hope. "Some of us more than others, eh, kid?"

A ghost of a smile flitted across the boy's mouth.

"See," Barry placed a hand on his grandson's shoulder, "what's really important is to be honest and stand up like a man or woman and take responsibility for your actions."

"You won't hate me?" Scotty said.

"Of course not. Mr. Scott, there's nothing you could do to make me hate you, understand?" Scotty nodded at his grandfather. "Okay, then. What's the problem?"

Everyone was silent and then suddenly, Scotty leaped up and rushed out of the room. His footsteps pounded up the stairs and into his room, then back down the stairs. A few seconds later he stood, gasping, in the doorway. With a swift flick of his arm, he threw his backpack onto the floor.

"It's in there," he said, before slumping with obvious relief into a nearby chair.

Charly picked up the backpack and peered inside. A jumble of books, toys and food wrappings met her gaze.

"Side pocket," Scotty breathed.

Charly unzipped the pocket and removed a slightly soiled envelope. It was stamped and addressed to their insurance company. Charly looked at her son and then at the stamp. It hadn't been cancelled. She ripped open the envelope and pulled out the check her father had written for the nursery's insurance.

Scotty dropped his head and booted the leg of his chair.

"You forgot to mail it," Barry said.

"So this's why you've been acting out lately?" Charly said. "Because you forgot to mail Grampa's insurance check?"

Scotty nodded slowly. "Lissa said we were broke and then Grampa had his heart attack and then I..." He swallowed, flushed and began weeping again.

"Now, now," Barry said. "Enough of that crying. If a man isn't honest, he's got nothing. Understand, boy?"

Scotty sniffled, but looked up.

"Same for a woman," Hope said.

"That's right," said Barry. "So, stand up and tell us what happened and apologize from the heart. You know the Good Lord will forgive you, and so will we."

Scotty looked around hesitantly.

"Go on, Mr. Scott," Hope said. "You can do it."

Scotty took a deep breath, and then stood and spoke quickly, as though the words were burning his tongue.

"I forgot to mail Grampa's check and didn't tell you, I mixed up the fertilizers, I punched out Alex, I left my bike in the driveway, I smashed the greenhouse, and I'm real sorry. My bad." He stood for a moment, rocking on his feet. "Mom, you're not gonna tell Grammie about it in your prayers, are you?"

"Come here," Charly said, opening her arms.

Scotty flew into her lap.

The others spontaneously broke into applause.

"Who wants another round of ice cream?" Faith said, already yanking open the freezer.

Thirty minutes later, as Faith and Hope were washing up and the children had gone to watch television, Barry cleared his throat.

"I've got something to say." His daughters and son-in-law looked at him. "I've known in my heart all along what I should be doing for Graeme, but I was weak and afraid." He coughed slightly.

"Can't lecture my own grandson about what it takes to be a man without acting like one myself. So, if Scotty can own up to his failing, then so can I."

Charly experienced a rush of love and pride for her father. She knew by the shine in her sisters' eyes that they felt the same.

"I've let you three do all the work on Project Heartsong so far." His expression hardened. "It's time I did some of the heavy lifting. However, I would ask one more thing of you."

"Of course," said Hope.

"Anything," Faith said.

Charly just smiled.

"Thank you. You see, I'd like to introduce myself to Sophie du Pont in person. Would one of you consider calling her first and setting something up? No details, just that I'm an old friend of Graeme's and would like to come by."

"Sure, Dad," said Charly.

Faith asked, "Who's going with you?"

Her father shook his head. "I'm going to ask God's advice on that. I'll let you know."

He stood, approached and offered each daughter a kiss on the cheek before heading to his room.

"G'night, Daddy," Faith called after him. She whirled and slapped a bejeweled hand on the table. "I'm making the call."

"No way," Hope said. "My turn."

The two turned to Charly. She didn't answer, glancing at Michael.

He quickly flipped up his palms. "Keeping out of it, thanks."

"Wimp," she said, only half-jokingly. Then she exhaled, closed her right hand and began pumping.

"One..." Her sisters followed suit. "Two, three!"

Their three fists flashed across the table. Both Charly and Hope choose scissors, while Faith picked paper.

"Aha," Hope said, "Scissors cuts paper. You're out, Faithie. Okay, Charly, go again. One, two, three!"

This time, Charlie stayed with scissors, but Hope chose rock. She jumped up. "Ha! Rock crushes scissors. I make the call. What's the number?"

"Hang on a sec," Faith said. "What're you gonna say?"

Hope hesitated, hand on the telephone receiver. "Just what Dad said."

"You're going to call this woman out of the blue and tell her a complete stranger wants to see her? And that, by the way, you're the stranger's daughter calling on his behalf?"

Hope chewed the inside of her cheek. "Hmm. When you put it like that...what should I say?"

"This's why I should be making the call," Faith said.

"Oh yeah? Okay, then, Miss Smarty-pants. Tell me what you'd say."

Faith spread out her arms dramatically. "How do I know? I'd sort of feel my way into it. Wouldn't I, my man?"

"You sure would, Faithie," her husband said.

Hope groaned and sat back down. "What do you think, Charly?"

"You're both right. Why don't you start with what Dad suggested and then take it from there? You'll think of something, and we'll be right here if you need help."

The sisters needn't have worried.

Hope made the call, calmly introducing herself and offering her father's explanation. She didn't have to ad lib much. In fact, Sophie du Pont agreed almost immediately to see Barry Shepherd the next evening.

As a somewhat startled Hope promptly relayed to her sisters, Sophie had quickly replied, "I'm so glad you called. It would be wonderful to meet someone who knew my beloved Graeme."

Chapter Forty-Two

I am fonder of my garden for the trouble it gives me.
Reginald Farrer

Charly wasn't sure how her sisters got through the next day. She was a bundle of nerves, couldn't concentrate on anything, and was actually appreciative of the crunchy clean-up task in the large greenhouse. It was monotonous but physical, and she swept glass and tidied for over an hour and was still barely finished in time for the glazier's arrival.

How is it, she pondered while teasing a fragment out of the back overhead fan, that bits of glass can fly an inordinate distance and hide in the smallest of cracks? The broken panel, as Hope had said, was less than four feet square, so its replacement was neither too pricey nor the repair too challenging.

Still, it was an additional unexpected expense against their already overdrawn bank account and another reason for her to discipline her son, however reluctant she was to do it. And to think that many of their customers regularly told her how wonderful it must be to live such a simple and uneventful rural existence!

Her father spent the day in his room and Charly only spoke to him at lunch. Though he was thoughtful and quiet, Charly sensed his underlying quiver of unease and anticipation. As she finished the lunch dishes, she wondered how she would be feeling in his place.

Pretty terrified, she concluded, but also encouraged and hopeful. She hadn't asked him if he had decided on having someone accompany him, and he hadn't offered. He had, however, suggested that she ask her sisters and Michael to arrive at 6:30.

After drying her hands, she made the phone calls. Her sisters were thrilled at the invite and eager to chat about all the possible permutations of who might attend, what Sophie du Pont would be like and what might be said. Charly wasn't keen on being pulled into these musings and ended both conversations more brusquely than she had intended. She made it through the rest of the day—whipping up chocolate-fudge brownies as a diversion—and making the Sloppy Joe dinner on automatic pilot.

It was easier than she had expected, as her father took center stage while they ate the still-warm dessert and told Melissa and Scotty everything. Not surprisingly perhaps, the kids' curiosity waned as they learned the full details. After all, Charly realized as she watched the boredom settle over their faces, going off to talk about the old days with an elderly stranger wasn't their idea of a good time.

Finally, just after six o'clock, Barry pushed back his plate and rose. "Please give me a call when the others have arrived," he said. "Going to lie down for a few minutes."

The trio watched him slowly leave the room.

"Is Grampa okay?" Scotty said. "He never lies down after dinner."

Charly wasn't sure how to answer. The boy was right.

"Hand me your plate. I'm sure he's fine. Just a little anxious about meeting Mrs. du Pont."

Melissa began picking up the used cutlery. "What's the big deal? It all happened, like, an ice age ago."

Charly smiled at her daughter's expression, took the proffered knives and forks and dumped them into the soapy water filling the sink.

"It's very important to your grandfather. That's all you need to understand. Okay?"

Melissa sighed. "Okay."

Scotty handed over the rest of the dirty plates while his sister picked up the milk-stained glasses. "Can we go now?" they asked in unison.

"Don't go far," Charly said, busy with the final tidying up.

Once finished, she poured a tall glass of skim milk, tossed in couple of ice cubes, cut a large brick of frosted brownie and stood sipping and munching and gazing out the window.

In no time, it seemed, she heard the roar of Michael's motorbike and then it blasted down the drive. Charly couldn't help laughing. Faith, dressed in her fashion goggles and pink helmet, waved merrily at her from the sidecar.

A few moments later, Hope's old red Jeep, with its convertible top down, shot into view. The two vehicles pulled to a halt next to one another.

When everyone was seated around the kitchen table, Charly went to her father's room and knocked gently. "We're all here, Dad," she said softly.

The door opened. Her father stepped out, dressed in the only new suit, dress shirt and tie he owned. His thick hair shone, he was freshly shaven and he smelled of Old Spice.

She reared back slightly in surprise. The only time he had worn the indigo suit was at his wife's funeral.

He clutched a soiled letter-sized envelope in his hand and as he tucked it into his inside coat pocket, Charly recognized it as the one that held the sheet music for Graeme's song.

"Okay, Charly," he said, with a just hint of embarrassment showing in the curve of his lips. "Let's do it."

Charly deliberately beat her father back to the kitchen and hissed out an order, just before he appeared in the entrance.

"Not a word about the suit!"

But Faith gasped involuntarily and Melissa cried out, "That's Grammie's funeral suit!"

Barry flushed slightly, took a couple of steps and brushed a finger along Melissa's cheek.

"Don't think she'd mind, honey. It's an honor suit and tonight, I'm honoring a fallen friend." For a long moment, he just stood, looking at them.

Finally, Scotty said, "You rock, dude."

Barry smiled broadly. "Thank you, Mr. Scott. Well, you all know what tonight's about. What you don't know is who's coming with me to speak with Sophie du Pont."

"Whatever you want, Daddy," Faith said. "We'll do it."

"Thank you, dear. I've thought and prayed long and hard about this. I'd like you all to come."

There was a stunned silence, which was broken by Melissa's voice. "Everybody's going, Grampa?"

He nodded.

"Sweet," said Scotty.

"Oh, one more thing," Barry said, as the others began pushing back their chairs. "I'd like Charly and I to go in first." He looked at Faith and then at Hope.

"I know you won't mind, dears. It was Charly's suggestion in the first place to help me out."

"Like Faith said, Dad," Hope said. "Anything you want."

Chapter Forty-Three

When speech comes from a quiet heart,
it has the strength of the orchid, and the fragrance of rock.
Stephen Mitchell

The sky-blue Bridgewater bungalow was modest, but as well cared for as Barry Shepherd's tools. The two vehicles pulled up and parked on the street beneath a huge Douglas fir. Melissa and Scotty jumped out, skipped over, and as previously arranged, clambered into Hope's Jeep.

Moments later, Barry and Charly stood on the top step facing the white door.

"This's it," Barry said softly. "Thank you, Charly, for helping me make this journey."

Charly squeezed her father's hand while he pressed the doorbell with the other. Sophie du Pont must have been waiting just inside. The door swung open as the bell sounded to reveal an elderly woman wearing a faded polka dot dress and a coral cardigan.

Charly knew she had to be of a similar age to her parents, but Sophie appeared much older. She was tall, stooped and extremely wrinkled. Still, Charly would have recognized her anywhere. She was now positive that Derek Burgess was Sophie's child. He had inherited her dimpled chin and lovely deep blue eyes.

"Good evening, Mrs. Du Pont," Barry began. "I'm Barry

Shepherd and this's my daughter, Charly. She's the main reason we're here. Thank you for seeing us."

Sophie smiled and gestured for them to enter.

Charly stepped in first. The living room was small but nicely furnished with a floral-patterned loveseat and matching wing chairs. A stone fireplace topped by a simple slab of wood commanded one wall. On it stood several framed photographs, right next to an old mantle clock. Along the opposite wall sat an upright piano with a broad bench.

"Welcome. Please, call me Sophie."

As Sophie stood aside to let Barry pass, she noticed the two vehicles in front of her house and frowned.

"The rest of my family," Barry said. "Was hoping to introduce them to you later, if that's convenient."

"Of course," said Sophie.

She waved at the vehicles, and Charly noticed that her knuckles were badly swollen with arthritis. As Sophie's hand fluttered down to her side, she looked for the Claddah ring that Faith had spotted in the old photograph but it wasn't there.

"We'll have them in for tea."

They settled quickly, Charly and Sophie on the loveseat and Barry facing them in one of the overstuffed chairs. Any fears Charly had that this greatly anticipated meeting would be awkward were brushed aside almost immediately. Her father and Sophie quickly fell into an informal chat about the past and people and experiences they had in common. Sophie was a charming hostess, both chatty and attentive.

After ten minutes, Charly hadn't said a word. She decided to close her eyes and just listen, delighted to hear the lively interchange between the pair of enthusiastic voices. It was as though two young people were just shooting the breeze, as her father would say.

Then her father's tone changed and she opened her eyes to find his expression had changed from animated to somber. Her stomach clenched, apprehensive about what he had to do.

"Sophie, may I ask, is Derek Burgess your son?"

Sophie smiled. "Why, yes. You know Derek?"

"He's my granddaughter's teacher. She thinks very highly of

him."

"I'm very lucky," Sophie said. "He's a wonderful son and father."

There was a moment of silence and then Barry cleared his voice and said, "I'm ashamed to say that I'm here because I...failed you and your son."

Sophie pressed a hand against the silver cross around her neck, and Charly saw something that stole her breath. The Claddah ring hung protectively round the little cross.

"I...I don't understand. Failed us, Barry? But we've only just met."

He swallowed hard. "You know that Graeme and I were buddies in Vietnam." Sophie nodded. "He was my best friend and he loved you with all his heart and all his might." A small smile itched at the corners of his mouth. "He talked about you all the time. Couldn't wait to get home to you and your baby-to-be. He had so many plans." This time the smile was loose and genuine. "Drove me batty."

Sophie sniffed and reached for a tissue from the coffee table.

"I'm very sorry if this's causing you pain, but I'm afraid I might be about to add some more." He partially rose and then dropped back down. "You see, Grae gave me something, something for you. Well, really more for your baby. I promised him I would bring it home and personally put it in your hands." He dropped his eyes.

"To my everlasting shame, Sophie, I broke that promise."

Sophie gasped softly.

Charly held her breath, not moving a muscle, wishing she weren't in the room. It was too painful, too personal.

Her father looked up and gazed directly into Sophie's deep-set eyes.

"My promise to my best friend. There're reasons why, Sophie, but no excuses. All I can do now is beg for your forgiveness and deliver a gift that's nearly four decades years overdue."

Sophie turned to Charly, her face rigid with confusion. Charly didn't know what to say or do, so she just nodded encouragingly.

Barry pulled the envelope from his pocket and handed it to Sophie.

She stared at it, running a gnarled finger along the soiled creases.

"This is from my Graeme?"

Eyes glistening, Barry nodded. "For you and your son," he managed to whisper.

Sophie gently moved back the flap and pulled out the yellowed newsprint within. Her eyes narrowed and she brought the paper close to her face.

"It's a foreign newspaper?"

"Turn it over," Barry said.

Sophie carefully flipped to the other side and peered. "Why, it's a musical score!" She glanced up at Barry, cheeks lifting in a brief smile.

"This is Graeme's writing!"

"He wanted you to know what it felt like to be a soldier far from the woman he loved." He nervously drummed the fingers of his right hand along his thigh. "One of the guys traded some cigarettes for a beat-up guitar. Once he heard Grae's licks, he just gave it to him. Graeme would play sometimes when it was safe, and all the guys would listen. One day, out of the blue, he told me he'd written a song for you called "Battlefield". 'Course, we had no paper, no music sheets, so he just scribbled away on this."

Without responding, Sophie stood and walked slowly to the piano. She settled on the bench, rested the music score on the stand and began to play. At first, her inflamed fingers moved awkwardly, but then she seemed to find her way and the room was filled with the haunting notes Charly remembered.

Sophie expertly played through the song once, and then something even more amazing happened. She began again, but this time she sang the poignant lyrics in a lovely, pure soprano voice. Charly was particularly taken by the song's chorus.

"The war grinds, on and on and on. You're my lifeline, compass and shield. In a whisper, I tell you what I've seen and done...on the battlefield."

It was a powerfully romantic song. Truly a heartsong, thought Charly.

When Sophie had finished, they all sat without moving or speaking and let the echoes of the soft notes of her voice and the piano continue to sweeten the air. Then Sophie dropped her head into her damaged hands and wept.

Charly and her father exchanged a dismayed glance. Neither did anything for a few seconds as the elderly woman continued to cry, and then Charly made a move.

Her father stopped her and he walked over to join Sophie on the piano bench.

After a moment, he put his strong arm around her slumped, thin shoulders and she turned quickly, like a child, and thrust her face into his chest and sobbed. After a time, she pulled back and moved aside. Barry handed her a tissue.

"Thank you, dear Barry," she whispered, dabbing her eyes. "You've brought him back to me, after all these years."

"Should have done it in 1973."

Sophie nodded. "Yes. I...it...would've been such a blessing. I...I felt so alone, then."

"Can you ever forgive me?" said Barry, his voice thick with remorse.

Sophie's eyes widened, but she didn't reply.

Barry's shoulders drooped and he sighed heavily. Charly wanted to run over and hug him, but Sophie surprised them both.

"Who's to say what should've happened?" Sophie stroked her necklace, fingering the Claddah ring and softly added, "None of us really know God's plan, do we?"

"Amen, and thank you," Barry replied.

Charly spoke for the first time. "When will you give the song to Derek?"

The wrinkles on the elderly woman's face tightened.

"You're...you're not going to?" said Barry.

"Oh, dear." Sophie put her hands in her lap. "You're not the only one, Barry, who needs forgiveness for a past indiscretion."

Charly and her father stared at their hostess.

"I've never told Derek about his father. You see, I left Silver Shores under difficult circumstances and moved here to start a new life. I met my first husband, Bryce Burgess, when Derek was barely two. He was a wonderful husband and father, bless his dear soul—he passed on almost a decade ago—and he raised Derek as his own."

She hesitated and glanced at the photographs on the mantle.

"Derek thinks Bryce is his biological father. And while Bryce was alive, I couldn't bear to tell him any differently. It would've broken Bryce's heart. And then when I remarried, it...it seemed even more difficult."

"You've thought about it, though, haven't you?" Barry said. "Hope you don't mind my saying so, but my dishonor's troubled me every single day."

Sophie nodded. "And if I'm honest, since Bryce's death, it's always on my mind. Not just for Derek, but for his two sons. I want them to know their birthright, but I haven't had the courage."

Barry rose and approached the mantle. After a few moments of examining the photographs, he picked one up and offered it to Sophie. Charly saw that it was a recent professional shot of the whole family. The two boys appeared to be about Scotty's age.

"Are you too upset to meet the rest of my family?" Barry said.

Though her eyes were red, Sophie said, "No. I feel wonderfully energized. Please, invite them in.

Barry nodded to Charly, who stepped outside. As she approached the Jeep, Scotty and Faith jumped down. They spoke simultaneously. "How's it going?" Faith said. "Can we go now?" Scotty said. "I'm thirsty."

"Come in and meet Mrs. du Pont," Charly said, before turning back to the house and ignoring the quizzical looks from the three adults.

She wasn't ready to talk about what she had experienced. She wasn't sure if she ever would.

Chapter Forty-Four

He that plants trees loves others beside himself.
Thomas Fuller

They all trooped into Sophie's living room. She looked up from the photograph, smiled and quickly stood.

Barry introduced everyone and then, with his hand resting on Melissa's shoulder said, "Sophie, I wanted you to meet them all, since they are the reason I found the courage to finally admit my failure and to fulfill my promise to Graeme."

Sophie was silent for a couple of moments as her eyes moved slowly across the new faces. Then she nodded and offered to make tea. Hope and Faith volunteered and the trio disappeared into the adjoining kitchen.

"How'd it go?" Michael hissed, in a voice barely above a whisper.

"Fine," Charly said. She was concentrating on her father's face and on the sounds drifting in from the kitchen.

"Great. That explains everything."

The kids sat together at the piano, and amidst bursts of laughter, plinked out *Chopsticks*. A few minutes later, Hope appeared with a tray filled with tall glasses of lemonade and thick slices of homemade pound cake. The children rushed over and were soon drinking and eating and teasing one another.

Sophie returned, trailed by Faith, who bore another tray holding a china teapot and several matching cups and saucers. Sophie busied herself with pouring and handing around the cups. Faith sat on the piano bench and beamed at her father.

"What a lovely family you have, Barry," Sophie said. "Three beautiful girls and such fine grandchildren!"

"Don't forget the outstanding son-in-law," said Michael, between bites of cake.

Sophie smiled. "Of course not."

"You're right," Barry said, wiping his mouth with a napkin. "My girls're the best, and the grandkids aren't far behind." Michael coughed. "And yes, Michael'll do in a pinch."

"Daddy!" said Faith.

Sophie laughed. "Thank you all for coming and for waiting so patiently outside. It may have seemed awfully rude of me not to ask you in immediately."

Hope held up a palm.

Melissa said, "No worries, Mrs. du Pont." She fingered the photographs on the mantle. "This Mr. Burgess?" she said, pointing to a black and white picture of a pudgy baby boy sitting on a blanket.

Sophie nodded.

"Can't wait to tell him I've seen him in diapers." She giggled, flung herself down beside Charly, and began telling Sophie about her band.

Soon, Scotty had joined in with tales of school, and then Faith, Hope and Michael were talking. It was like being at the Shepherds' dinner table, with several conversations happening at once.

Charly watched and listened, but she wasn't taking much of it in. After a while, she realized that both Sophie and her father looked preoccupied and tired, and were no longer participating.

She cleared her throat and stood. "Think we should be going now," she said firmly. The others stopped chatting, briefly taken aback. "Say goodbye, kids."

Scotty and Melissa bounced up and thanked Sophie. Faith, Michael and Hope followed suit—the sisters kissing Sophie's cheek— and took the children out the front door.

Charly turned to Sophie and reached for her hand. "Thank you so much for meeting us. You don't know what it means to our father and to us."

Sophie smiled up at her and gently pressed her palm. "Oh, I believe I do." She touched the cross around her neck.

"It means the world to me, too. Thank you for bringing your father and your family."

Charly stepped outside into the chilly night air and let her father say his goodbyes in private. While she waited, arms wrapped around herself and staring up at the muted stars, she whispered a little prayer of thanks and told her mother all about the evening.

When her father finally joined her on the front step, he was pensive.

"She going to tell Derek?"

"No idea. Said she'd think about it," he said, taking her arm. "Not an easy decision to make, dear. It'll change all their lives."

They strolled toward the truck. The others were piled into the Jeep. Hope had raised the top and started the engine to keep them warm. Charly hesitated, but only briefly. She had a lot of questions, especially about how her father felt, but there would be time for that. But she was desperate for one answer.

"Did she forgive you, Dad?"

"Yes, hon." He gave her a peck on the cheek. "Let's go home."

Chapter Forty-Five

*Growth takes time. Be patient. And while you're waiting, pull
a weed.*
Emilie Barnes

For Charly, the next two days played out more like two weeks. She maintained the family's routine—breakfasts and dinners with the kids and nursery and housework in between—but time dragged horribly. It didn't help that the most pressing job was potting up hundreds of flowers. Though she, her father and Michael toiled nonstop, the work was dull and dirty and the minutes barely crept by.

Adding to her frustration, her sisters phoned several times, pressuring her for details of the conversation between Sophie and their father. Charly resisted. Her father had made only one quiet comment when he had joined the rest of the family outside Sophie's house two nights earlier: "She's a lovely lady and I'm very grateful to her. She listened to my story. I think she understood my situation, and thank the blessed dear Lord, she forgave me." Faith and Hope wanted more, but their father just shook his head.

Now, as Charly pulled seedlings and pressed soil, she discovered she had never realized how much time there was to think while tending her plants. In the past, her mind had just happily skipped from subject to subject, enjoying the freedom. She felt burdened by this new awareness, especially since her inquiring thoughts consistently snapped back to Sophie du Pont and her family, as if she were connected to them by a rubber band. Would she find the courage to tell Derek? Would he ever be able to forgive her father and her family? How would he treat Melissa now, and later, Scotty? Would Sophie ever call?

By late the second afternoon she was cranky and distracted. She knew she had no right to push Sophie, or even hope that the widow would do anything just to appease her father's regret. Sophie du Pont was the injured party in all this, she and Derek.

Charly then tried to imagine what it would be like to be told, at her age, that she had been adopted. That her parents, her sisters, her history were all just a facade. That she had come from somewhere else, from someone else and that she wasn't really a true part of the Shepherd family.

She was positive she would be devastated. It meant so much to her to be the natural daughter of Eileen and Barry, the two people she admired most in the world. Not just to have been blessed with their DNA, but with their fine sensibilities, old-fashioned values and unique history, and to have all that passed down to her children. Though she barely knew Derek Burgess, she instinctively believed he would share her reaction, and she felt uncomfortable and wrong for wanting his mother to alter his life, his understanding of himself and his family.

A slight cough caused her to cry out in surprise.

"Sorry!" Michael said, brushing dirt off his gloves and pushing back his baseball cap. "You've been out of it the last coupla days. Still worrying about whether Sophie told her son?"

Charly looked at her brother-in-law, frankly surprised at his intuition. "That obvious, huh?" She motioned to him to follow her to the family picnic table nearby, then *you-hooed* at her father to join them.

Charly and Michael sat across from one another and silently gazed at the garden beds. Their vast array of plants, most in six-and ten-inch plastic pots, were bushy, multi-budded and nearly-ready-for-sale. Soon, the next phase of the Sweet Shepherd Nursery business would take over and their property would be overrun with eager green thumbers.

"Just can't get it out of my mind," Charly finally admitted. "I know it's really none of my business, but..."

"I understand where're you're coming from," Michael said as Barry crunched toward them. "Sometimes I'd get all caught up in a case, usually one that was over, but finished on a sour note." He slapped the wooden top. "Hate not being in control."

"One of life's trials," said Barry as he clambered in beside Charly. "And sometimes, the result can be a great enlightenment."

Michael scowled. "I wasn't much enlightened by guilty perps who got away."

"No," Barry said. "That would be difficu—"

The ringing of the family phone interrupted him. Charly scrambled off the bench.

"I'll get it!"

She raced inside, pounded into the kitchen and nearly yanked the phone off the wall in her haste. "Hello?"

"Hellooo!" a man's deep voice blasted her ear. "Izzat one of Barry's gorgeous girls?"

Charly stood still, jaw dropped with surprise, and yanked the receiver away from her head. It took a few seconds for the voice to stop reverberating between her ears before she was able to reply.

"Uhhh, this's Charly Shepherd speaking," she said tentatively. "May I ask who's calling?"

"Are you there? Hello! Hello! It's Stan Hubenig. Er, don't ya know my voice, girlie?"

Stan Hubenig? Charly played the name over her tongue, but no matching face came into her mind's view. She put the receiver near her mouth.

"Uhh, I'm sor—"

"Stantheman! Your Dad's ward mate," the voice boomed. "From the hospital!"

Charly cringed from the noise. "Of course, Mr. Hubenig," she finally shouted into the phone, now picturing the elderly man with the large pair of hearing aids, whose hospital bed was next to her father's.

"Hello. How are you?"

The sound of hoarse coughing *rat tat tatted* in her ear and then Hubenig said, "Well enough for a dying old man. I want you to help me."

Heartsong

Charly bolted upright, her attention hijacked by his first sentence. "What? I'm sorry...you said you're...you're *dying*, Mr. Hubenig? Should I call 911? Where are you?"

"What? 911? What'n tarnation for, girlie? Don't want those nosy parker ambulance types trooping up my stoop."

Charly dragged the phone and cord over to the kitchen table and slumped down. This was insane...like a Monty Python sketch. She didn't know what to say so remained quiet.

"Girlie!" thundered the voice. "You there?"

"Here!" she sang out, feeling like laughing at the absurdity of their conversation.

"Your father told me about your aim to help folks. Said you're callin' it some sorta project."

Astonished and suddenly breathless, Charly couldn't respond. Her itch to laugh vanished as the ramifications of Hubenig's statement spun round her brain.

Dad told you, someone he barely knows, about Project Heartsong?

"Well, girlie, I'm someone in need of your help." He coughed heavily again, wheezed and roared, "Real soon."

Charly stared at the receiver for a long moment, expecting it to explode with more deafening sounds at any second. When it didn't, she swallowed and spoke loudly and clearly, "Please, Mr. Hubenig, call me Charly. Uh, and yes, my sisters and I are helping our father with...something."

"No need to pussyfoot round it, girl...er...Charly. Barry told me all 'bout it."

Charly slumped back into her chair, glad she wasn't standing. "He what?" she squeaked, when she finally found oxygen.

"Folks talk real close to the heart when they're lookin' right at the ol' Grim Reaper. Ain't no surprise. Anyways, that's Barry's affair. Mine's all together different."

Still stunned, Charly whispered, "Oh?"

There was a pause in their earsplitting conversation and then Hubenig bellowed, "What? Hey, you still there?"

"Here, there, everywhere!" Charly shouted back, unable to help herself. She covered the receiver and roared with laughter. This was

272

morphing into a Robin Williams' skit!

"Made up my mind when that red-headed sawbones told me my chances were less 'n fifty fifty."

Charly almost choked on the disparity between the sensitive nature of Hubenig's last few words and the shocking volume at which they were delivered. She sputtered and then finally found her breath.

"Wwwhat can I do for you, Mr. Hubenig?"

"You can rustle up those beeeuuutiful sisters of yours and find me my li'l girl, Louanne."

Charly's mouth went dry. She sagged against the hard kitchen chair. Her ears rang, her throat ached and her mind spun like a whirligig. Isn't this what you wanted? she asked herself. To help others? Well then, why the big hesitation?

"This ain't no charity, mind you," Hubenig's voice continued to boom. "I'll pay you girls whatever you ask. This may be a sight personal to me, but I understand it's business to you 'n yours. So, when can you start?"

Business? Charly had never considered this. Was it possible?

"Ssstart? I'm sorry, Mr. Hubenig. I...I'm not real sure what to say. I...well, my sisters...we haven't..." Her voice trailed off. How could she explain to him when she hadn't really even figured it out herself? She straightened. *Oh for heaven's sake, Charly, the man's waiting. Get it together!*

"You still there, Mr. Hubenig?"

"Far's I know!" came a boisterous reply.

Charly grinned. "Look, can you give me a little time? I'll talk to my Dad and my sisters, if that's okay? And get back to you in a few days."

"Make it two...don't have all the time in the world, y'know."

"I'll...I'll try, Mr. Hubenig. Goodbye." She hung up the phone and then fell back into the chair.

What've I got myself into? Oh dear Lord, you've got to help me. Help me to do the right thing.

The telephone rang again, disrupting her thoughts. Presuming it was Mr. Hubenig calling again, she jumped up, reached for the receiver and said, "Look, I'm sorry, but I said I needed a few—"

"Excuse me?" said a hesitant voice. "Is this the Shepherd

residence?"

It was a woman's voice, one that she recognized. Charly's tongue twisted, but she chewed out a reply, "Oh! Please forgive me! I thought you were...oh, it doesn't matter. Yes, this's Charly Shepherd. Sophie? Is that you, Mrs. du Pont?"

"Yes, dear. I was wondering, do you think I could come by sometime with my family?"

"Come by? Well, of course! Anytime. How about tonight?" Charly knew she was pushing the envelope, but couldn't stop herself.

"Tonight? Why yes, Charly, I suppose that would work. Derek and the boys'll be here anyway. They're coming for dinner."

"Would seven be okay?"

"Fine. Now, don't go to any trouble, dear." She paused, and added softly, "I would just like my grandsons to meet your family, especially your father."

"Did you tell Derek?" Charly asked on impulse and then panicked. "Oh, please, don't answer! It's none of my business, Sophie. I'm sorry. Shouldn't have asked."

"That's quite all right." Sophie's voice was calm, but Charly thought she heard sadness. "Yes. I told him."

"Is...is everything all right?"

"It will be, dear. Given time and the good Lord's help. Thank you."

She hung up, but Charly remained in place, holding the receiver and staring at the wall.

~~~

"I...uh...I spoke to Stan Hubenig this afternoon," Charly said as she handed her father a plate to dry. She eyed his profile reflected in the kitchen window. With all the excitement surrounding the arrival of the Burgess family, Charly hadn't had the opportunity to bring up Hubenig's call.

Barry's outstretched hand dipped slightly and then he firmly grabbed the plate. "Was wondering when he'd call."

Charly scrubbed a mug for a couple of seconds. "Why didn't you tell me?"

There was a momentary clatter as Barry placed the plate onto a pile in the cupboard. He turned and looked at his daughter.

"Wasn't aware that I had to run everything in my life by you."

Charly's throat tightened, taken aback both by her father's brusque statement and his taut facial expression.

"Uh...I'm sorry, Dad!" she said, rushing to fill the awkward void between them. "Of course, you don't answer to me on anything. It's... it's just..." She dropped her eyes and focused on scouring out a tea stain at the bottom of her favorite china mug.

"I didn't know you had told anyone else, especially a stranger, about our idea...about Project Heartsong."

She felt her father's warm fingers on her shoulder and twisted to meet his gaze. This time, he smiled slightly, though his face remained somber.

"Sometimes it's easier to tell a stranger details we have a hard time telling our loved ones."

Charly nodded, tears brimming in her eyes.

"It's a terrible thing, dear, to...." Barry Shepherd swallowed, then continued hoarsely, "To think you're going to face your Maker and wish you'd been a better man."

"Oh, Dad..."

With a soft moan, Charly pushed herself into his arms and hugged fiercely.

~~~

At 7:07 that evening, Charly opened the door and welcomed Sophie and her family inside. Derek Burgess was solemn. Heavy shadows curved under his deep-set eyes, but his air improved when he saw Scotty and Melissa. The pair immediately took the Burgess boys into the backyard, while Derek re-introduced himself to Barry.

There was an awkward hesitation.

"I believe you knew my...my, uh, biological father," Derek said finally, avoiding his mother's anxious glance.

"Yes," Barry said, firmly shaking Derek's hand. "Graeme Walker was a great guy, a true friend and an American hero. You look a bit like him." He clapped an arm around Derek's shoulders and led him down the hall.

"And from what I hear, you're as good a man as he was."

Barry stopped at the entrance to the living room and turned. He stood ramrod straight and spoke with poise and emotion.

"Son, I owe you an apology. I broke your father's trust, and for that I will be eternally ashamed. I hope that, like your dear mother, you may one day find it in your heart to forgive me."

Derek observed Barry for a heartbeat. "Thank you, sir," he said. "Have to be honest, I'm not sure what I feel at the moment." He rubbed his chin. "It's...it's been a bit of a shock."

"Of course. Please, come, sit down."

The two men disappeared. After a moment, Charly overheard Derek ask, "What do you think of his song?"

Her father's reply was loud and enthusiastic. "I think it's fantastic. As they used say in my day, 'Number one with a bullet!'"

Both men chuckled and fell silent for several seconds. Then Derek's deep voice said clearly, "Please, Mr. Shepherd, would you tell me about Graeme Walker?"

Charly felt Sophie's paper-thin hand in hers and she squeezed gently. She felt immensely satisfied by her efforts and profoundly fulfilled by their results.

Charly Shepherd whispered a prayer of thanks to her mother as her own heart sang with joy.

The End

Nicola Furlong

BATTLEFIELD

Roadside bombs split the sky, Hell's doors open wide.
And dreams are pulverized into sand.
One clear thought echoes true, The love I have for you
It's enough to get me through this wasteland.

The war grinds, on and on and on,
You're my lifeline, compass and shield.
In a whisper, I tell you what I've seen and done...
On the battlefield.

This old jargon's tasting stale. Is morale the Holy Grail,
and glory just a nail in the chest?
I'm way too young to feel this old. My blood runs hot and
cold.
This soldier's weary soul needs to rest.

© Glynne Turner, 2012

CHARLY SHEPHERD'S CHUNKY COOKIES

Ingredients

1 cup salted butter, softened
¾ cup brown sugar, packed
½ cup granulated sugar
1 egg
2 tsp vanilla extract
1 tsp baking soda
½ tsp salt
2 cups bleached or all-purpose flour
1 cup semi-sweet chocolate chunks or chips
1 cup milk chocolate or 1 cup white chocolate chunks or chips
1 cup pecan pieces

Directions

Preheat oven to 375°F (190°C)

Using a mixer in a large bowl, beat together butter, sugars, egg and vanilla extract until light and fluffy (about four minutes).
Add baking soda, salt and flour. Beat to combine.
Stir in chocolate and pecans.

Drop dough by tablespoon chunks onto ungreased cookie sheet.
Bake in center of oven for 8-10 minutes.
Cool on wire racks before eating. (This rarely happens in the Shepherd household!)

If you enjoyed *Heartsong,* You may enjoy Nicola Furlong's other books.

Teed Off!, Dark Oak Mysteries, 2014
The Sad Clown Affair, Guidepost, 2002
Plots and Pans, Guidepost, 2002
No Safe Arbor, Guidepost, 2002
The Unwelcome Suitor, Guidepost, 2001
The Angel's Secrete, Guidepost, 2001
No Safe Arbor, Guideposts, 2002
The Nervous Nephew, Guidepost, 2001
A Hemorrhaging of Souls, Salal Press, 1998

FRANKFORT FREE LIBRARY
123 Frankfort St.
Frankfort, NY 13340
(315) 894-9611